May God bless you in all you do.

[signature]

SEED OF SEERLING

SEED OF SEERLING

AMY KENNEDY

VMI Publishers • sisters, Oregon

Scripture taken from the *Holy Bible,* New International Version ®. Copyright © 1973, 1978, 1984 International Bible Society. Used by permission of Zondervan. All rights reserved.

The "NIV" and "New International Version" trademarks are registered in the United States Patent and Trademark Office by International Bible Society. Use of either trademark requires the permission of International Bible Society.

Published by
VMI Fiction
a division of
VMI Publishers
Sisters, Oregon
www.vmipublishers.com

ISBN: 1933204656
ISBN 13: 9781933204659
Library of Congress Control Number: 2008925267

Printed in the USA.

Cover design by Juanita Dix

I dedicate this book to the idea man.

Dan, you are my rock. I am still profoundly amazed
that you chose me to be your wife. I thank God for blessing me
every day with such a wonderful best friend.

I also want to thank dear friends Denise, Glenda, and Kathy,
who were my first editors.

A very special thank you goes out to Susan Lohrer
who did a fantastic and patient job of professionally editing
for this new author.

Chapter One

It's a tiny foot," Sallian cried above the noise of her daughter's screaming.

The young priestess panted and let out another shriek. "Can't you turn the child," she cried through panting breaths.

"It's too late now, Isilian." Her words were lost as the next wave of pain caused her daughter to bellow. Sallian smoothed Isilian's saturated hair back from her face. "We're going to have to make do."

The night wore on with the young priestess writhing in pain as her mother worked to bring the new life into the world. The sun was barely peeking over the horizon when Isilian let out a final grunt and birthed a healthy baby girl. Sallian held the baby close then stepped back to allow a smaller woman to busy herself with cleaning up.

"It's a girl," she beamed, giving her daughter a better view. "You have birthed a daughter, Isilian."

Pride showed on the tired face of the young woman as she reached out her arms to hold her small babe. "A priestess, mother. I have birthed a priestess." She sighed then closed her eyes, overcome by the deep sleep of one who has worked tirelessly.

A dark cloud spread in Sallian's heart as she stood staring over her sleeping daughter. Reaching down, she picked the baby up and cradled her. She knew the babe would soon need to nurse but for now she would relish this time alone. She kissed the soft down of the white head and smiled deeply into the perfect gray eyes of her first grandchild.

Holding the baby close and walking from the room, Sallian whispered a prayer over her. "May you be blessed by the One True God, the Maker of heaven and earth. May He and only He direct your paths."

One full sacrifice had ended and another approached quickly. Astril was not yet old enough to be weaned, and Isilian was late again for her feeding. Sallian held the baby as she read from her copied scrolls. She knew by the small fussing noises that the child was getting hungry. Isilian had left hours before to go about her regular temple duties. It worried Sallian that her daughter worked such long hours in the temple in service to the High Priestess and took only a few short breaks daily to feed and care for her own child.

Isilian rushed in the room just as the infant was beginning to howl in hunger. Sallian lifted the squirming baby.

"My dear, you are here. Astril is so hungry. I gave her a small piece of bread, but she needs her mother's milk."

Isilian looked slightly annoyed as she unlaced the front of her Priestess gown and reached for her crying daughter. Sallian noticed that she barely even looked at the baby as she put her to feed.

"When will I be able to wean her, Mother?"

"Why not for many moons still." Sallian spoke slowly to hide her shock at the question.

"This is becoming more and more difficult. I have too many responsibilities in the service of the Great Goddess to run home so often."

Sallian had quickly hidden her scrolls when Isilian entered the room; now she played nervously with them in her pocket. "You could always take her with you as the other women do."

"You know that I cannot. The High Priestess would never allow it." Isilian's voice held a hint of anger. She sighed then went on in a softer voice, "It won't matter much longer anyway."

Sallian turned her head away from her daughter, and they sat in silence for some time while Isilian fed the child.

It was Isilian who broke the silence. "I have very good news." She smiled as her mother only raised an eyebrow in response. "My aunt told me that since she has been unable to have her own daughters, she looks to me to become High Priestess one day."

Sallian ignored her daughter's words and instead looked out the window.

"Mother!" the younger woman roared, setting Astril to fretting. "Didn't you hear what I said? I am to become the High Priestess one day."

"I heard you. I was just wondering why my sister has chosen to abandon her lifelong hope of having her own daughters."

Isilian rolled her eyes and snorted. "She says she is past her prime. She looks to me now to bear many daughters to replenish the line of priestesses. And for my obedience, I will succeed her as High Priestess."

Sallian jumped to her feet, "And at what cost does this honor come?"

Isilian's reddened eyes blazed. "I hope you remember that if it were not for the generosity of the High Priestess—your own sister—you would still be in exile. She brought you back home even though it was your disobedience that destroyed her ability to bear her own children."

Sallian worked hard to hide her anger as she thought back to the day when her own mother had forced her out of Seerling land because she would not give Isilian to the Great Goddess as a Keeper so her older sister, Ruman, would be blessed with children. Ruman was to succeed their mother as High Priestess, but when she was found to be barren, Sallian was called upon to conceive and bear a Keeper. One who could be given to the service of the Great Goddess. Sallian's sacrifice was to have brought honor to the Great Goddess, who would in turn bless the eldest daughter, Ruman, with her own children. Sallian had not been pregnant five phases of the moon when she realized she could not give her own child up. Her refusal to give Isilian at the birth for her sister ignited the High Priestess's rage, and Sallian paid for it with a long scar on her forehead and banishment from her homeland. She did not see her daughter again for fourteen sacrifice years. By that time, Isilian had been indoctrinated into the old ways of the Great Goddess and was lost to her forever.

Sallian's silence only fueled Isilian's rage. "And with that gift in mind, no price is too high to cover up your mistakes."

"Would the price of your own daughter's life be too high for you to pay, Isilian?"

Isilian sat quietly, looking straight through her mother as if seeing some glorious paradise in the distance, then breathlessly answered, "No price is too high for the service of the Great Goddess and the High Priestess."

"You know what happens to those who are chosen as Keepers, Isilian. Would you subject your own daughter to such a fate?"

"The Keepers are honored and revered. The power they hold within themselves can be used only for the Great Goddess. It would be an honor to have a child of mine chosen for such service."

Sallian stood, nauseated. "Do not spout those false words to me, Daughter. We both know what the Keepers are forced to do."

Isilian ignored her mother's words and stared down at the floor while the child nursed noisily.

A loud rapping at the door jolted both women out of their thoughts.

As she had done so many times in the past, Sallian hid her frustration at her daughter's loyalty to the goddess and went to answer the call.

She had no more than reached for the handle when the door was flung wide open. Towering over her was her sister, Ruman. The High Priestess, of exceptional height for a Seerling, looked frighteningly beautiful with her dark yellow hair flying freely about her round face and caressing her shoulders like a luxurious cape. She enjoyed the great fear her appearance left in the eyes of those she encountered and used it to intimidate her subordinates. Her deep green gown, specially created for her as all her clothing was, emphasized the small flecks of green in her dark blue eyes.

Wearing only a white, floor-length dress, Sallian's humble attire was no match for the grandeur of her sister's. As High Priestess, Ruman wore an elegant, lightly beaded garment that flowed ethereally behind her tall, thin frame. Each of her gowns was of the same cut and made in the colors of the earth; opening at the neck to just below the shoulder.

"Sallian, dear sister," the High Priestess cooed in an irritatingly high-pitched voice. "How very nice to see you." She then turned and gestured to an Olden crone behind her. "And you remember Thauma the mystic." Sallian nodded her head in recognition. Thauma was a member of the Olden race and was the caretaker for the Keepers. It was she who chose a new Keeper each year from among the thirteen tribes, and she who whisked the Keeper away to higher grounds just south of Seerling. Thauma stood head and shoulders above Ruman despite her deep hunch. Her skin had the color and appearance of hardened, dark leather. The Olden people were a mysterious group, seemingly friendly but suspicious of all, including Seerlings.

The old mystic acknowledged her with a slight squint of her wrinkled eyes, an action that left Sallian's blood running cold.

"Were you planning to allow us entrance?" Ruman's cooing voice was laced with annoyance as she pushed her way past Sallian and into the hut.

Sallian opened the door wider and allowed Thauma to enter as well. Then walking behind them, she slowly entered the room where her daughter still sat nursing Astril. *No, Father. Do not let Astril be chosen. I beg You to protect the child.*

"I'm sure you are both wondering why Thauma has agreed to visit here today." Ruman paused, not so they could answer but for her own glory, then added, "Isilian, I have been planning for much time for you to become the next High Priestess. You have learned your lessons well and have kept nothing from me or from the Great Goddess. Your magic is growing stronger every day, and I look to you to bear many priestess daughters. We must take action now to ensure the safety and strength of our line."

Isilian smiled at her aunt and then sent a smug look in her mother's direction.

Silently, Sallian prayed as she waited for the abominable request her sister was sure to unveil.

"The annual sacrifice of our best animals as a tribute to the Great Goddess approaches. The Great Goddess also commands that a Keeper be chosen and given to her service." Hard pleasure rang in Ruman's voice, and Sallian knew if she showed fear for the child, it would only increase her sister's delight. She held her tongue. "In return for our worship, she has protected our people and granted our line, the line of the priestesses, long life and great magic."

Ruman paused for a brief moment, then looked hard at Sallian. "She asks for so little of us, and we have tried our best to provide everything she desires. However, we have let her down and are now suffering. You, Isilian, were once chosen as a Keeper, but your mother refused to offer the sacrifice and let you go. Because of your mother's disobedience, the Great Goddess rejected you, and another from among the people was chosen. No child since you has been born to our line." Picking up Astril, Ruman looked down and smiled. "This child is our hope of redemption."

Sallian took a sharp breath in and sat roughly down on her chair. Everyone in the room ignored her actions.

Ruman returned the child to Isilian then looked down at her niece. A mask of false love, ambition, and greed warred across her features. "Thauma has come to read your child's future. Her reading will determine whether she is to become this year's Keeper." Ruman ignored the small cry that escaped from Sallian. "If she is the one the Great Goddess desires, we will be blessed with many daughters to replace her."

The look of delight that passed over her daughter's face filled Sallian with grief. With great sadness, she folded her hands in front of her. *One True God, I pray Your protection over this small babe. I pray You will hold her in Your loving arms and give her the chance to live freely. Give her the chance to make a change in our people; to take our land away from evil and enter into Your great light.*

Continuing her silent vigil of prayer, Sallian opened her eyes to watch the actions of the mystic who had knelt to the floor in front of Isilian and the baby.

Thauma spread a length of leather on the floor and shook ten small toad bones from a leather pouch that was tied about her immense waist. The portentous bones clicked against one another as they tumbled onto the leather. Then taking a dagger from the folds of her skirt, she seized the baby's tiny hand and sliced through the newborn skin. A gusty scream erupted from the child as a torrent of blood poured from the wound. Thauma then squeezed the child's hand above the bones and chanted a series of unintelligible words. Astril wailed, and Sallian closed her eyes to the evil display.

Finally pushing the babe's hand away, Thauma took up the sides of the leather and shook the bones together with the blood. Then laying it out again, she knelt to review the images only she could see.

After many minutes, Thauma croaked out her reading. "This child is not the Keeper you seek. She is a seed." The old crow then stopped, moved a few bones around on the leather. "The seed." Her gruff whisper rattled to every corner of the room.

High Priestess Ruman knelt down beside her and stared at the bones in awe. "What seed?"

Thauma squinted her wrinkled eyes at the High Priestess then looked up at Isilian. "This is the child who will rule and bring peace to the Seerling tribes. She will be the seed that will lead her people out of slavery by Harkonian hands and into a great light."

Ruman jumped to her feet and cried out in joy as Isilian sat smiling proudly down at the infant who whimpered and flailed by her feet. She flicked the hem of her dress out of reach of the tiny, bloodied hand.

"This child will bring our people deeper into the light of the Great Goddess, Isilian," Ruman cried. "With her in the lead we will rule over all the lands and take from the Harkonians what is truly ours."

Ruman laughed aloud at her own exclamation. She whirled about the room with her arms held high above her head then suddenly stopped to stand in front of her sister.

Leering down, Ruman gloated. "You thought you could change your path and the path of your child, didn't you, Sister?" She grabbed Sallian's arms, pulling her to her feet. Her green-flecked eyes glittered with malice.

"Don't you know that the Great Goddess will take whomever she desires, and in whatever way she wishes? You are powerless to change anything." The High Priestess's mirth rang long and loud, and her fingers dug into Sallian's upper arms with bruising force.

Sallian pulled away from her sister's iron grip and turned to stare at her daughter, who swayed as if drunk. In a dreamy voice Isilian whispered, "Yes, one day my daughter will take their lands for our own. We will indeed grow rich under her light."

Ruman and Isilian celebrated with laughter the great deeds they believed Astril would do in the name of the Great Goddess. The High Priestess resumed her gyrating dance around the room, and Isilian sat down in a drunken stupor, finally picking up the crying child in her arms. The mystic sat back on her heels in silence, perhaps waiting for quiet to resume so her continued revelations would be delivered with greater effect.

Sallian stepped out of the way of the celebration and quietly thanked her God for answering her prayers. *Thank you for saving her life, One True God. May she truly be the one to lead our people into Your light and abolish the evil's of the Great Goddess.*

Then she looked to her own daughter. Perhaps now Isilian would love her.

The young priestess still appeared to be overcome by the news when she turned her gaze upon the mystic and with slurring words asked, "When will I see her do these things?"

Thauma hunched over the bones once again, moved them around slightly, and stared, then rocked back on her heels. A grimace bared her few remaining teeth. "Not one of you will live to see these things come to pass."

All exultation vanished from the room. Thauma exited as quietly as she had entered. The only noise that could be heard came from the baby, who lay in her mother's haphazard grasp, whimpering and sucking her injured hand.

CHAPTER TWO

Toren, riding the great steed Calton, raced through the woods in pursuit of a large boran despite his father's warning to slow down. As a boy of ten harvests, Toren had already experienced more than a dozen boran hunts. The average Harkonian boy was not allowed to go on the hunts until he had reached at least eleven harvests. Toren was no average boy. The son of Prince Verne and Princess Emile and grandson of Harkonian King Kortan, Toren received many pleasures his playmates only dreamed about.

"Slow down, Calton!" He screamed as the newly broken steed fled past the boran and drove farther into the woods that bordered the land of Harkan.

Toren yanked hard on the reins, turning his head to see the snorting boran trot in the opposite direction. His frantic mount tensed under him, muscles bunching. Toren clamped his legs around the horse's ribs. Calton reared and wheeled, Toren fought to keep his seat while avoiding the many branches that lashed at his face. The impetus jerked Toren from the back of the steed, sending him headlong into a prickly bush. The frightened animal exploded into a headlong gallop, his hooves pounding as he fled.

"Stupid beast," Toren grumbled. "I should have listened to Father and ridden Gomer."

He rose slowly and checked himself for injuries. Realizing he had only minor cuts on his face and arms, Toren looked about to orient himself. One tree looked like the next, and the crossroads of his land lay far from where the blasted Calton had thrown him.

Toren knew from previous hunts that Harkonian land lay north of the crossroads. "But which direction do I take to get back to them," he muttered. After debating with himself for a short time, he decided to stay put and wait for the hunting party to find him.

After only a few minutes of sitting near the bush, Toren heard a rustling of leaves a few feet to his left. The air suddenly filled with a musty, foul smell, while at the same time a loud snort rumbled behind him. Jumping to his feet and grabbing his dagger, he leaped sideways—out of the way of the charging boran.

"The one I was chasing. No doubt he's come back to finish me off." Toren screamed, "You'll not do me in, you foul beast!"

The boran turned back and scraped a forehoof on the ground, leaving a deep gouge in the rich earth. Its breath huffed, and a cloud of moisture sprayed from its snout. It lowered its tusked head and charged him again. With a quick thrust of his hand and a jerk of his right leg, Toren slashed his dagger deep into the side of the beast. The wound, not immediately fatal, incensed the beast further. It snorted and charged again. The boy jumped backward and out of the way only to fall in the bush, tangling himself with his flailing. Once again the boran charged. Toren raised his dagger defensively as the beast rushed toward him.

A deafening boom and flashing white light pounded his senses as the boran caught his left leg with the sharpened horns of its head.

Toren lay blinded, ears ringing, entrapped in the bush. Nearby, the boran screeched its pain and offense at the noise and light. Even after many long moments, his own eyes could no longer see anything but the white of the flash.

A soft rain began to fall, and he felt cool hands rip the cloth of his pants and gently probe his bleeding leg. Then an arm supported his shoulders. Someone tried to lift him to his feet. Toren screamed in pain as his body crumpled back into the prickly bush. A smothered voice whispered, "I'm sorry." He felt himself being dragged by the arm out of the bush, each movement knifing through a haze of pain. He quickly drifted out of consciousness.

The fog of sleep lifted from Toren's head, but he was still unable to open his heavy eyelids. From the itchy feeling on his face and arms, he knew he was lying on a bed of hay. He could not identify the smells around him but the shuffling sound of feet told him he was not alone. Grunting loudly and moving his head, Toren tried again to open his eyes.

"Don't move," commanded a soft voice hovering over him.

Toren obeyed and sank back into a deep sleep.

He was not sure how much time had passed before the fog began to lift again. This time he was able to open his eyes slightly. He made out the blurry image of a fire burning. He slowly began to raise his upper body, and a draft swept across his chest. Looking down, he realized he wore no clothing. Grabbing the fur that covered his hips, Toren desperately tried to adjust his eyes to the human form floating before him.

"Where are my clothes?" he demanded.

The blurry image knelt down before him and tried to push him back on the hay. "They were wet. I had to take them off so you would not catch fever."

He snatched his arms away from the peasant's insolent grasp. "Give them back now,"

"No, you are not recovered."

Exhausted, Toren leaned back heavily on the bed of hay. He rubbed his eyes in an attempt to see better as the image leaned closer in to inspect his wound.

Panic flooded over him as he understood it was a girl who cared for him. "You're a girl!" he cried while reaching again to cover his body with the fur blanket.

"You are observant," replied the mocking voice of the girl as she wrapped his wound tightly with cloth.

Toren dug the heels of his hands into his eyes, desperate to clear the haze. "Why can't I see?" he demanded.

"I'm sorry. I may have accidentally wounded your eyesight while I was trying to injure the boran." The girl stepped away from him and then held a clay mug to his lips. "Drink this. It will help improve your eyesight."

"I had everything under control with that beast." Toren demanded. Then curiosity made him ask, "You are the one who caused the flashes of light?"

"Yes."

"How did you make the lights?"

She turned her face away from him. "Magic."

"Magic?"

"Yes, magic." She shoved the mug at him. "Now drink this or you may never see well again."

Toren sulkily drank the heavy, bitter liquid, wondering at the thought of someone actually doing magic. Within minutes, his eyes recovered their sight, and he was able to see clearly. Sitting near his feet was a very thin girl with the straightest light-colored hair he had ever seen. She wore a brown leather tunic that left her arms indecently bare and fell just above her knees. Underneath the tunic, she wore pants of the same color leather. She took the clay mug from his hand, set it down, and turned deep gray eyes toward him.

"How do you feel?"

Still staring at the strange girl, Toren replied in a grumpy voice, "My leg hurts. What was that I drank?"

"It's no wonder your leg hurts. The boran gouged your thigh pretty deep," the girl answered while ignoring his question about the drink.

"Who are you?"

She let out a long sigh and again turned large gray eyes toward him. "My name is Astril."

"That's a funny name." Toren laughed and then let out a groan as his leg jerked with the motion.

"It is not. It's a beautiful name. I am named after the star that sits above the throne of the Great Goddess."

Toren sat bolt upright. "You're a Seerling!"

"Again, you are observant for a little boy," she whispered.

"I am no little boy. I am Toren, son of Prince Verne and grandson of King Kortan of the Harkonian people. You are my sworn enemy."

Astril's large eyes lit up with a fire of anger. "Enemy? Would an enemy save you from a charging boran, drag you to her dungee, dress your wounds, and nurse you back to health?"

"You are a Seerling," Toren replied slowly. "We are enemies."

Astril closed her eyes briefly then gave him a forced smile. "I am not your enemy, little boy."

"I'm not a little boy. I have already seen ten harvests. In my country I am almost a man." The forcefulness of his defense and the effort of the conversation left him dizzy and tired.

Seeming to recognize the effort he expended, Astril gently pushed him back down on the bed of hay. This time he did not resist. "I'm sorry I offended you." She fingered one of his brown curls and whispered, "You remind me of my little brother." Pain filled the girl's face as she held the curl softly between her fingers. "He had your hair color."

"Oh," he managed to whisper as she again stroked a brown strand that lay just below his ear.

Astril turned wet eyes away from him, and lifting the vines that closed the opening of the dirt hut, exited.

Toren knew the girl was suffering but did not have the energy to worry after her. He lay his head back down and slowly drifted into a fitful sleep.

When he awoke, the smell of boran meat filled the dungee, and Astril was sitting at his feet sipping from the clay mug.

"You are awake again," she said as she emptied the mug, cleaned it in a jar of water, and filled it with the same heavy liquid as before. "Here, drink this."

Toren obeyed without question this time then lay back down to look at her more closely. "You're strange looking," he said softly.

Astril turned a haughty gaze upon him, "That's a fine thing to say to someone who saved your life."

"No, I—I'm sorry…" he stammered. "It's just that girls in Harkan look different. They wear dresses, not pants like men. Your hair is light colored, and theirs is dark and they're clean and—"

She uttered a muffled shriek. "I'm clean! Why would you say that?" Then springing to her feet, she stared down at him. "You're a mean little boy."

The hurt look on her face made Toren shake his head. "I'm sorry. I didn't mean it. I only meant that they would never live in such a place as this, nor would they cook their own food as you have."

Astril bared her teeth at him. "I do not live here. I built this dungee because it is tradition. I will leave to go back home once you are well enough to be taken to the crossroads, which I hope is soon."

Toren tried to turn the conversation back to a safer topic. "What tradition would cause you to stay in a cave so far from your home?"

He held his breath as the thin girl stared down at him.

"You are filled with questions." She sighed, and her posture relaxed. "This is a dungee. Every Seerling girl leaves her home and goes deep into the woods after twelve sacrifices. She builds a dungee and waits for the Great Goddess to come and commune with her. After that she is considered to be a woman and is able to return home and begin whatever service the Great Goddess has given her."

"And has the Great Goddess communed with you?" Toren asked.

"No," Astril responded without blinking.

Toren turned his face away from her, "You worship a false god."

"I worship no god," she quietly replied.

Surprised by her words, Toren turned back and studied her face. He saw discomfort there. "But you are a Seerling. I thought…"

Astril sat down, closed her eyes, and hugged her knees tightly. "I refuse to worship a god who demands such a high price of her servants. Since I will not worship her, she will not come to me."

"You are not like any Seerling I have ever heard of."

"I am not so different from you." She laid her head down on her knees in a gesture that implied a great sadness burdened her heart.

Toren felt sorry for the girl and wanted to touch her hand in comfort but only had the courage to ask, "What price have you paid?"

She opened her eyes, which were glistening with tears and again turned away from him. The smell of the burning meat caught her attention, and she reached to take it from the flame.

Setting the meat down to cool on a flat stone, she busied herself with the meal. "I am from the womb of Isilian, who has become High Priestess to the Great Goddess. High Priestess Ruman died before the last sacrifice and left her the position. Every year, the High Priestess must make a blood sacrifice to appease the Great Goddess. The people bring every large animal they can find, and some they have raised, to the High Priestess, and she spends the entire night sacrificing. The fragrance of death and burning flesh fills the air and goes up to please the Great Goddess, supposedly filling her with life. The life within her comes back down to the High Priestess and is said to flow through her body, giving her greater magic. This year's sacrifice was well in hand when…" Shaking her head, Astril fell silent.

Unease pricked at Toren's mind. "My grandfather told me that you Seerlings kill one of your own people every year in tribute to your goddess."

Astril shook her head emphatically. "No. I can never remember a time when the High Priestess offered a Seerling on the sacrifice stone."

"But I was told that human blood was the only thing that would please your goddess."

Astril's eyes filled with tears. "Then she was certainly pleased with this year's sacrifice."

"Why?"

Turning her face away from him, Astril stood up and walked to the other side of the dungee. "Isilian took the position of High Priestess when Ruman died because there was no one else. Our line is diminishing. My mother birthed me, then a sister who was chosen as a Keeper." Her thoughts seemed to turn inward for a few moments. Then she twitched her shoulders as if to shake off some unknown discomfort. "Much time passed before she birthed again, and when she did it was a brother. She also birthed a third sister, but has not birthed another child for the line. This was the first year that my mother performed all the sacrifices alone. It was far into the night and the smell of burned meat filled our camp. My mother left the gathered group to reach a higher level of consciousness, then returned to complete the sacrificial service. Every elder from every tribe of the Seerlings was present in honor of the night of sacrifice. It was my job to watch over my younger brother and sister. I failed…"

Astril's voice broke again. "My brother got away from me just as mother was raising her hands in worship to the Great Goddess. He was teasing me as he did so often and laughing and looking back. He didn't notice that he had entered the sacrifice circle. He interrupted the service with his laughter. Mother had reached a high level of consciousness by that time and was speaking to the Great Goddess. She told me later that his laughter sounded to her like the snorting of a boran. She thought he was one of the sacrifice animals that had escaped and hurled her knife at his heart. Only after it left her hand did she see what she had done. His death shocked the gathered crowd and ended the night of sacrifice."

Toren shuddered in horror to think of a mother doing such a thing to her own child.

Astril stared down at her hands and cried, "I didn't move. I saw what was happening, and I didn't do anything. I only stood there staring at him as he died."

"Did she feel bad for what she did?" Toren asked quietly.

"Oh, she mourned his death if that's what you want to know, but then claimed that it was the very will of the Great Goddess that he died. She claimed that the priestess line has been weak for too long, and my brother's death was a precious gift to the Great Goddess. Mother says that it will soon be my time to enter the priestess service and give my own precious gift."

"Will you?"

"My mother gave her second daughter up as a Keeper to the Great Goddess without any effort or feeling. She accidentally gave her son in death to the Great Goddess. She was taught to believe that no price, even the price of her own children, is too great to give in service. I am not my mother, and I never will be." She looked down at her shaking hands and whispered, "If only it could have been me instead of him."

Toren wanted to ask so many more questions but knew he had exhausted the poor girl. "I'm sorry you lost your brother. You must have loved him."

"Of course I loved him! Do you think we Seerlings are beasts?" She grabbed a handful of hot meat and thrust it at him. "Eat this and go to sleep." She then left the dungee and Toren alone with his thoughts.

Startled at her outburst, he chewed the burned meat. After he'd eaten, he wrapped the small fur that covered him around the lower portion of his body and hobbled to a section farther back in the cave so he could relieve himself. He completed his task and dragged himself, exhausted to the point of falling down, back toward the main portion of the dungee.

His foot banged into something hard. "Ow!" Looking down, Toren saw a large orange rock amid many different types of herbs; some he recognized and some he did not. He also saw a bowl full of orange powder that appeared to have been crushed from the same rock he had banged into.

"Realgar," he muttered. "So that's how she made the flashes of light. Some magic." Leaving the rock where he had found it, Toren hobbled to the bed of hay and fell fast asleep.

He awoke some time later to Astril shaking his arm.

"Toren, wake up. It's time to take you to the crossroads."

"What?" He groggily raised his head.

She thrust his dry clothes in his face. "Your people are looking for you. We must get you to the crossroads before they leave the area."

Toren glared at Astril until she turned around to give him semiprivacy to dress. It took a lot of effort to force his limbs into sleeves and pant legs, but he accomplished the task as quickly as possible. Once he was fully clothed, she placed his arms around her thin shoulders and gently lifted him to his feet.

"I did not realize you were so short." She giggled. "I thought all Harkonians were supposed to be giants."

Toren gruffed, "I'm not short. I just haven't grown into my full height yet." Then he grinned. "Besides, I was told that all you Seerlings were short as stumps."

Astril smiled at his supposed insult, then grew serious. "You are going to have to try to walk with one arm around my shoulders and support some of your weight on your own. You're just too heavy for me to carry. I dropped you earlier."

Toren gave her one last glare at her admission and then allowed her to half drag, half carry him outside. After he'd lain in the dimness of the dungee for so long, the bright sun blinded him.

It took some moments before his eyes adjusted to the daylight. Astril waited patiently as he leaned heavily upon her for support.

"I found your so-called magic," he gloated.

"You're a little too observant for your own good, little boy."

Toren chose to ignore her insult. "Realgar is a rock, not magic. Do you even know real magic?"

Astril stopped and looked him full in the face. "So you know the truth. I told you we are not so different from you. Now, get moving, or we'll miss the search party and who knows when they'll be back this way."

Slowly, with her support, Toren was able to manage the pain in his thigh and maneuver through the heavy foliage. It was not long before sweat began to drip off his forehead and dizziness almost overcame him, but he continued on. Soon they could hear the barking of hounds in the distance. The sound of horses' hooves pounding alerted him that they were getting close to their destination. Astril slowed her step and stooped down, forcing him to crawl beside her.

"What are you doing?" he hissed in her ear.

"Quiet!"

They crept on in silence until they reached the bridge just before the crossroads. It was apparent by the dust clouds that the search party had passed over the bridge only moments before their arrival.

"This is where we part." Astril's whisper tickled the hair above his ear, sending an unfamiliar yet pleasant shudder through his body.

"You're going to leave me?" he asked aloud.

"Shhhh. Do you want them to take me as a slave?" She slowly backed away. "Stay here and yell if you like, but only after I have gone."

"No one will hurt you. You have my word," Toren whispered.

"I do not trust the word of a little boy," Astril said over her shoulder as her nimble feet stepped silently, taking her even farther from him.

"Wait!" Toren commanded. But she disappeared into the woods without looking back.

Chapter Three

Astril's encounter with the boy left her with mixed feelings. In her heart she knew she had done the right thing, but her head kept accusing her of being a traitor to her people. "I can never tell anyone that I saved his life," she whispered to herself while traveling home. "Mother would have expected me to leave him to die or even to kill him myself."

Smiling to herself, she went on. "Well, Mother, I guess you can't control everything, can you?" With those freeing words spoken she walked out of the woods, ending her three-day journey back home. In the distance she saw her younger sister, Gallian, playing a game of pretend. Astril recognized immediately that Gallian was playing the part of their mother, the High Priestess. Waving her arms wide above her head and screaming, Gallian ran in circles, trying to create a magical windstorm. Astril watched for a moment, dreading the thought of her sister one day following after their mother. A darker dread filled her heart as she watched the young girl at play; remembrance of what had happened to her brother. Mother had all ready shown a heavy hand with Gallian and when she took the cybin that allowed her to reach higher spiritual levels, she was unpredictable and dangerous.

"Perhaps my decision to not become a priestess will force Mother to cherish Gallian."

Looking up from her game just as her sister approached, Gallian broke into a run, screaming, "Astril's home, Astril's home."

Walking up and taking the hand of her sister, Astril laughed. "All right, Gallian. I think the entire world heard your pronouncement."

"I missed you," the little girl said with a giant smile that revealed two missing front teeth. "You were gone longer than all of the other girls."

"I had more to do than they did," Astril responded. "Now, I am craving a real bath, and my hair is itching to be washed thoroughly. How about you go and get me the soap." Astril began peeling her clothes off at the side of an ancient green pool. The pool, which had been dedicated to the Great Goddess, was built when Astril's great-great-grandmother was High Priestess. The inner lining of the large round pool was green and gave the water a dark, mysterious look. It was purported by many Seerlings to possess healing powers and was the only source of water that was used to clean the High Priestess's body before and after each sacrifice. No one was allowed to enter the pool for any other reason.

"You're going to take a bath in the Great Goddess's pool?" Gallian's deep blue eyes grew even larger at the thought of such a rebellious action.

Astril knew that entering the pool was forbidden to even members of the priestess family, but at that moment she didn't care. She understood in her heart that she had betrayed her mother by caring for the Harkonian boy, and the thought of swimming in the forbidden pool brought a small sense of freedom from her mother's tyrannical rule.

She smiled widely at her younger sister, cohersing her into the rebellion. "If you're a good girl, I'll wash your hair too."

Gallian squealed in delight at the thought of joining her sister in the pool. She was always ready to get attention from Astril and quickly ran off to find the soap.

"That girl," Astril sighed as she undressed and jumped into the pool. "She's a handful." She smiled as she anticipated sharing these few moments with the precocious little girl; their bond had always been stronger than that of other sisters, perhaps because Astril often filled in the role of their mother.

It only took a short time for Gallian to return with soap. She followed the lead of her sister, and undressing, jumped into the cool waters of the pool with a happy scream.

Her head popped up through the surface. "What if mother sees us?" she asked through jittering teeth.

"Calm down, Gallian. Mother won't know unless you tell her. You're not going to tell her are you?"

"Mother knows everything, Astril." Gallian responded in a matter-of-fact voice just before she dunked her head underwater again.

The two girls spent the next hour swimming and laughing.

"We better get out now," Astril said. "Rinse your hair so we can get back. Mother will want to see me soon."

Gallian smiled broadly. "She's been pacing back and forth for two days waiting for your return. She said she's anxious for you to start your training."

"I'm not going to do my training," Astril said quietly while helping her sister back into the traditional clothing. All common Seerlings wore similar light-colored tunics made of boran leather. The sides of the tunics were tied together at the base of the neck, allowing free movement of the arms. Beneath the tunics, each Seerling wore tanned boran-hide pants. The comfortable outfit, called a mauklan, allowed every extension of the body to move freely, unhindered by excess cloth. It was also durable and protected the covered skin from the harshness of the land. Seerlings were mainly animal herders who delighted in working the land through their small farms and using the provisions of the earth to efficiently care for themselves.

Gallian's eyes grew large when she heard her sister's quiet admission. "Mother is going to go into a rage when she finds out that you won't train."

"I know," Astril responded while hurrying to dress.

"You better go see her right away."

Astril sighed and smiled down at her sister. "I think I will go see Grandmother first."

Gallian callously snorted at Astril's words and blurted out, "She's dying."

"What!"

"Yeah," Gallian said, while dancing in place and laughing loudly. "Mother said it's about time that the old crazy woman goes to be with the Great Goddess. She's very angry with Grandmother."

Fighting to keep her calm, Astril grabbed her sister's shoulders to stop her dancing. "Did she tell you why?"

Gallian was still delighting in the attention she was getting from her sister and gleefully explained, "Grandmother has been calling out to some strange god. Every time she says his name, the magic in mother rages throughout the entire room. It's frightening," she added with a gleeful twinkle in her blue eyes and a small shudder of her shoulders.

Astril looked at her sister with despair. *Gallian is so much like Mother. She delights in discourse and pain.* Then she thought to herself, *Grandmother must be in very bad shape if she is allowing Mother to hear her pray to her god.*

"Gallian," she said, "Go and tell Mother I am home and am with Grandmother."

She was already running toward her grandmother's secluded hut when she heard Gallian yell after her, "Mother isn't going to like this."

"Let them praise His name with dancing and make music to Him with tambourine and harp. For the One True God takes delight in His people; He crowns the humble with salvation," the dying woman whispered.

"Grandmother, do not say such things," Astril pleaded with the sick woman.

"Astril, my love, is it truly you?"

Bending her ear close to her grandmother's face, Astril said, "Yes. I am here."

Sallian opened her eyes and smiled softly. "There is a man named Augur…"

Astril interrupted her grandmother. "You need your rest." She then patted her grandmother's hand and reached to give her a glass of water.

Waving the glass away with a weary hand, Sallian urgently said, "No, listen! I have been waiting for your return. I have only this one chance to tell you. Go to Augur, Astril. Learn from him."

"Who is Augur, Grandmother?" Astril asked, again bringing the cup to the older woman's lips.

Sallian pushed it away a second time and breathlessly whispered, "Augur is a good man. He will teach you…" She paused to cough softly. "The truth." She then turned pleading eyes to her granddaughter, and taking the child's hand in her own, begged in an urgent voice, "Vow to me, Astril. Vow that you won't take the priestess training. Vow that you will go to Augur."

"Grandmother, I—"

"Vow!" The older woman urgently demanded.

Astril wiped the tears from her face. "I vow it."

"What do you vow?" Gallian asked while entering the sick woman's room.

Looking up from the face of her grandmother and staring at her curious young sister, Astril shook her head. "Nothing." It was then that she noticed the fierce, red handprint etched into the small cheek of her sister.

"Oh Gallian," she cried, running to the child. "What happened?"

Gallian raised her hand to her cheek. "Mother was not pleased with your choice to come here first." Her lower lip quivered.

"I am so sorry," Astril whispered while hugging her close. "Please forgive me. I should never have sent you with such a message."

Gallian melted into her sister's hug and the bravery from before disappeared as she cried into Astril's tunic. After a moment she looked up and asked, "Why doesn't Mother ever strike you, Astril?"

Astril felt horrible as she looked into the deep blue eyes of the girl. "I don't know, Gallian, but I am so very sorry." Then turning back to her grandmother, she whispered, "Please stay with Grandmother, Gallian. I am going to see Mother."

Her younger sister nodded, and Astril briefly placed her hand on Gallian's injured cheek before exiting the room. A muffled sob made her look back.

"I am tired of being the one who always faces mother's rage." Gallian's voice shook with anguish, and her eyes had turned hard and cold.

Astril stormed toward the white temple of the Great Goddess. Upon approaching the building, she stopped and stared at the black sacrificial altar stone that stood in front of a giant iron statue of the goddess. A shudder coursed through her shoulders as she remembered her brother's death.

She forced her gaze past the dark granite of the stone to that of the giant statue. The iron Great Goddess, taller than any hut in the village, was the main focal point before reaching the temple. She was depicted sitting on a wheat-covered mound that represented the land of the Seerlings. In her right hand she held the lifeless body of a boran, and in her left she held the sun. These symbolized the yearly sacrifice and the promise of prosperity. Above the statue's head was the image of the bright, glittering star, Astriala, which means *promise*. The Seerling people were taught as young children to believe this star would bring about the promise of a new life.

There was a time when Astril felt proud to bear the name. Now, even her name reminded her of her loss. A deep-seated loathing began to grow inside her spirit as she stared up at the perfectly formed metal face of the statue. Allowing only a moment to relish the hate she felt inside, Astril turned and quickly continued her walk toward the temple, going up the white stone stairs and through the great columns, stopping before two large, gleaming doors. It took all of her might to push them open and enter the evil sanctum where she knew her mother waited.

The darkness of the temple was shocking in comparison to the bright sunlight of outside. Astril closed the doors that allowed natural light to enter and paused to allow her eyes to adjust to the dim candlelight. Once she could see somewhat clearly, she forced her body to move forward from the entryway and through another set of white doors. These doors lead her into a hallway that twisted in a circular labyrinth of walls, ending in a center room that highlighted a golden statue. This smaller version of the Great Goddess sat in the middle of the inner room surrounded by torches that made the pure gold glisten as though alive.

It was in this inner room that her mother carried out her daily rituals as High Priestess. The room was heavy with the smoke of the candles. Astril paused and looked around. One of the Seerling soldiers stood chained to the wall. Knowing that was one of the kinder methods the High Priestess used in resolving disputes, she shuddered and gave the older man a sympathetic look. Then entering the room, she walked on toward the statue where her mother knelt worshipping.

Isilian was as frighteningly beautiful as every other woman of the line of priestesses. She was tall by the standards of Seerlings, and her long blonde hair waved in lovely layers around her delicate face. She wore a long, flowing tan dress that was opened at the neck to expose slender shoulders. Much care had gone into the creation of the simple gown, covered at the scooping neck with small, multicolored gems. Each priestess was attired in such a way daily. It showed a separation of herself from average people. Seerling women wore simple gowns on special occasion but none wore dresses of the grandeur of the priestesses'. Astril looked down at her own traditional mauklan outfit and smiled at the thought of never having to wear the garments of a priestess.

She cleared her throat to alert her mother to her presence.

"I know you are here, my child," Isilian said without turning.

"Mother, why did you strike Gallian?" Astril's voice coursed with the tension she felt. "She only delivered the message that I spoke."

Turning to her daughter with fierceness in her eyes, Isilian waved her hands slowly above her own head and chanted. The action created a gust of wind that flew through the walled room and snatched at their hair. "How dare you go to that unfaithful woman before me," she screamed.

Astril hunched her shoulders against the buffeting of the wind for a moment and then found the courage to straighten herself. "How can you call your own mother unfaithful?"

Isilian's rage slowed in its intensity, and the forceful wind died down as she walked closer to her daughter. She took Astril in her arms and kissed her cheek in a loving way. "Because she is unfaithful, child. She has been unfaithful to her line, to her daughter, and more important, to the Great Goddess."

Astril stood her ground despite her mother's hug, knowing that it was only a ploy to soften her heart. "I want you to stop taking your anger out on Gallian, Mother."

"The girl needs to be brought under submission, Astril. She has much hate living within her."

Astril untangled herself from her mother's arms and walked a few paces away. "She has evil within her because you put it there."

Her mother's mouth curved in a cold smile, and she walked back to the statue. Astril also turned to the statue and stared up at the golden form. They stood there for long moments, side by side, one with a look of love and one with hate.

Isilian turned to her daughter and beckoned her closer. "I think you should begin your training right away."

"Mother, I..."

Cutting off her daughter's words, Isilian went on, "I know you are younger than tradition says, but you have shown much promise to be great in the true magic. You must begin your training now." Her passion for Astril to begin her training brought forth a magical gust that whipped through the room.

Astril stood as straight as she could, summoning her bravery to stand up to the taller woman before her. "I will not take the training."

With a flick of her hand, Isilian forced the raging wind to quiet, though it still simmered unsettled in her gaze. "You will take the training. You are the chosen seed to protect our people." She then turned and looked back at the statue, pointing to the star. "Astril, you are named after the star Astriala. Do you know what that means?"

"Yes, Mother. I know that it means *promise.*"

Turning back to her daughter, Isilian passionately cried, "You are the promise, Astril. The seed! You must begin your training."

Astril threw back her shoulders, blindly reaching for a strength far beyond her tender age of twelve sacrifices. "No. I am not that seed. I choose to not train."

The wind within the High Priestess erupted in a giant torrent that slammed Astril backward onto the stone floor.

"You will train!" she screamed, pointing down at her. The evil wind whipped Isilian's hair about her face, and her gown tore wildly around her body. Astril's defiance evaporated as she stared up at her mother in fear.

Her mother's expression softened. "Ah, my beloved daughter." She slowed her rage, bringing her arms down to her sides. She knelt before her daughter and reached out her hand in a gentle manner. "Perhaps you are still too young to begin the training. We will wait until after the next sacrifice."

Astril stood to her feet, ignoring her mother's hand. Shaking, she started to say she would never take the training.

Gallian ran into the room. "Grandmother has died!"

"Finally," Isilian muttered.

Heartsick, Astril ran from the room.

CHAPTER FOUR

Six harvests had passed since the last time Toren rode over the bridge to the crossroads that separated Harkan from the land of the Seerlings. Times had grown desperate, the Seerlings had grown bolder than ever with their attacks on Harkonian farmers. Many farmlands were lost to the evil High Priestess and her people. Under her rule, the battle over Harkan and Seerling land grew fiercer. No part of the crossroads was safe, which made it the perfect place for young Harkonians to test their manhood.

The nine young men on their steeds considered themselves very brave and had chosen that day to ride three miles into Seerling land and back. Each of the young men rode with an air of dignity and pride, hiding the mounting fear that stuck in the back of his throat. They had all heard the tales of the Seerling magic, and although Prince Toren confessed the secrets he had found in the cave of the girl, none believed him. To Harkonians, the Seerlings were evil heathens who used their mystical powers to overcome and kill their enemies.

Prince Toren rode upon his purebred horse, Calt and was in the lead as the young men raced toward the crossroads. Just as Toren's cousin Ard passed him on the right, Calt reared his front legs in protest to the quick pace and promptly slowed to a trot.

"Why haven't I had your throat slit?" Toren muttered. "You are the most unfaithful beast in the palace stables, even worse than your father was." Calt was the only offspring Toren's first horse, Calton, had sired.

His face showing his concern for the safety of his cousin and friend, Ard slowed his steed to match the pace of Toren's. "Are you all right?"

Toren berated himself out loud for his choice of steeds then looked to his older cousin. "Yes, this isn't the first time this stupid animal has let me down, and it probably won't be the last. His father had a knack for it too." He leaned forward and dug his heels into Calt's sides, but instead of surging forward, the horse jolted to a halt. "You obstinate, inbred—ughh!" Toren yelped as Calt merely sidestepped to the verge, tore up a mouthful of grass, and chewed placidly.

"Why don't you just have the beast destroyed?" Ard questioned as their seven companions quickly thundered past them in a flurry of hoof beats. The two young men watched them go, then turned to each other and laughed.

"I guess they aren't worried about our safety," Toren observed as he dismounted his horse to let him graze at will in the green grasses just off the road. Ard nervously looked around and then did the same.

As they watched the animals eat, Toren let his mind wander back to the day six harvests earlier when Calt's foolish father had taken him far inside the woods. It was strange how he could still see the dungee in his mind, he could still remember the smell of the burnt meat and the face of the girl who'd saved him. The way her breath tickled the hair on his ear when she whispered...

"Toren?"

His mind snapped back from the vision of large gray eyes.

Ard put a concerned arm around his cousin and asked, "Are you still thinking about going into the priesthood?"

Toren rubbed the side of his cheek, feeling the slightest hint of stubble, and smiled. "It is a decision that I'm going to have to make soon," he replied.

Ard picked up a large clump of grass and stared straight in front of him sullenly. "You certainly are thinking about it a lot. Just make up your mind already."

Toren smiled at his friend, knowing Ard's impatience with indecision. "Well, this time I wasn't thinking about that."

"Really?"

"I was just remembering when Calt's father threw me off, and I was attacked by the boran. That was the last time I was in this part of Harkan."

Ard chuckled. "You know, no one ever really believed your story about that Seerling."

"I know, but I swear it's true. She did save me."

"Well, no Seerling has bothered to try that again. Only yesterday I heard of twenty hunters who were accosted by Seerling women. Only one escaped. He said they were fierce fighters. I don't believe his eyes have yet recovered from their magic fire," Ard explained.

"Realgar." Toren stretched back. "It wasn't magic, just realgar."

Ard cocked his head. "What's realgar?"

"Remember what I told you about the flashing light that Astril used to frighten off the boran?" Ard nodded his head as Toren went on, "She made it out of ground rock and special salt. I found it all in her cave. She didn't even seem to care when I told her that I found it. It's not real magic." He sat and thought for a moment. "If we could find a way to block the realgar light from hurting our eyes, we could stop them."

Both young men sat engrossed in their own thoughts before Ard finally asked, "Was she ugly?"

Toren glared at him in surprise and stuttered, "What? No, of course not. Why would you ask such a thing?"

Ard chuckled nervously. "Well… the hunter said that the Seerlings he saw were all women." He stopped talking and played with a glade of grass.

Toren looked at him impatiently. "And…"

Looking up at him, Ard grinned. "Well, he said they were smaller than our women, you know, shorter. He said they were all very thin and had long, light hair. He said they were… well… strangely beautiful. What did the girl who saved you look like?"

The abrupt question threw Toren off. "Uh, I don't know." As he chose his words, he picked up a pebble and tossed it on the ground near Calt, whose only response was to twitch an ear. "She was a girl. She had lighter hair than I have ever seen and deep gray eyes that flashed when she got angry. Why do you care anyway? I thought you didn't believe my story."

Ard's face turned bright red as he dug his left toe into the ground. "Oh, I don't know. I was just wondering."

Toren sighed slowly and stood up. "Well, it's done and over, and I'm not likely to ever see her again. It's best to think on things that matter now, not events from the past."

"Things like Morgan, perhaps," Ard teased.

Now it was Toren's turn to be red faced. "Morgan is only a girl."

"A very pretty girl." Ard smiled.

"Pretty, yes. Smart, no. She is not someone I want to spend much time with."

"If your grandfather has anything to say about it, you'll spend more than time with her, Prince. I think he wants you to marry her."

"Marry Morgan? Me?" Toren sputtered, "You've got to be kidding. I am not planning a marriage anytime soon. In fact, I'm going to go to my father today and request a chance to train under Priest Augur."

Ard looked incredulously at his prince. "When did you make that decision?"

Toren smiled at him mischievously, "Just now. I'm tired of waiting. I'm going to train for the priesthood as soon as possible. Perhaps I can even leave at the end of this season's harvest."

"No prince of Harkan has ever been allowed to study under a priest. You're supposed to train in the army. How will you ever gain permission?"

Toren reached his hand out slowly and squeezed the arm of his cousin and childhood friend. "I've been training with the armies since I was able to mount a horse. Now, it is time to train my spirit. I feel in my heart that I am meant to do this. If it is the will of the One True God, then it will happen. Come, they will wonder where we've gone."

The two young men mounted their steeds and with a slap of the reins galloped toward home.

Later that evening Toren stood in the doorway of his parents' chambers after long minutes of pleading his case.

"Father, I feel a calling to train under Priest Augur at Helgard. I won't be deterred." With those words he turned on his heel and walked toward his own room.

Prince Verne hastened to walk beside Toren and laid an arm across his shoulders. With startlement, Toren realized his father had to reach up to do it. The elder prince cocked an eyebrow at his son's broadening shoulders and smiled proudly. "I know. I felt this same calling around your age, but King Kortan forbade me, and I am sure he will forbid you as well. He expects you to take my place and rule over the armies one day."

"I understand that. I know the war rages on against the Seerlings every year, but my taking a few harvests to train under Priest Augur will not change anything except my spirit." He halted, facing his father. "It will make me a better soldier and leader."

With concern flooding his dark brown eyes, Prince Verne regarded Toren. "I am not the one to convince."

"Yes, Father, I know. I have already made an audience with the king." He squared his shoulders. "I believe I will be able to convince him."

Prince Verne's gaze softened. "How tall and strong you have become. You will make a better king and a better leader than either myself or my father."

A light touch on Toren's arm caused him to turn. His mother, Emile, stood at his father's side. Taking her in his arms, Verne smiled down into her lovely face and swept an unruly brown curl of hair from her cheek as he bent down to kiss her furrowed brow. Unbidden, a vision of pale hair and a smooth brow over serious gray eyes filled Toren's mind. He pushed it away. A future Harkonian king had no business fretting over a Seerling girl.

Verne gazed at Toren for a moment, then turned his eyes once more to Emile. "Do not worry, my love. Our son is far braver and much smarter than I have ever been. He will do what is right. Even if the king's answer is no."

Her brown eyes smiled into his as she reached up to kiss him back. "He is growing so fast," she whispered.

"Yes, too fast."

The royal couple, rapt in their adoration for each other, turned from Toren and hand in hand walked into their chambers.

Toren stared after them while slowly rubbing at a knot forming in the back of his neck. The king would be well within his rights to refuse his request.

Bright and early the next morning, Prince Toren stood before his grandfather. While Toren's father was tall but slightly built, King Kortan was both tall and muscular. The dark, burly king had once been a mighty warrior, defending the honor of the One True God in a short war against the Gernons. He and his troops easily defeated the weaker, smaller race and scattered them from the borders of Harkan. The few Gernons left were now bounty hunters and mercenaries who roamed the eastern mountains.

"I believe this is what I need to do, Grandfather," Toren said. "I have made my decision."

King Kortan roared, "Last I checked it was the king who made decisions in Harkan and not young princes."

Toren flinched slightly then stiffened his back. "Yes, Grandfather, I understand. I meant no disrespect to you. I only ask that you give me two harvests to train."

King Kortan became very quiet and looked around the room, settling his gaze on his only grandchild. "And you will come back to lead the armies once you have fulfilled this quest of yours?"

Hope sprang full in Toren's chest as he nodded.

The King made a loud rumble in his throat. "Very well. I will grant my permission for you to train under Priest Augur for two harvests only." He then stopped and rubbed the side of his cheek. "Extending your knowledge by training with the priest just might be the answer we are looking for in removing the Seerling Priestess Isilian. She is a growing threat that needs stopping in whatever way possible."

Toren smiled, "I will work hard for you, Grandfather."

King Kortan raised his hand impatiently. "That is not all. I have plans for you to marry young Morgan when you return."

"What!" Toren yelped. "Grandfather, I do not wish to marry that girl."

"You will do as you are told. Now go before I change my mind about your training under the priest." The King dismissed him with a curt wave.

Toren trudged from the room as if the weight of the world had crashed down on his shoulders.

Within one phase of the moon, Toren and his company of forty men were on the road to Helgard to train under Priest Augur.

CHAPTER FIVE

hile Prince Toren trained under the priests at Helgard, Ard stayed behind and continued his training in the armies. The last two harvests had been good to him, and he had grown in both mind and stature. His brute strength won him every award in the contests held for the soldiers. He was easily the largest and most muscular in the troops and was quickly rising up the ranks to become a general. Well respected and envied, Ard was a giant of a man. As he approached a particularly ravishing young lady walking ahead of him, he flexed his biceps and admired the bulge of muscles from the corner of his eye.

With words dripping honey the fairer sex swooned for so readily, Ard spoke to the enticing creature. "Your looking especially lovely today, Miss Morgan."

Halting for only a second in her steps, the brown-haired beauty turned, gave an alluring smile, and thanked him for his kind words.

Feeling a surge of encouragement, Ard pushed his way in front of her, forcing her steps to stop. He then mischievously yanked a curl free from her hairpins. "Do you miss Prince Toren yet?"

Megan batted his hand away from her face, and lifting her nose to the air, walked past him briskly. Ard believed he saw a slight smile play at her lips as she crossed in front of him. His breath caught deep in his chest as he watched her walk through the corridor and into the kitchen.

"Master Ard," beckoned a servant who had skulked nearby, watching the exchange with envy.

Forcing himself to breathe normally, Ard turned his attention to the servant.

"King Kortan requests an audience with you."

Ard turned on his heel and quickly headed for the main hall. He knew that the polite word *request* from his great-uncle, the king, meant he had better hurry.

Upon entering the main hall Ard stopped, straightened his waistcoat, and walked toward the king's main hall attendant.

The scrawny main hall attendant gave Ard a snooty look that showed his jealousy. Ard deliberately gave the attendant a haughty smile as the man announced his name. "Your Majesty, Master Ard has come."

King Kortan quickly turned from his advisors and shooed them away with a wave of his hand. Then he addressed his nephew with pride. "Ard, my boy, come here. I want to speak with you about a matter of great importance."

Feeling his forehead bead up with sweat, Ard quickly walked toward the throne and knelt before his king.

After what seemed only a few moments, Ard was ushered out of the main hall to go and pick out his troops.

"Did the king really give me my own troop of men?" he whispered to himself. Then reassuring himself that he remembered correctly, Ard stood straighter and smiled. "To think, I am only twenty-one harvests old and already a general with the command of thirty men." With that thought Ard hastened his pace.

After choosing the best young men he could find, Ard reentered the castle grounds and marched toward the servants' quarters to find an attendant. Not far from his destination he changed his mind, turned direction, and headed toward the women's chambers.

"After all, I have to tell someone the king has finally paid tribute to my talents," he said with a laugh.

Finding himself at the proper door, Ard knocked twice. A female attendant opened.

Flashing a bright smile at the girl and forcing his hand to stay at his side rather than stroke her bare arm, he said, "I am here to see your mistress." At the servant's questioning look, Ard added, "Please tell her that *General* Ard is here."

After a short wait, Morgan entered the room, looking striking in an emerald gown. He noticed with satisfaction that the color of the dress helped emphasize the small green specks that hid within her brown eyes.

"General Ard?" she questioned in a teasing tone, then seating herself at the table, waved a hand for the young servant to bring tea. "Would you care to join me, General?"

Grinning wide to display his splendid teeth, he sat down. Although attempting to be on his best behavior, Ard, making sure that Morgan was not paying attention, couldn't resist allowing his right forefinger to brush the bare arm of the servant as she placed the steaming cup in front of him.

Morgan dripped a small amount of honey in her own tea. She returned his smile. "So, when did King Kortan make you a general?"

With a swelling of his chest in pride, Ard went on to tell Morgan about the commission he had been given and how he was going to pick out just the right men for his mission.

"And what is the mission that the king has sent you on?" Morgan politely asked.

"He has appointed me to take my men and spy on the Seerlings on their own land."

Morgan demurely touched her hand to her throat. "My, that will be dangerous, and you so young."

"The king has great faith in my ability, or he would not have given me such an opportunity." Ard envisioned the battles he would soon lead his men into, and the victories that would be his. Everyone would know his greatness. Morgan would be his.

The two went on for a while longer, speaking of his upcoming adventure and plans for spying on the evil Seerlings. Ard confided in her the plans that Prince Toren had sent him that laid out the directions for making eye guards for the men and horses.

"If these work, we will have an edge in our battles against the Seerlings." During the conversation Ard prided himself on leering at the pretty servant only twice while Morgan wasn't looking.

All too soon, Morgan stood and politely motioned him toward the door. She held her hand out to wave him good-bye. Instead of simply leaving as he would have before such an auspicious promotion, he took it and kissed the tips of her fingers.

"Ard," she stuttered, snatching her hand from his. "That's improper."

Ard laughed. "What is improper between such good friends?"

A cloud passed over her face as she whispered, "You know the king has kept me away for Prince Toren. I must keep myself for the prince and none other."

At the mention of Toren's name, Ard's joviality soured. He grabbed hold of Morgan's waist and pulled her tightly against his own body. "And would you keep yourself for him if I told you that Toren doesn't want you?"

Morgan braced her arms against his chest and pushed him away. He gasped at her audacity. Didn't she understand how important he was? How powerful? She took only a second to glare straight through him then scurried inside and slammed the door.

"Stupid girl," he growled.

Bolting the door tightly and leaning her head against it, Morgan felt true fear for the first time in her life.

"Miss Morgan, did he hurt you?" asked the servant.

Gaining her composure and turning to Lea, who had been her faithful companion and friend for more than ten harvests, she answered, "No, I am not hurt. Only a little shaken."

"What has gotten into that man?" muttered her servant. "He knows better than to touch you, let alone do what he did. If the king knew about this, he could have Ard put to death."

"I have always believed him to be a merciless flirt until now." Morgan said, still shaken. "What am I going to do?"

Lea walked over and placed her arm around her mistress's neck. "You did nothing wrong. Do not fear for your own safety. He is the one who stepped out of line."

"Yes, I know." Morgan sighed. "But that doesn't change what happened." She then sent a shaky look to her friend and added, "If only Prince Toren were here, Ard would behave better."

Sadness replaced the fear in Morgan's heart. "How can the prince justify staying to train under a priest during such a terrible time of war as this? No man I have ever known has done such a thing."

"I heard that the fighting is desperate, especially in the area of the crossroads. The Seerlings are becoming very brave in their attacks so close to our land, and King Kortan has twice sent for Prince Toren's return."

"Good, perhaps then Ard will behave himself better," Morgan replied.

The servant sat down beside her mistress and gently took her hand. "I hear from the main hall attendant that Prince Toren refused to come home."

"Doesn't he know how desperately he is needed at home?" Morgan clenched her fists in the silky fabric of her skirts. "Perhaps Ard is right after all, and the prince does not want to marry me."

"What prince wouldn't want to marry you, Miss Morgan?" questioned the faithful servant. "You have been in training since the day you were born to be Prince Toren's wife. Of all the eligible families who had daughters, you were the only one to be picked by the king himself. You are beautiful and have learned your lessons well. You know all of the prince's likes and dislikes and will make the perfect wife for him. He would be a fool to not love you."

"Oh, Lea, the things you say." Morgan chuckled, encouraged by the compliments. "Still it is going be difficult to marry a man I do not love, but how can I marry one who does not love me?"

"You do not know that. Those are the words of a vile young man who desires you for himself. He would say anything to keep your heart from Prince Toren," replied the servant. With sadness in her voice she added, "Unfortunately, I do not believe this will be the last time you have to face the advances of *General* Ard."

Morgan swallowed the fear that crept back up her throat and looked to her friend. "I believe you're right," she choked.

They sat in silence for a short time before Morgan teasingly added, "For your sake though, I think we should invest in long-sleeved smocks from now on."

Both girls covered their worry and fear with an outburst of laughter at the brazen behavior Ard had displayed.

Chapter Six

Streaks of sunlight blazed across the eastern sky as Astril held the lifeless body of her beautiful nephew. She cried out in anguish as she sat on the steep rocks just outside the cave where the Keepers worked. The sacrifices had ended. Isilian and Gallian had both been in a high spiritual state for many days thanks to the cybin they had taken.

Several days earlier, as the morning approached after the night of sacrificing, Astril watched Thauma, the mystic from the land of Olden, choose Corin, her nephew, as a Keeper. He was proudly displayed for all to see, just as every other Keeper had been. The people called out chants in his honor, and Isilian kissed his head for the first time in his very short life. The child was very pleased by the attention and smiled throughout the entire ceremony. He even smiled as Gallian cut all his golden hair from his head. Gallian had been so proud, but Astril's heart held caution so she made the decision to find out where he had been taken and see for herself what would become of him.

It didn't take Astril long to track out the path that Thauma had laid with Corin. The mystic walked with a heavy limp, favoring her right side, and the barefoot steps of Corin made their winding way easy to follow. She tracked them far into the wooded land south of Seerling, a place Astril had never gone before. Their tracks traveled up a large mountain and onto a rocky land. It was steep but she was able to maneuver her way up the rocks, arriving in a cleared area at the base of a large cave. She could hear the pinging sound of metal on rock as she entered and walked into the dim light of the cave.

"You should not be here," a hushed voice whispered close to her ear.

Astril jolted around to stand face-to-face with a young woman her own height.

The woman, her baldness indicating she was a Keeper, grabbed Astril's arm and forcefully pulled her out of the cave and back into the daylight. "This is not for you to bear. You must leave this place now," she whispered again.

Astril stared at her. "You—you look just like me. Who are you?" Even with a bald head, the woman's resemblance to Astril couldn't be ignored. Could this be her sister? But no, the woman was so aged. Still, her sister had been chosen as a Keeper when Astril was still very young. She didn't even remember her own sister's name.

The young woman touched her own face then reached and stroked Astril's hair. Her lovely gray eyes were darkly smudged and her hands were knarled by the heavy work she had endured for so long.

"I am called Elan," she whispered. "Now you really have to leave. You do not belong here."

"I'm looking for my nephew. He would be your new Keeper."

Elan turned her face to the side and coughed loudly. Once her attack had ended, she looked back at Astril and sighed. "I'm afraid he was too young to be brought here." Again, Elan turned her head to a large pile of rocks and coughed loudly.

Astril's eyes followed the gesture and widened as she beheld the crumpled body of Corin. "No!" she screamed, rushing toward him.

Elan followed closely, shushing Astril while other Keepers emerged from the cave to see what had made the sound.

Astril picked up Corin's lifeless body and cried. She then turned angry eyes upon Elan. "What happened to him?"

Elan looked around at the growing crowd of Keepers. "He was too young." She stared down at Astril, her tone cool. "He fell on the rocks. There was nothing any of us could do."

Astril looked around at the other Keepers all huddled closely together staring down at her where she sat holding the child. They all had shaven heads, hollow faces, and knarled bodies that had faced long years of hard labor. The horror and the evil smell of death turned Astril's stomach as she buried her face into the child's chest and wept.

"Corin," she cried holding his body close. "Oh, Corin, to be cut down so young."

"You must leave this place now," Elan whispered again in an agitated voice. If Thauma finds you here it will not be good."

Astril stared up at the girl then looked around at all the other faces of the Keepers. She knew their images would haunt her for the rest of her life. Drying her eyes, she picked Corin up as she stood "How can I help you?"

Elan shook her head and smiled, revealing broken teeth. "Just seeing one of our own kind has given us hope." Reaching out her hand, she touched Astril's hair again then grabbed her arm and pulled her out of the rocks. "Please leave."

Astril nodded her head and wept even harder as she walked through the small group of Keepers still carrying Corin's dead body in her arms. She looked back at them as she reached the steep cliffs. "I will return for you. I will free you from this."

The Keepers all stared at one another as Astril climbed down the cliffs while holding on to the tiny body of her nephew.

Once she reached the woods, Astril dug a shallow grave with her hands and buried the body.

Then with a fierce determination on her face she screamed aloud to the Great Goddess. "I will never give you anything!"

"Yes, you will," whispered an evil voice deep within her head.

"Where is the body of the child?"

Elan heard the heavy footsteps of the old mystic approaching and chose to ignore her question, opting instead to pretend to sleep. She braced her body against the kick she knew would come and then moaned loudly as if awakened by the pain.

"Did you want me, Thauma?" she asked innocently.

"You heard me, Elan. Where is the body?"

Again Elan feigned innocence. "What body is that you seek?"

A sound kick met her midsection, and she doubled over in pain. The knarled old mystic seized her arm and yanked her to her feet.

"Do not toy with my intelligence. Tell me now what you know and perhaps it will go easy for you."

Elan knew better than to stall any longer. She had seen what happened to those who didn't obey. "A… a girl," Elan began stuttering in fear. "A girl with hair that glistened with the rays of the moon and eyes the color of rock took him."

"Astril!" the gravely voice of the old woman exploded.

"Astril," Elan whispered softly to herself. The name felt right on her tongue, but she couldn't remember why.

A sound slap to her face brought Elan out of her daze and back to the evil reality of her situation.

"And you helped her?" questioned the mystic.

"I only told her to leave."

Thauma nodded her head slowly and then let go her hold of the young woman. "So, the seed is beginning to grow," she whispered angrily. "It won't be long now." She turned to leave but then stopped and turned abruptly around. "I have been soft on you for too long. You will no longer oversee the workers but will begin working in the mines again."

Elan shook her head fiercely, and the motion sent her into a coughing fit that left her gasping. She clasped her hands over the deep, abiding ache in her chest. "Please, Mystic, punish me in another way."

"Maybe you will survive the mines and maybe you won't. Perhaps you should have thought of that before you decided to help your sister."

Elan watched in amazement as the mystic hobbled away.

The knowledge of what her future held could not dampen the unexpected stirring in her heart. It was a feeling she had never experienced. It was the feeling of love.

"Sister," she whispered softly to herself. "Astril is my sister." She lay down with her head on a rock and stared at the stars above. "I have a family out there somewhere. I have a sister, and she promised to come back for me."

Many moons after Astril's return home, Isilian called for her eldest daughter's company.

"Astril," she began. "I'm not going to ask where you have been all this time."

"Then I will tell you anyway, Mother." She had promised herself that the next time she had an audience with her mother she would tell her everything, not caring what the outcome would be. "I followed the tracks of the mystic and found the land of the Keepers."

Isilian turned her head away from her daughter and muttered, "That was a very foolish thing to do."

"Do you know what I found?"

Isilian ignored her daughter and began lighting incense around the golden statue of the Great Goddess.

"Corin is dead."

At her abrupt words, Isilian turned and showed genuine concern on her face. It was the first time that Astril had ever seen such an emotion cross her mother's face, and it caused her to pause for a moment.

"He was killed climbing the steep rocks."

Isilian's hand shook slightly as she touched her face then looked back up at the statue. "These things happen," she replied in a soft voice while keeping her eyes focused on the statue.

"These things happen!" Astril cried as she crossed to stand in front of her mother. "Elan was there, mother. Do you know how they are treating her?" Astril watched her mother's face closely as recognition at the name crossed over it, causing it to take on a bluish, sickly color. It was that look that put a new resolve in Astril's heart and convinced her completely who Elan really was.

"So she lives," Isilian whispered while staring over Astril's head.

"You call that living!" Astril screamed. "How could you send her there? How can you send any of the Seerling children there? They believe that the Keepers are noble and highly treated. They're all just slaves."

"They serve a higher purpose, Astril."

"Oh, really! What purpose would force them to mine the mountain caves?"

Isilian cried out with despair in her voice, "How do you think we get the realgar for our magic lights, Astril? How do you think we get the cybin that we use to commune with the Great Goddess? Sacrifices must be paid. You may think it is tragic, but there is no other way. It has always been thus."

Astril stood shaking her head as Isilian sidestepped her and then stared devotedly up at the statue.

"It's wrong," Astril cried out. "How can you serve a god who commands such heavy prices from her people?"

Isilian raised her arms. Astril knew that the evil on her mother's face would lead to a harsh reprimand, and she closed her eyes and braced herself against the expected blow.

It did not come. When Astril opened her eyes, Isilian let her hands drop to her sides and merely sighed. "I did not call you here to repeat old arguments, Astril. I have a far more important topic to discuss with you."

Astril opened her eyes and stared up at her mother, who had taken on an unusually calm demeanor.

"I understand you have refused your training as a priestess yet again."

Astril nodded. Every sacrifice since the time of her grandmother's death, Astril had rejected her training. She chose instead to live her life as a soldier. She worked hard to develop her skills and learned a mastery over the staff that surpassed even the most seasoned warriors. The staff had become an extension of her body. It had become so natural for her to wield the staff that she was rarely seen without it. Young and old, Seerlings flocked to Astril for training in the art.

"The Harkonians have become very bold recently. They have sent their spies deep past the crossroads into our lands. This cannot be allowed." Isilian's eyes glittered. "You will take your company of fighters and make an example of them once and for all. Kill all the Harkonians you find close to the crossroads. Do not leave even one alive."

"May I speak, Mother?"

Turning a questioning look at her daughter, Isilian slanted her eyes then nodded.

"I believe the attacks are taking place because you ordered the soldiers to remove all Harkonian farmers that were close to our lands," she said. "You ordered us to cross their lands first."

"Astril, do not question me again, only do as I have said." Isilian stalked away. She stopped mid stride and jerked her head back toward her daughter, "I do not care that you are widely known as a great soldier, Astril. That accomplishment means nothing to me. You have let me down many times. Perhaps you will one day redeem yourself. Until that time, go and make yourself useful. Annihilate every Harkonian that crosses your path."

Astril knew it was worthless to argue further, so she nodded her head in compliance and quickly turned to do her mother's bidding.

As she left the inner room, her mother hissed her name.

Astril paused, her battle plans already half formed and the promise she'd made to her sister shining before her.

"Do not ever return to the land of the Keepers."

It took three long days for Astril and her company of thirty male and female fighters to reach the crossing where Seerling land met Harkan. They had not seen anyone during their journey but had found horses' tracks heading southwest.

Astril knew the marks were days old and made the decision to wait for their return. She sent four of her soldiers to stealthily approach the bridge before the crossroads and prepare a firestorm of realgar bombs, which they would use for the attack.

Turning to one of her men, Astril laid out her plan. "It won't be long before they return. There is nothing southwest of here except forest. They will be tired from their journey and will not expect an attack so close to their own border."

The soldier nodded his agreement and turned to fulfill her order.

"Tell them also to not throw their bombs until they hear my cry." Astril surveyed the dense brush that concealed her highly trained warriors—not a staff or blonde head could be seen. "Once they are blinded we will bring them down. My mother wants proof, so take an ear off of each man you kill."

"Yes, Astril," the man replied as he silently melted into the landscape to tell the others.

She waited in the seclusion of a bush with only her staff and line of realgar bombs. The company of Seerling fighters waited through the early morning hours and into the afternoon, never leaving their positions. Seerlings were taught as young children to ignore their physical needs in order to remain in complete silence for long periods of time. It was a game they played that prepared them for battle as adults.

From her position, Astril heard the sound of hooves approaching the bridge. She waited until the final horse and rider crossed before giving the call for attack.

"Now," she screamed, throwing her bombs in succession toward the Harkonian army. After the last of the flashing lights had subsided, Astril jumped up and used the end of her staff to propel her body through the air. Flying feet first, she kicked a Harkonian soldier off of his steed.

The Seerlings were used to being outnumbered in their attacks against the Harkonians; with the realgar lights, one Seerling could easily cut down ten or twenty enemies. Yet these Harkonians advanced in brutal waves, each man wearing a dark covering over his eyes.

"Fight on," she screamed to her people while taking down a Harkonian that rushed toward her.

Through the lines of approaching enemy soldiers, a massive man rushed her way. His muscled body was bigger than any she had ever seen. With dark eyes, he glared at her as she took down two more men with a high swing of her staff. Using the staff again, Astril propelled her body into the air, flying past the behemoth. The cries of fatally wounded soldiers drew her attention to her right. Hope kindled—surely her fighters had regained their advantage. She spared a glance in that direction. Horrified, she saw five of her people lying pooled in their own blood.

Grasping a second staff from one of the dead, Astril propelled herself again, crashing feet first into the giant Harkonian. She attacked in a similar manner two more times before he was able to grab hold of her long hair. The action caught her off balance and sent her crashing to the ground. As she scrambled to get up, his heavy body fell upon her with crushing force, pinning her to the ground.

Laughing at her through the blood that coursed down his face, the dark soldier plucked her up and confined her against his chest with one heavily muscled arm. She flailed and bashed her fist into his nose.

"Now, I have you, heathen," the bear of a man roared while strangling her into submission.

"Take the living heathens back to King Kortan," he ordered his men, then gripped Astril's chin and forced her to look at him. He smiled full in her face. "That was the most pleasurable fight I have ever had."

Fury fired her thoughts as she fought with all her might against the hard body of the giant. She felt herself falling back to the ground as he doubled over from the impact of her well-placed kick.

"Get back here," he grunted, grabbing Astril's waist just before she escaped. Then turning to his men, he yelled, "Tie her arms behind her back. We will take her along with the others back to the king."

Chapter Seven

I want to stay and train longer." Toren spoke softly to Priest Augur. "I have learned so much about the One True God, and I want to know more."

"Prince," the priest said, "you have fulfilled your time that was promised. Your grandfather expects your return soon. Besides, your father and mother are anxiously waiting. With your father's illness coming on so suddenly, you are needed at home."

"I know. My heart is torn. I want to fulfill my duty to them, but I know there is so much more I need to learn from you." The prince's shoulders slumped.

The old priest extended his hand to the younger man. "You cannot go against your grandfather again. This is the third time he has beckoned you, and I do not believe his patience will last much longer. You are strong and have learned much. I know you will do the right thing."

Toren gave him a shaky smile. "I will leave for home tomorrow."

"Finally, a break through the lines of the enemy." King Kortan chuckled in delight as he reviewed the slaves. "Although they are smaller than I imagined, this is a fine group of Seerlings. However did your men manage to capture so many, Ard?"

The victory still heated the blood in Ard's veins. He threw his shoulders back. "My king, the cowards sought to ambush our troops as we passed the crossroads, and under my leadership our men were ready. Once I told them the flashes of light and loud booms are not magic, they were able to shake off their fear and fight. We now carry with us specially made visors that protect our eyes from the flashes of light of the Seerling trickery. Even our horses have been outfitted with flaps that can be turned down over their eyes for shade." He grinned. "The Seerlings run fast when they're scared, but we rounded up this lot without much trouble."

"Well done, well done," laughed the King as he stood closely reviewing each new slave. He smiled devilishly as his gaze stopped on a taller female. "I'm sure Prince Toren will be greatly pleased with your conquest upon his return."

The king knew very well who had first learned of the Seerlings' use of realgar, and Ard was not about to be caught taking credit and thus risk the king's indifference.

"Thank you, my Lord, but I cannot take the credit alone." Ard quickly explained, "It was Prince Toren who wrote me, giving clear instructions as to how to make the visors and horse flaps. Before he left for training, he taught me to not fear their so-called magic. I merely saw that my men implemented the plan." The king would no doubt realize Ard was a man of action, while his cousin had merely whiled away two harvests at the feet of a priest. Toren had always chosen to favor intellect and spirit over brute force. Ard knew that his own passion for fight was favorable to the king, and he wanted to make sure he kept that favor.

The King smiled in further delight as he fingered the hair of the female Seerling before him. "Prince Toren, you say. I shall have to reward him dearly." The King, seemingly oblivious to his failure to reward the one most deserving, then turned to Ard. "Take these dirty heathens to be washed. Now that they are under submission I think we can put them to use in the fields."

Holding back his resentment, Ard warned, "You will need to keep them chained at all times, my king. Even though we have mercilessly beaten them down, I believe they pose a great threat if freed."

"Yes," said the King absently, still fingering the unusually light hair of the Seerling girl before him. "You are right. Still, take them to be bathed. I don't want filth of this magnitude on any part of my land." He paused to leer at the girl. "This Seerling has unusual hair. Wouldn't you agree?"

With a large smile and a knowing look, Ard answered, "Yes, my lord."

"I think I would like to have it." King Kortan smiled back at him. "Take her to the women. Have her cleaned thoroughly, wash this hair three times, and then chop it off. Bring it back to me." He laughed at the flashes of hate that ran deep in the large, gray eyes of the Seerling girl. "That feisty nature will soon be beaten out of you, heathen." The king's open hand met her face in a loud slap.

Ard grabbed the girl from behind and with the assistance of his men herded the slaves out of the royal conference room.

"Toren, you're home." Princess Emile dashed toward her son in a most unladylike manner that made him chuckle. "Oh, how I've missed you. Come, your father and grandfather will want to see you too."

Toren allowed his mother to drag him into the palace, through the main hall, and into the royal conference room. A loud cheer went up among the men in the room as he entered and smiled in the direction of his father, who sat stooped over at the right of the king. Large black circles could be clearly seen under the soft brown eyes of the elder prince.

"The prince has returned," cried his grandfather's attendant, running down the stairs to greet Toren.

"Ahem." His grandfather scowled, his twinkling eyes belying his disapproval. "You are later than I had expected, young prince."

"I'm sorry, Grandfather."

His grandfather smiled down upon him. "If it were not for the good news I have just received, I would not forgive you."

Toren smiled and waited.

"I hear I must reward you rather than punish your disobedience."

Surprise filled Toren as he looked to his grandfather. "A reward?"

"Yes, a reward for the wondrous plan you came up with to ward off attacks from the Seerlings. Because of your ingenuity, Ard's men captured fifteen Seerlings for field slaves."

Toren wisely guarded the cloud that flashed over his eyes. During his time with Priest Augur, he had come to despise the practice of keeping an enemy as a slave. His parents had never liked the practice and even spoke about it in their own chambers while Toren was present. However, it was not until his two harvests with the priests that he began to understand how selfish and degrading slavery truly was.

The King continued his praise. "As a reward for your faithful service while away—and in the hearing of all this company—I grant you, Prince Toren, a gift of your own choosing."

Toren laughed. "A gift of my own choosing?"

The King looked around the room at his loyal subjects and proudly exclaimed, "Yes, any gift you so choose, even up to a quarter of the realm to rule. Think long and hard over your decision, my son."

Toren was reflecting on the fact that his grandfather had called him his son when a servant entered the room from the left, and walking over to the King, held out a silver tray for approval.

King Kortan removed the lid. "Ah, Emile, now this is a fine sight you might like." Laughing, he picked up the item and handed it to his daughter-in-law.

"What is it, my lord?" Princess Emile studied the glistening, rope-like object.

Prince Toren approached the throne from the side, recognition slowly registering in his mind.

"It is a braid of hair, my dear," the King chuckled. "I had it washed and then cut off an especially challenging young Seerling girl."

"It is such an unusual color," Princess Emile commented while a look of horror flashed across her face. "Not quit the color of wheat and yet not white." She held the braid between her thumb and forefinger.

"Yes, I know. All the other Seerlings have a dirty color to their hair. But this hair is quit beautiful," said the king. "I think I might have it braided into a rug for my bedchamber floor. It is especially soft, don't you think?" The king then made a comment about keeping the girl alive to grow more hair, which brought a chuckle up from the rulers in the room.

The princess nodded her head then turned slightly away from the offending object in her hand and gave it back to the king.

"Tell me what has become of the Seerling who donated that hair to the king," Toren whispered into the ear of his grandfather's attendant.

The attendant shrugged. "I suppose she has been sent to the fields with the other slaves."

Toren glared down at the shorter man. "Take me to her."

Toren waited impatiently in the kitchen quarters until three men dragged a Seerling waif into the room. Her thin stature did not match the fierceness of her struggle as she fought against the strong arms of the men.

"She's a wild one," the servant observed loudly.

"Bring her here," Prince Toren ordered. "And do not hurt her."

The men firmly held the girl in place and forced her to stand before the prince all the while flinching at the painful jabs she occasionally landed.

Toren closed his eyes and sighed as the fighting continued. It was some minutes before the guards were able to subdue the small young woman.

Two men stood at her sides and one stood behind, forcing her head downward in a sign of submission to the prince.

Toren waved the third man off and gently ordered the girl to look at him. When she ignored his command and kept her head down, the soldier behind her yanked her shoulder-length hair.

Toren grabbed his arm in a vise-like grip to prevent any further harm. "Don't!"

Again, the prince spoke gently, and asking the girl to look up at him, took his forefinger and lifted her chin.

He took a step backward in shock as familiar gray eyes flashed hate in his direction.

"Astril?"

It took only a moment for the hate in her eyes to transform into confusion and then recognition.

"Astril, I am so very sorry," he said gently then ordered the men to release their hold on her. All three of the guards looked at him incredulously but obeyed.

Once free, Astril did not turn to run. Instead she glared around at the guards who had held her in place. While staring at the guard on her left, Astril unexpectedly and violently struck the prince with the back of her hand and with venom in her voice screamed, "I should have never saved you."

The viciousness of her words and the slap to his face caused the guards to again rush to grab her. Toren raised his hand to ward off their quick approach then wiped the blood off his lip.

Staring up at him, she continued with pain in her voice, "You used what I told you against me. If it were not for the betrayal of my words so long ago, my people would not be enslaved now." She hung her head in defeat.

Pity for the girl flowed through every vein in Toren's body. She looked so small and frail standing before him; such a contrast to the tall, bold girl he remembered. Once she had stood taller than he, now her head barely reached the top of his shoulders. His desire to protect her over whelmed his common sense and before he even thought about consequences he spoke, "Astril, I can save you."

Reaching out, he took her slender arms in his hands. She fiercely pulled away from his touch and slouched against the cool stone wall.

Toren raised his hands and slowly backed away from her. "My grandfather has promised me any gift I want for…" He halted his words then promised, "Because of what you did for me I will save you."

"Save me?" she questioned with a raised eyebrow. "My life is worth nothing because of the traitorous act I committed. Save my people and have me killed. That is what you can do in return for the *gift* I gave you."

"No, my grandfather would never allow fifteen rewards in return for the gift I gave him. He will allow only one," Toren explained as he grabbed her hand and dragged her past the guards and through the hall. His quick action startled her so that she did not fight on the way to the royal conference room. By that time the guards had caught up and ominously walked beside them, blocking any attempt she may have had to run.

The prince burst through the doors, shocking the entire party inside the meeting room.

"Toren, what are you doing?" thundered the king.

Toren dragged Astril in front of the throne, and making a quick bow of his head, forced her to stand at his side.

"Grandfather, in the company of these people, you promised me one gift for my actions while away in training."

A gleeful leer passed before his grandfather's eyes as he looked at the young prince and the slave. "I suppose you want this slave as your gift."

Toren glared at his grandfather, and holding Astril's wiggling form tightly at his side with one arm, slowly nodded yes.

"Toren!" his father gasped. Both of his parents looked horrified at the unusual action of their son. He knew they abhorred slavery but tolerated it in the fields. His request was a great disappointment to them, but he could think of no other way to save the girl.

Toren ignored his parents' reaction and forced himself to swallow, then said to his grandfather, "King Kortan, I ask only that you give to me this slave as my reward for faithful service."

The king laughed outright, showing obvious pride in the actions of his grandson. "I grant you your gift, my son. Now, why don't you tell this company why you would choose a slave over a quarter of the realm to rule."

Toren gulped again and regained a tight grip on the fighting girl. "This is the girl who saved me from the boran when I was only ten harvests old."

The laughter in the eyes of the king quickly disappeared. "This is Isilian's daughter?"

Toren could only nod as he fought to hold Astril's violently thrashing arms.

A gasp went through the room and silence followed as all waited to hear the response of the king, who trembled in obvious fear.

Slowly he stood and walked down the steps of his throne to approach his grandson. With a look of awe and dread, he stared at the girl then cleared his throat. "Prince Toren, I promised you a gift of your choosing, and you have chosen. Take her, she is yours." Then he gave a nervous laugh. "Take care you do not leave her unguarded for long. She may slice you in the night." At that he picked up Astril's braid of hair and threw it to the floor.

"Take her out of my sight," the king ordered as he turned to walk back up the stairs to his throne.

Toren did not move but only stood watching the king.

"Is there something more?" King Kortan bellowed out.

The bravery he had displayed before drained from Toren's face, but he stood his ground. "I would like to make a decree in the presence of this company."

All was extremely silent as Prince Toren spoke. "In the presence of this company, I, Prince Toren, do decree that this Seerling slave, who has been given rightfully to me, is now free."

Astonishment flew through the room as rage flashed over the king's face. "No!" he roared. "This I will not allow." Shaking an angry fist in Toren's direction, the king bounded down the stairs as if he were a young man again and grabbed the girl around the throat. "This is a threat to my kingdom, and it shall never be set free."

Astril fought his grip. Breaking free, she fell to the floor, and Toren quickly grabbed her by the arm and dragged her to safety behind him. "It is my right, Grandfather. She is my property now, and I choose to set her free."

His mother gasped in fear as the king's jowled face purpled and shook in anger. Trying to regain his composure, the king pleaded, "Toren, she's the daughter of our enemy and cannot be released to return to her homeland."

Prince Verne slowly rose to his feet. Every action stopped in the room as the failing prince, with the assistance of a servant, walked down to make peace between his father and son.

"My Lord," the elder prince haltingly said. "Perhaps Toren could send her to a far portion of our land. Blindfolding her for the journey will keep her from keeping her bearings or being able to return to her homeland or here." Taking a deep breath, the older prince continued, "If Toren hires an attendant and some guards, it is likely that the girl will enjoy a sense of freedom."

"I do not care for this heathen to enjoy any freedom," the king declared. "She is the daughter of my enemy. An evil of this magnitude should not be allowed to live. If the prince will not keep a close watch on his slave, then I shall have her destroyed as soon as possible."

Prince Verne held up his hand to block any retort his son might have had. "Father, I believe that the One sent her to us for a purpose. Killing her will only ignite further anger in their High Priestess," he reasoned. "Just look at the rage we ignited from her when our farmers delved too close to her lands." He shook his head. "No, I believe we should send her far from here. Perhaps she will prove useful if there is to be another battle."

Nodding his head, King Kortan reluctantly agreed. "Yes, I suppose you are correct. Killing her will only cause more problems." Then angrily looking to his grandson he said, "We can not allow her to have freedom though!"

Prince Verne waved his hand for help from the attendant and whispered, "The best course of action is to send her far from here, Father."

The king looked to his sick son with a slight nod. "That is the only thing we can do. Toren, you may take this heathen away from my sight. Take her somewhere that even I can not find her and do not let her go."

Toren looked down at the girl with compassion flooding his face and knowing that he could do no more, nodded his agreement.

King Kortan drew himself to his full height. "When you have her secure, come home and begin your service with the armies."

Chapter Eight

Toren took a deep breath after escorting Astril to the hall. "I'm sorry I could not do more for you."

Turning hate-filled eyes upon him, Astril spit out, "Why did you do that? I told you that my life is worth nothing now." She turned away from him, leaned her forehead against the wall, and let out a strangled moan.

Toren stared at the strange young woman and was desperately trying to sort out the confusing feelings he felt inside his heart when a servant interrupted. "My lord." The man extended his hand, bearing the braided length of Astril's hair.

The prince accepted the braid that the servant had retrieved and dismissed him with a curt wave. He offered the shameful item to Astril and whispered, "I'm so sorry they cut your hair."

A look of disgust spread over her face as she turned back to him; she grabbed the braid and threw it to the ground. "How can you think that this would be important to me," she hissed. Her head drooped. "My life is forfeit. Once my mother hears what happened to me, it won't take her long to find out what I did. She will never stop hunting me."

Ignoring the urge to reach out and lay a comforting hand on her shoulder, Toren replied, "She will not be able to find you where we are going."

"You do not know my mother." Astril's slender form shuddered. "She has ways of finding things out. Because of the capture, she will know that someone betrayed our people, and it won't take her long to find out it was me."

"You were only a young girl helping a boy. You didn't know that this would happen. If your mother finds out, she will understand." Toren shook his head. It was impossible for him to believe that any mother, no matter how evil she appeared, could intentionally harm her own offspring.

Astril gave him an incredulous look just as Ard rounded the corner of the hall.

"There you are, old boy." Ard laughed as he pummeled his cousin in a huge bear hug.

Untangling himself from his cousin's firm grip, Toren forced a smile and shook hands with his relative and friend.

Noticing Astril for the first time, Ard nodded in her direction. "This is a fine Seerling, don't you think? You should have seen her before the king had me cut off her hair. Long and lovely, it flowed about her face like a fine, white curtain." He then smiled broadly and addressed the girl. "But it was your downfall, wasn't it?"

Forcing himself to remain calm, Toren hissed, "You did this, Ard?"

"Well, yes. The king told me to." The confusion that had spread over Ard's face quickly disappeared as he threw back his shoulders and tensed his jawline. "As a general, I do everything I am ordered."

Grabbing Astril by the arm, Toren pulled her away from Ard and beckoned for the two guards that stood in the hallway to follow them. He then gave them orders to have the female servants attend to her wounds, feed her, and give her a soft bed to sleep in for the night.

"We leave tomorrow," he said to Astril then returned his attention to the guards. "Give her a hardy breakfast and then have her dressed in boys' clothing. We will leave at first light."

The two guards flanked Astril on either side and took hold of her arms. Imploringly she glanced up at Toren then dropped her eyes to the floor. She looked so small and frightened, like a wild animal caught in a trap; a trap of Toren's making.

"Everything will be fine. I promise." He lightly placed his hand on her shoulder, and she shied away. A motion that brought even deeper feelings of sympathy out of him, strengthening his resolve to save her.

Straightening his back, Toren turned to the guards and ordered, "Protect the door to her room and do not hurt her."

"Prince Toren is home, Miss Morgan," Lea gasped as she ran into their chambers. "He is far more handsome than before. His hair has gotten darker and the boyish curls have all but disappeared, and he's almost as tall as General Ard."

Morgan sat up on the bed and smiled at her servant. "Calm down, Lea. Now help me get dressed. I will wear green because it is his favorite color," she ordered.

Within a few hours, she was presentable enough to go searching for her prince.

***

"He did what?" Morgan questioned Holan, the king's main hall attendant. "When does he leave again?"

"I'm not sure, but he seemed to be in haste to remove the Seerling from here." The attendant winked as though he shared a juicy bit of gossip.

Morgan turned away from the attendant and slowly walked back to her own room. She was deep in thought over the tale she had heard and did not take care to guard her posture. She was tall even for a Harkonian woman and had to really take care not to stoop. When she was caught stooping as a young girl her mother would place a long stick in the shoulders of her gown and force her to walk around for hours.

"What has caused such a downcast look upon your lovely face," a deep voice murmured, tickling her ear.

Wishing she could pick up her speed and run away from General Ard, Morgan politely slowed her pace, her face frozen in a stiff smile.

He leered at her. "Have you heard the news?"

"Yes," she replied. "But I am puzzled over it all. Why would Prince Toren care about the life of a Seerling?"

Ard boldly looked her up and down until she regretted the effort she had made to look pleasing for the prince. "I have just found out that the slave is the one he raved about for so long." At her puzzled look he continued, "Remember, the one who he claimed saved his life from the boran."

Catching her breath and throwing her hand to her mouth, Morgan shuddered. "She was real?"

"I suppose so," Ard replied. "And exceedingly beautiful. Uh, for a small Seerling, of course."

Heat rushed to Morgan's face, and she looked down, pretending to adjust the sleeve of her gown. "Do you suppose he is in love with her?"

Ard gave her a long, appraising glance then shrugged his shoulders and chuckled.

"I told you before that the prince does not love you." His words were like a harsh slap to the face. Shaking her head, she was still reeling from their impact when he pulled her toward him in an embrace. Whispering in her ear he asked, "How long will it take until you give up your hope in him?"

Morgan gasped at his bold actions and jerked free of his hold. "Do not touch me again, or I shall tell the king." She ran with all of her might down the hall and into her chambers, locking the door behind her.

Safe in her room, she mulled over her situation. With Prince Toren gone, Ard would surely continue his advances. She cringed. How long could she ward him off? She knew she had to figure out a way to get him far from her.

And what of Prince Toren? Not one of her lessons had prepared her for the possibility that he might fall in love with another. At dinner that night, she would employ every teaching she had ever learned to beguile her distracted prince.

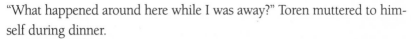

"What happened around here while I was away?" Toren muttered to himself during dinner.

"My lord, did you speak?" Morgan asked as she seductively fluttered her long eyelashes.

Looking her full in the face for the first time all night, Toren settled his gaze on her red lips. *Is that her natural color,* he thought while continuing to take in the beauty of her face. He looked down at her bare arms and felt an itching in his hand to stroke the soft, white skin. *Marrying her wouldn't be so bad, would it?* Toren realized for the first time that the young Morgan had grown into a great beauty—and was available to him at any time he so chose. The realization sent a shudder through his spine, and heat lit up his face. *After all the time I spent in the training of the priests, how can I have such thoughts? he berated himself. You do not love her, Toren. She is not your wife yet. Thinking such thoughts is evil. Just be nice and pay attention to her. After all, it's what your grandfather wants.*

No matter how hard he tried to concentrate on the attentions of the dark-haired beauty beside him, his thoughts went back to the poor, desperate girl he felt compelled to save. *Is it wise to take Astril across the country, all the way to Priest Augur? The war is far worse than I knew, and I need to be here fighting. No, even Grandfather agreed that her presence here will make things far worse for Harkan, and I won't send her back to her mother. The only thing I can do is take her to the priests,*

His tortured thoughts were eased for a moment as a servant approached to his left. Reaching to take a letter off of a silver tray that the servant held out, Toren half listened to the prattling words of the young woman beside him. Politely smiling at her, he slightly turned his body away and opened the letter.

My Dearest Son:

I realize this letter will come as a shock to you. I can not believe I am writing it myself, but I must ask you to take heed of my words

*and take Ard with you on your quest tomorrow. Please do not ask me
why, only do as I bid.*

*I am in constant prayer for your safety. I know you will make
right decisions no matter what the challenges may be.*

In the name of the One True God,

Your mother,

Emile

Toren closed the unusual missive, and forcing a smile again at the girl
beside him, turned his face just in time to see a dark cloud settle over the
eyes of his old friend Ard.

Chapter Nine

S tanding outside in the early morning hours was not a habit of Morgan's, but she felt it important to say good-bye to the prince; her future husband.

It's too cold out here. I wish I were tucked snugly in bed, she thought. The sight of the extremely large general made her breath catch in her throat and her shoulder shudder in remembrance of the horrible look on Ard's face the night before when he was told that he would accompany Toren on his quest to remove the Seerling slave from Harkan. *He must know I told.* She shuddered. *Well, it's not my fault he can't keep his hands to himself. It serves him right, and maybe now I can have peace.*

Morgan stood with her servant, Lea, at her side waiting for Prince Toren to usher out the heathen. Her sleep last night had been often interrupted with thoughts of the slave. She knew by the tenseness of the castle staff that everyone was itching to have the girl removed from their presence. Everyone realized that keeping her close was a threat to their safety. *I know it's important that Prince Toren get her away from here, but why can't he just let Ard take her?*

Morgan's thoughts were interrupted by the sight of five soldiers surrounding a small, thin girl walking out of the side door of the servants' chambers.

"Why is there a need for five of them? She seems so small," she pondered quietly.

"What did you say?" Lea asked.

Turning to face her loyal attendant, Morgan pasted a fake smile on her lips and answered, "One can hardly see what she looks like, all closed in among those men."

At that moment a man's yell went up, and two other soldiers rushed forward. Morgan and her servant stood transfixed as seven men pounced upon the savagely thrashing girl a mere five feet in front of them.

Once they had her well in hand, Morgan was given a clearer view to observe the unusual girl.

"Ohhhh, she's lovely," Lea stuttered, then catching her words sent her mistress a look that pleaded forgiveness.

Morgan shook her head and gave a small wave of her hand as if batting Lea's words away from her ear. She had to admit that the unusual-looking young woman was lovely even though she was small and thin. Her striking features were emphasized by the halo of light-colored hair that had been cut short to her shoulders. Absently reaching a hand to her own long, brown curls, Morgan shuddered as she remembered the story of what Ard had done for the king.

As the soldiers stopped to await the carriage that would transport the slave, Morgan was able to review her features more closely. The defeated girl before her had a thin face with very high cheekbones. Morgan stood amazed at how tan the slave's skin was compared to her own ivory complexion. She was still staring intently into the girl's face when large, gray eyes looked toward her. Brown eyes met gray as the two girls stood staring at one another. The intensity of the look made Morgan feel as though the girl could see right through to her very soul, and the thought filled her with fear. Still, she could not turn away.

It was not until Prince Toren strolled between them that the spell broke. Toren, with Ard by his side, seemed oblivious to what had taken place between the two women.

"Miss Morgan," he said with a hint of concern in his voice, "what brings you out of your comfortable bed so early in the morning?"

Morgan tore her gaze from that of the Seerling. She seductively approached her prince and took his arm, pressing her body into his side. "I came to say good-bye to you, my lord," she said with a breathless air.

"How nice, but not necessary," he responded with kindness.

Why does it have to be so cold out here? Morgan thought while staring up into the prince's dark brown eyes. All of her years of training to be his wife had taught her well how to hide her own feelings and appear to focus entirely upon him. Still she could not keep herself from shuddering slightly due to the cold. *Lea should have given me a heavier shawl to wear.* She resisted the urge to send her maidservant a rebuking look and instead smiled sweetly up at the prince in an attempt to keep his focus away from the Seerling.

"You're cold. Perhaps you should go back inside the castle before you get sick," Prince Toren spoke with a calm concern in his voice.

Still smiling up at him, Morgan lightly touched his chest with her right hand and giggled. "I could never be cold when you're around." She chose to ignore the annoyed look that quickly passed over his face. It was a look that she was becoming accustomed to seeing. *That will change when we're married,* she silently reassured herself.

"She's to be his wife, you know. Don't they make a cute pair?"

Astril knew without turning that the deep, sarcastic voice belonged to the giant who had originally captured her. Every fiber of her body burned to get away from the strong arms of the two soldiers who held her in place. The large body of the dark man pressed into her from behind as his deep voice muttered close to her ear, "A Harkan prince would never allow himself to love an evil Seerling."

It was at that moment that Astril felt the grasp of the soldier to her right go slack, giving her just enough room to jump high in the air and throw her head backward in a quick motion. She was pleased to hear the loud *crack* of the giant's chin and the curse that escaped his lips. Her unexpected jump startled the two soldiers who held her in place and allowed her to free her left arm. With it she gave a quick jab to the stomach of the soldier on her right. He doubled over in pain, bending his knees slightly. She used his knee as a vaulting post, propelling her body into the air and coming down hard on his head with her elbow. An enraged roar erupted behind her, and a hard object struck the back of her head. Pain ricocheted through her body. The giant grabbed her around the waist, turned her around in midair, and threw her over his shoulder. The hit to the head and spinning motion left Astril stunned and dazed.

"Ard," Toren screamed. "What are you doing?"

Astril could hear the disgust in Ard's voice as he told Toren, "She tried to escape."

She twisted her head around and stared at Toren, who had a look of compassion on his face. Shaking his head at her, he ordered, "Put her in the carriage. Gently."

Ard carried Astril, still squirming, to the carriage, where he opened the door and threw her down on the cushioned seat. Slamming the door behind him, he leered down at her with a triumphant look on his face. "It's going to be a pleasure to break you into submission." He then brusquely chained her hands and feet with the shackles screwed into the floorboard of the carriage. After completing his task, Ard pulled a linen cloth from his pocket and crouched over her, dangling the cloth in front of her face. She felt her eyes widen, and his cruel mouth curved at her fear.

"I really wish the king hadn't made me cut off all that lovely hair," he whispered, with breath hot against her cheek.

Astril sank as far into the cushioned seat as possible, trying to get away from his touch. He stroked her cheek with his finger.

"I've never been this close to a Seerling before."

Ard was still staring intently in her face and stroking her cheek with unsettling gentleness when Astril abruptly jutted her head forward, cracking her forehead into his mouth.

"Ow!" Grunting, he wiped the blood from his mouth with a deliberately slow motion. "You little heathen." He raised his hand, and a fleeting expression of hurt clouded his gaze. In silence, he dropped his hand then picked up the linen cloth he had dropped when she struck his mouth. He tied it around her eyes before leaving the carriage.

With the scuffle settled, Toren entered the carriage and sat on the seat opposite Astril. The carriage lumbered forward. "I wish you would stop fighting. I'm trying to do what is best for you, and you are making this so much harder than it needs to be." He rested his hand for a moment on her shackled wrists.

Her only response to his touch was a slight stiffening of her posture.

"Fine." He crossed his arms over his chest. One of the women in his life wouldn't leave him alone though he'd expressed no interest in her, and the other stubbornly refused his every offer of help though she desperately needed it. Who could understand such creatures? "It seems this is destined to be a quiet trip after all."

Astril rode in silence equal to Toren's, refusing to give him pleasure by complaining of the discomfort her bonds and the lack of movement caused her. Half the day had gone by when he finally thumped the roof of their jolting conveyance.

"Stop the carriage!" he shouted to the driver, and the vehicle began to slow down. She heard him get up from the seat opposite her own, then smelled the slight scent of rain-covered woods, which unexpectedly caused her stomach to flutter softly. It was the same smell that had filled the dungee while she cared for him when he was a boy. She sensed his nearness just before his hands softly stroked her hair as he removed the linen rag from her eyes. "We will rest for a short time and take our noon meal here. Do you need to go into the woods?"

Seeing pity in his dark eyes as he removed her eye covering only fueled her anger, causing her to mull over a possible escape. She nodded her head slightly and pondered which way she would need to go. Astril had, in vain, tried to determine what direction they had been traveling for the past few hours.

Toren interrupted her frantic thoughts as he sat down on the seat beside her and with pleading eyes asked, "Can I trust you to behave if I release you from your chains?"

A mere nod of her head would give her freedom from the bonds and ensure a quick escape. But as she stared deeply into the brown pools of his eyes, she knew she could not lie and instead turned her face from him in defiance.

With his features set and unreadable, he moved to the door and ordered a length of rope. Securing her hands behind her back, he walked her out of the carriage and into the bright afternoon light. "I'm sorry. You will not be allowed to go into the woods alone," he said after ordering two soldiers to attend to her needs.

After giving them strict commands to take her into the woods and give her the privacy she needed while holding tightly to the rope, Toren walked away shaking his head.

Her humiliation was nothing in comparison to the knowledge of his disappointment in her.

"You know, she's taking a long time back there," the taller soldier said.

The shorter, stockier man looked up at his friend and snickered. "Well, who knows how she's managing with her hands tied behind her back."

The two laughed together and waited a few more minutes.

"I think we should check on her," the cautious soldier spoke while pulling hard on the rope. "She's way sturdier than she looks. I can't even get the rope to budge."

Realization flooded their faces at the same time, and they ran back to where Astril had tied the end of the rope to a tree.

"How did she... ?" The stocky soldier untied the rope and gawked at it like he'd never seen one before.

"We better find her quick," the other answered as they ran in different directions looking for Astril.

Having watched the entire display from the safety of a tall tree, Astril chuckled to herself. One of the first lessons she had learned as a girl was how to untie ropes that bound her hands together. No rope had ever been able to hold her. As a girl, she had thought it a fun game. Now the game had come in handy.

She waited until she was sure the soldiers were far from the site then jumped down and ran in the farthest direction from camp. After a short time, she stopped to check for signs as to where she might be. Shading her eyes with her right hand, Astril looked up toward the afternoon sun in an attempt to find the direction of home. She knew that Harkan land lay north east of Seerling but had no idea how far they had come or what direction they had taken.

"It's hopeless," she whispered out loud. "Where do I go now?"

Astril's attention was temporarily distracted by the sound of a twig breaking behind her. Turning back to flee from the noise, she slammed face first into the chest of the dark giant.

"I thought those two were going to need some help," he sneered down at her. Taking her by the arm, Ard tried to pull her back toward camp. Astril punched him hard in the face with her free hand and kicked him soundly in the thigh. He grunted in pain and clamped his giant arms around her.

"Stop fighting. I don't want to hurt you," he shouted just as she jutted her head forward, smacking him hard in the jaw.

Fierce anger raged over his face as his fist made contact with the side of her head. She heard the sound of someone saying, "General Ard," and felt the sensation of her body being lifted into the air just before her world went completely black.

Astril could feel a wet cloth being pressed to her head and a soft cushion beneath her. Though a light breeze and a nearby twitter of forest birds suggested she was outdoors, a squeak of springs and the stomp of a hoof told her she was back in the carriage. Her breath caught deep in her chest as she opened her eyes to see Toren's face closely hovering over her own.

"You're awake. Good." He dipped the cloth in water and wrung it out. "You shouldn't have run off like that. It's a good thing Ard found you lying in the forest. You must have hit your head on a tree while running."

Astril stared up at him with disgust.

"You need to eat something," he said while continuing to administer the wet cloth to the side of her face.

Pain shot through her head as she pulled herself upright and maneuvered her body as far away from the prince as possible. The sad sigh he let out touched her heart, but she refused to pay it any attention and instead turned far from him and huddled in a corner of the seat.

"Astril, you have to eat," he pleaded. "I don't care if you refuse to speak to me, but it's a long journey, and I don't want you to get sick."

She turned away from the bread he held to her mouth and stared at the strips of heavy cloth that draped the carriage windows.

"I will only make you wear the eye covering through tomorrow, and then I think we will be far enough away to remove it. However, the chains will have to stay." He gently covered her eyes with the linen, and sitting back on his seat, ordered the carriage driver to go.

Sighing again, Toren whispered, "One True God, am I doing the right thing here?"

Astril strained her ears to hear more of his prayer, but gave up as he let out a soft sigh. Could it be that Toren prayed to the same god her own grandmother had loved? How often had she heard that same prayer uttered? Memories of her grandmother's last request of her flooded back, and she leaned heavier against the seat back. Her heart cried out in anguish as she realized she had not kept her word to seek out the man called Augur.

What more can I do for this girl? I wish I could trust her to stay put. Doesn't she realize this is for her own good? Besides, if what she says is true about her

mother, this is the only way I can save her life. Consumed by these thoughts, Toren rode out the rest of the day in stony silence.

Many hours later he ordered a stop for the night. After the carriage slowed its pace to a halt, he removed Astril's eye covering and ordered four soldiers to assist her to the woods. This time she made no attempt to escape and gave in to the order to return back to camp, where two soldiers chained her feet and hands back inside the carriage.

The prince reentered the musty old carriage after a short time and offered her dinner.

He tensed in frustration as she again refused to eat.

"There was once a time when you didn't hate me so much," Toren reminded her as he unchained her feet and laid a pillow down so she could rest for the night.

The hate that he was becoming accustomed to seeing in her gray eyes all but disappeared. By the look she gave him, he knew she remembered their time together as children. Watching her closely, he could almost see her heart begin to soften as she sighed deeply, looked to the floor, and then lay down on the seat to sleep.

Somewhat encouraged, he gave her a small smile. "Tomorrow will be a better day. I promise." Then, with his growing admiration for the Seerling girl warring with his desire to get home and protect his family's kingdom, Toren left the carriage to sleep under the stars.

Chapter Ten

K ing Kortan sat alone in his bedchambers eating his morning meal of fresh-baked wheat biscuits with a variety of jams and jellies when his attendant opened the door and rushed to his side.

"My lord," the attendant choked. "Prince Verne is missing."

Confusion registering on his face, King Kortan dropped his biscuit, smearing strawberry preserves down the front of his white tunic. "What?"

"He left this morning to seek treatment from a neighboring Olden family, my Lord. His steed returned without him only a few moments ago."

King Kortan jumped out of his chair, and wiping the sticky residue from his tunic, rushed from his chambers to the main hall, where a flurry of activity greeted him.

Several hours later, the king was in deep discussion with two of his generals concerning their unsuccessful attempts to find the prince when a white-faced servant entered the hall.

"K-King K-Kortan..." He jerked his head back over his shoulder, eyes rolling. "Isilian, High Priestess of the Seerlings, has come to see you."

"Isilian is here?"

The side doors to the hall burst open, admitting a gust of chilly air. Immediately an extraordinarily tall Seerling woman swept into the hall, her ageless face contorted in fury. Long, dark blond hair waved freely about her. Her tan gown seemed to have a life of its own as it swirled in the magical breeze and sparkled in the firelight of the hall. She was frighteningly beautiful. She fixed the brilliance of her gaze on Kortan.

"Give me back my soldiers!" Her thundering voice sent icy shudders up his spine.

Gaining his composure in the face of the unexpected threat now buffeting his own hall, King Kortan leaped to his feet. He straightened his frame to its full height and glared down at her, ordering his men to attack. With only a small wave of her left hand, Isilian created a gale that leveled the attacking soldiers to the ground and slammed Kortan back onto his throne.

"I will not warn you again." She stilled the gust with a flick of her finger. "Give me back my people!"

King Kortan again stood and roared down at her, "I shall give you nothing."

Isilian sauntered closer to the king's throne.

Behind her, Princess Emile ran into the room. Kortan's body stiffened as he pointed his finger. "No, Emile. Get out."

Following the gesture of his hand with her eyes, Isilian glared over her right shoulder and produced an evil smile. In a movement so fast that no one had time to react, Isilian transported herself halfway across the room and trapped Emile in a cruel chokehold. Kortan's daughter-in-law gasped and clawed at the powerful woman's forearm.

Smiling at the struggling woman, the evil priestess sneered, "I can see that you are a princess among this people. Perhaps even the wife of the sick man I now hold in my possession?"

A gasp washed through the room as Isilian allowed the fainting princess to fall to the floor in a heap.

Isilian stared down at her, contempt dancing in her eyes. "Your women are useless."

She then turned her attention back to King Kortan. "I am waiting!" The force of her anger sent a tremor through the great hall, and as Kortan watched, a zigzagging crack split the tiled floor from one side of the room to the other. A supporting column teetered slightly as the crack grew larger, but it held firm, keeping the ceiling from crashing down upon them all. Kortan stood helplessly by as the tapestries depicting his many victories fell from the walls.

For the first time since he was a young man, King Kortan shook with fear. He waved a cautious hand to his servant and ordered him to bring the slaves to the main hall, all the while working to gain his composure.

Standing in the center of the room, Isilian began an unintelligible rant. She stood in place with hands to her sides, whispering words no one understood. Her eyes were half closed, but it was clear by the rigid way she held her body that she was prepared for anything and ready for battle. No one but the king dared look into her stern face. All others stood with their white faces turned away from her. The moments that passed seemed like an eternity as the king worried what the demonic woman would do once she discovered her heir was missing.

A team of soldiers ushered the ten female and four male Seerlings into the hall. Isilian waved the soldiers away with a twitch of her hand. Victory shone over her countenance as she closely reviewed each of her people.

The triumphant look on her face quickly faded as she turned from reviewing her people to face the Harkonian king. "Where is the girl?" she roared.

King Kortan sat back in his seat and folded his arms in front of him. Looking to his attendant he innocently asked, "What girl do you suppose it is that she's looking for?"

A fury of wind exploded in the room, snuffing out the fire in both fireplaces and causing Isilian's hair to fly about her face. "Do not test my patience, Kortan. Where is she?"

The king was too afraid of her reaction to lie to her about the girl and was very glad at that moment that he had never asked Toren where he was taking her. *How dare this heathen ask anything of me. Besides, it was her own daughter who betrayed her, not me,* he thought ruefully to himself. *I don't have to give her anything.*

"You can either tell me where she is or die right there on your throne." Isilian glowered at him with hands raised high above her head, ready to make good her promise.

"Ah, you must be talking about that lovely little thing that betrayed you?" he replied with a forced snicker desperately hoping she would put her powerful hands back down to her sides and leave his kingdom quickly.

Panting, Isilian looked from the king to her people, one of whom gave a slow nod of his head.

With a scream that threatened to bring the rafters down upon their heads, Isilian cried, "My daughter? Betray me? Tell me where she is now."

King Kortan drew upon every inch of bravery he could muster and truthfully answered, "I do not know."

Isilian's body writhed as she shook her hand toward the king and screamed, "Your son's life is forfeit just as is my daughter's."

Again the King mustered his bravery. "If you harm my son, your people will suffer." He nodded his head at his generals, and his soldiers placed their daggers at the throats of the Seerling slaves.

Seeming to realize that further use of her magic would endanger the lives of her own people, Isilian glared at him and folded her hands demurely at her waist.

"Your sickly son is being held at the crossroads between our lands," she said to the king. "Once I have safely reached the bridge with my people, I will order his release. Although I doubt he will live much longer anyway."

The loss of the Seerling slaves would cause little hardship to his lands. They had been nothing but trouble with their constant rebellion, but how he hated to let Isilian have the upper hand. Fear of what the woman would do if he refused her won out.

"Release the slaves." His chest ached with frustration. "We will escort the Seerling priestess and her people back to the bridge at the crossroads, where we will let them go free. I want Prince Verne back here safely."

Isilian whirled from the room and stalked out of the palace with her people in tow. Kortan and his soldiers followed at a safe distance, keeping a close eye on their every move. Upon reaching the bridge, Kortan watched in desperation as more Seerlings than he could count emerged from the foliage. Among them was his son, face ashen and body doubled over in pain.

Once past the bridge, Isilian turned her steed around, and creating a terrible dust storm with the waving of her arms, disappeared.

Only a stumbling Prince Verne remained to fall face forward on the road.

Isilian's anger drove her and her people faster than normal through the Seerling forests toward their own homeland. She forced the group to travel at great speed even though all were exhausted. More than one steed was lost to the brutal pace, but Isilian raced on with no regard for her own needs or those of her people.

Once back at the temple, she continued her rage, throwing constant questions at the exhausted soldiers before her.

"I understand that the crime was committed while she was in her time many years ago," quavered one of the women. "She must have saved the life of their young prince while he was being attacked by a boran. Sometime during the nursing process she revealed our secret fire to him."

A second soldier continued the tale. "We were captured because that same prince found a way to shield his soldiers' eyes from our realgar bombs."

Quieted for a moment, Isilian allowed her thoughts to be heard by those around her. "She left for her time angry with me over the death of her brother. It was a tragic accident, but she refused to forgive me."

"Astril would never intentionally betray you," another Seerling boldly spoke. "She was only a young girl at the time."

Glaring at her recently freed people, Isilian waved them away and turned to her daughter Gallian, who had recently been named a priestess although younger than Astril.

"Your sister has indeed committed a heavy crime, Gallian. What do you suggest I do?"

"Mother, it is obvious that Astril has never desired to fulfill her duties to become a priestess for the Great Goddess," she sneered. "You have put up with her refusals to train for far too long. She has openly defied you, has committed crimes against you, and now this, the betrayal of her own people..."

Waving a weary hand before her daughter, Isilian responded, "You are right." Sadness flitted over Isilian's eyes for only a moment as she thought of her oldest child. She knew that truth rang in the words that Gallian spoke. Astril had done everything in her power to avoid the trainings to become a priestess for the Great Goddess, but still in her heart Isilian held on to the prophesy given about the girl.

"Mother, let me bring her back here. We should sacrifice her on the altar stone. Give her to the Great Goddess."

Isilian looked hard at the dark blond woman before her. She knew that Gallian was faithful to the Great Goddess, and that Astril was not. The differences between her daughters could not be more pronounced. One had all the passion and desire to do anything for their god while the other had nothing but contempt for the old ways. Still it was Astril who owned the prophesy.

Shaking her head in frustration, Isilian made her choice. "Find her, Gallian. Bring her back to me alive. We will let the Great Goddess decide her fate."

"Yes, Mother," she said as she walked out of the temple gate. Stopping at the door and smiling she added, "She will make a wondrous sacrifice."

Sadness filled Isilian's heart as she watched her younger daughter walk out of the inner room of the temple. She reminded herself that Gallian had embraced the training; taking on the rightful role of the eldest daughter. For her efforts, Gallian had been rewarded the rights of a priestess during the last sacrifice. Allowing herself to go through the final training process to become impregnated, Gallian had valiantly given her own son to become a Keeper. She had done this because Isilian had asked her to in an attempt to force Astril into her training. At the time, Isilian believed that Gallian's sacrifice would be a blessing to her eldest child, but Astril still refused her training and had even gone to the land of the Keepers, a heavy crime in Seerling.

And to top everything off, Astril had intentionally kept herself pure, refusing to take a mate and bear a child. As an untouched child of a priestess, Astril would indeed make a great sacrifice to her goddess. No human blood had ever intentionally been spilled on the sacrifice altar, and the thought caused Isilian's shoulders to shudder in despair. Was this Astril's true destiny and the meaning of the prophesy? Isilian shook her head slowly, staring up at the face of the Great Goddess, searching for an answer.

"I thought she was to be the savior of our people," she whispered into the air.

CHAPTER ELEVEN

Astril woke in the early morning hours to the sound of a soldier screaming, "We're under attack!" Swords clanged, bellowed commands pounded the air, and arrows whizzed past the carriage. A fire arrow blazed through the window, embedding itself in the seat across from her. With a quick motion she reached for the jug of water Toren had left her earlier and doused the flames only to be met by another fire arrow flying to the floorboard. Choking smoke filled the small space. Air was becoming precious, and her sight was impaired as she desperately stamped at the fire with her bare feet. A quick rush of cool wind and a flurry at the chains on her arms told her that someone was releasing her from captivity. Fighting back the darkness that threatened to take her under, Astril felt her body being lifted out of the burning carriage.

Through burning eyes, she could make out the square jaw of Toren's face set firm in determination. Holding her tightly to himself he raced passed fighting men, winding his way into the brush far from the burning conveyance. Setting her down gently, he inspected her arms and torso for burns.

"Are you all right," Toren whispered while tenderly checking her bare feet. She had taken her boots off to rest for the night and had stamped at the fire with naked feet. Surprising them both, her feet were deeply black-ened by the soot of the fire, but no burn marks were found.

Astril nodded and stared up into his caring eyes despite the deep pain she felt in her chest.

At her reassuring nod, Toren smiled tensely. "If you are hurt, Priest Augur will know how to help you." He then jumped to his feet, grabbed his sword, and ran full thrust into the massive fight.

Did he say Augur? Is it possible that this is the same priest I promised Grandmother I would find? She scooted out of the way just in time to avoid being squashed by a falling, red-skinned man. The stench of sweat and blood permeated from his body as he clawed viciously at the wound at his throat. Astril crawled quickly out of the way, her stomach turning as she heard him take his last strangled breath.

She knew by the small, squat stature and dark red skin that the fallen enemy was a Gernon; a bounty hunter. *Are we close to their border? Why else would they attack?* Her thoughts raced. Looking up and locating where Toren was, she saw he was overwhelmed fighting four Gernon warriors. She couldn't just sit there and let him be killed!

Making her decision, Astril rose to her feet and tore loose a wooden pole that was attached to the now quickly burning carriage. She jabbed it deep into the chest of a Gernon approaching her from the side. With a few quick moves, she took down four more Gernon warriors. Masterfully using the pole as if it were a staff, she continued to fight. It was not long before she found herself standing back to back with Toren. He gave her a sideways glance as he slashed down a large Gernon warrior with his sword. Still fighting the enemy and using each other's backs as shields, Toren and Astril brought down an impressive number of enemy fighters.

The last Gernon fell to the ground in defeat as the sun climbed high in the morning sky. Exhausted, Astril knelt down and watched Toren interrogate the only enemy left alive. She watched in amazement as he ordered the man to be tied down and watched by the guards. The Seerling way was to kill all enemies and take no prisoners.

Would Toren keep him as a slave? Once he had gotten as much information as possible out of the beastly man, Toren turned and looked straight into her eyes before coming to stand in front of her.

Conflicted by her own thoughts, Astril fought the desire to run into the woods away from the approaching prince.

⁀

Why would she fight for us? Toren walked toward the slumping girl. No man he had ever seen could bring down a well-armed enemy with only a pole in his hand.

"Where did you learn to fight like that?" he questioned while checking to make sure she was not hurt.

Ignoring his inquiry, Astril rose to her feet and looked him square in the eyes. "You promised this would be a better day."

Toren felt a flicker of pleasure at her argumentative words. "So you are speaking to me now?"

At her shrug, he went on, "Why would you fight for us?"

Astril turned her face away from him.

Taking her by the forearms and forcing her to look at him, he whispered, "That was your opportunity to run off. Why didn't you?"

"It seems destiny is bringing me to this priest of yours. Who am I to fight it?" she said with a shrug of her shoulders.

Toren released his hold on her and took a step back. Was this a ruse? Why would she change her attitude so quickly? His throat choked off the air to his lungs when she innocently smiled up at him then turned and walked over to help one of the wounded Harkonian soldiers.

He stood for many minutes watching her gentle movements in caring for the man.

⁀

Toren and his company trudged on toward Helgard at a much slower pace. Although they had lost only one man to the attack, there were many wounded, including their prisoner. Even at the slower pace, the badly wounded Gernon died the following day.

Ard approached Toren and Astril as they sat around an afternoon fire eating a small meal. "The only thing he said before he died was *gallian.*"

Astril had shown little emotion and refused to speak throughout most of the trip, but at the sound of the word her eyes grew wide, and she inhaled a sharp breath.

Her reaction startled both men and Toren asked, "Do you know what *gallian* means, Astril?"

Her large gray eyes pooled with tears before she stood to walk away from the men. Ard took two quick steps in her direction, and grabbing her arm, forced her to sit back down.

"Ard, let her go." Toren walked in between the two and gently placed his hand on Astril's shoulder. "Have you heard this word before?"

She nodded her head, stood back up and then hardening her expression, glared past his shoulder at Ard.

"I told you my life is forfeit."

Still holding her gently by the shoulder, Toren asked, "Astril, what is it?"

Her face contorted in a painful expression, making it obvious to Toren that she was fighting overwhelming emotions. Closing her eyes and allowing a single tear to fall slowly down her cheek, she replied, "Gallian is my younger sister."

At her words Ard gave a loud snort and laughed then sat down and stoked the fire.

Turning flashing eyes upon him, Astril cried, "She is a priestess under the Great Goddess and has already begun her training in the real magic. Although we may seem small in your eyes, there is a great magic that dwells within her. She is very dangerous!" She then turned her face away and choked, "And not one to be laughed at."

Toren knew his face showed his confusion, and he couldn't help but ask, "I thought your people couldn't really do magic?"

"My people cannot do the real magic," Astril said levelly. "But the priestesses can. Gallian is young but very strong."

"So why can't you do this magic?" Ard sneered out the words while taking a large bite of meat.

Emotion played across her face. "I never took my training."

Toren watched her closely, taking in every word. "Why would a Gernon speak the name of your sister?"

She shrugged. "I imagine she has placed a bounty on my head." Slightly turning to glare again at Ard, she added, "and upon the heads of any who are with me."

"Your mother must know by now that you were captured by the Harkonians," Toren observed. "But how would the Gernons know you would be with Ard and I?"

Astril looked deeply into his eyes. "They wouldn't have known and wouldn't have cared. The bounty on my head must extend to all Harkonians as well. No one is safe as long as this bounty is in place."

Realization at what her words implied sank deep into Toren's heart. He shouted to his men, "We must get to Helgard quickly. Move out. Now!" With those words he hastily mounted his steed and dragged Astril up behind him, then urged the horse into a gallop toward Priest Augur's home.

I should have run away during the fighting, Astril thought while riding behind the prince. *Doesn't he realize that sending me back to my mother would cancel out the bounty? Although, with Gallian in charge, no Harkonian is safe with or without a bounty.* Pondering all of Toren's strange actions, she tightened her grip around his middle to avoid falling off the steed as they raced on toward his priests.

She cast a sideways glance at the large dark man riding at full speed to their right. A shudder involuntarily coursed through her. *Can't Toren see that Ard's blood runs evil?* She held even tighter to him as the relentless speed of the horse increased yet again.

Toren thought from the shudder he felt go through her body that Astril was cold. *I don't have time to stop and take care of her needs right now,* he thought guiltily to himself. *She probably wouldn't accept the help anyway.*

He could feel a tightening of the thin arms that held his middle and wished there was something he could do to relieve the cold that afflicted her.

Can't she see that I am only trying to fulfill the promise I made her when we were children? I can keep her from being hurt. Why can't she see that she is safe with me?

Shaking his head and then casting out all thoughts, Toren drove his steed faster in an attempt to reach Helgard before nightfall.

"One True God, please protect the priests," he muttered as he pushed his horse further on.

The full moon hung low in the western sky as Astril and Toren rushed through the open gate of a large, dark wall that surrounded several small houses. In the center of the houses stood a large building with steep stairs ascending to the door. The salty scent of big waters dwelled heavily in the air, and Astril could hear the crashing of waves in the distance. The last of the soldiers entered the compound when a tall, thin Harkonian walked out of the door of the center building and smiled down on them. He was dressed in a dark brown tunic that fell just past his knees where the same colored pants could be seen going down to his booted feet. At his waist hung a bronze-colored star with a cross in the center.

With a huge smile spreading over his face, the tall man greeted the dusty travelers.

"I did not think you would return so soon, Prince Toren," he shouted with outstretched arms.

Toren rounded his steed in the open clearing in front of the center building then jumped down to greet his mentor and friend who was quickly descending the stairs. His quick action threw Astril off balance, and she slid sideways, clutching at the saddle of the huge steed. Ard shot his hand out and grabbed the reins, giving Astril a smug smile that said he knew she'd almost fallen.

Turning her nose up at him and jumping down without assistance, Astril went to stand behind the prince.

"And who is this?" The thin man asked, staring down at her. She could tell by the look he gave her that he was confused by her presence but there was also the slightest hint of recognition that crossed over his face then faded away just as quickly as it had come, replaced by a brief stab of what she thought was pain.

Toren took two huge strides and gave the priest a giant hug. Then he turned and gestured to Astril. "I have brought you a new student, Priest Augur."

At the flustered look on the face of the older man, Toren continued, "This is Astril. I will tell you all about her soon, but now we need to get these gates closed quickly."

The priest motioned for the gates to be closed while still staring down at her with the same pained expression spread across his features. He then slowly turned his gaze back toward Toren. "I see you've heard about the attacks by the Gernons and Oldens."

"The Oldens are also attacking?" Toren incredulously asked.

"Yes, it is the strangest thing. We have lived in peace with the Oldens for as long as I have been alive. They have always been a suspicious but peaceful people. Now to face these attacks…. I just don't know," answered the priest. "There has been no direct attack on us. The villagers, however, have not been so lucky."

"The Oldens are loyal to the High Priestess," Astril interjected then squirmed slightly under the weight of the priest's stare.

Just as Toren was about to respond, a flaming arrow hissed past his ear and embedded itself in a pillar of one of the houses.

"We're under attack," Ard screamed as a non-flaming arrow spun him about, and Astril suspected from the sound of the impact, it had pierced his left shoulder blade.

Three painted Gernons frantically notched arrows to their bows just outside the closing gate. A few more arrows made their way into the court-yard before the gates were fully shut.

"Go out the side exit and do whatever you have to do to catch those mercenaries," Toren yelled at his men, who were all ready in pursuit.

"This is because of me," Astril cried turning to Toren. "Give me to them, and the bounty will be called off."

"No!" he screamed rushing to the aid of his fallen cousin then looking up to Astril and the priest cried, "Please help him." He looked down at the big man whose eyes had begun to roll backward. "I have to go, Ard. Astril and the priests will take good care of you."

"Toren, give me to the Gernons, and no one else will be hurt," Astril insisted after running to his side.

Shaking his head fiercely, Toren stood up, and rushing out the side exit with his sword in front of him, disappeared. Ard struggled to get back to his feet and attempted to follow the soldiers but ended up falling to the ground in a heap. His face turned ashen as he rolled over to his back and stared unseeing up at the sky.

Astril looked down at the dying man without moving an inch. Rushing toward him, the priest knelt down and imploringly addressed her. "I can't help him, but I know you have the power to heal. Please help me." His eyes pleaded. Relenting, Astril assisted the priest in his attempt to lift Ard to his feet.

It was impossible to lift the heavy man, but they were finally able to drag him to a bed in a side building.

"This is an unusual reaction to being struck in the shoulder by an arrow," Priest Augur commented with worry in his voice.

Tearing Ard's shirt away and grasping the arrow with both her hands, Astril broke the shaft off, leaning in for a closer look. The embedded object rose and fell rapidly with his panting breaths. Blood seeped slowly from the wound, which had become red and irritated.

"Ard, do you feel a tingling in your tongue and mouth?"

The huge man nodded his head only slightly then let out a loud, pain-filled moan. Ard's eyes grew wide as he turned and vomited up everything he had eaten for days.

"Just as I thought," she commented under her breath. "The arrow was poisoned with thung."

"What's thung?" Priest Augur said in a tone that was not completely trusting.

"Aconite… monkshood…" Astril tried to explain, then losing patience said, "those blue-hooded flowers you have growing all around your property."

"Oh," he breathlessly replied, then started praying for the man's healing.

This rambling man was the priest her grandmother had regarded so highly? "Praying to your God won't help him. I need sea plants now!"

"We, uh, I…" stammered the priest.

"I know we are near big waters." Astril worked hard to keep her patience in check. "I can smell it. Send one of your attendants out to gather as many sea plants as possible. I would prefer them to be dried, but we don't have the time. If we work quickly, we might be able to save his life." *Not that I should save him. He's such an evil man. It would be better for everyone if he died.* Astril stared down at him contemplating dark thoughts when she remembered the pained look he had given her when she rejected his touch in the carriage and how he had not wanted to hurt her in the woods after her unsuccessful escape. Even though he had punched her when she fought him, could there be some good there? *No, I can't be like my mother. I will not let this man die. I won't hurt Toren like that.*

Priest Augur looked at her with delight in his eyes. "We routinely dry kelp to be used as a seasoning on our meat. Would that work?"

"Yes, bring it here quickly." Astril deftly moved out of the way as Ard lost his stomach contents again. As the priest turned to leave the room, she added, "Bring as many cool wet cloths as you can find. He's growing a fever. And bring a sharp knife. We're going to have to dig that arrowhead out." She smiled slightly to herself then felt a stab of shame as she realized that the thought of causing him pain was not entirely unappealing to her.

CHAPTER TWELVE

*W*ell *that was a wasted trip,* Gallian thought ruefully. *Now not only do I not have Astril, but I don't even know where else to look.* Gallian and her team of soldiers had scoured the countryside as far around Harkan as they dared without turning up even one clue to her sister's whereabouts. It had been many moons of hard travel. All she wanted was a hot bath and the comfort of her adoring friends. *At least they'll know how to treat me as the priestess I truly am.*

Gallian knew that no matter what her own desires were, she had to go immediately to the temple and face her mother's wrath. It took all her courage to dismount her steed and walk over to where the High Priestess knelt in worship.

"Have you brought her home?" Isilian did not bother to turn from her prayers to the iron Great Goddess that stood guarding the temple doors.

My trip went well, thank you, Mother, Gallian silently griped. "No, High Priestess."

Isilian jumped from her kneeling position in front of the statue in an unnaturally quick motion. Slapping Gallian with the back of her hand, she screamed, "Fool child. How long must I put up with your failures?"

Holding her hand to her face in an attempt to hide the anger seething within her, Gallian lowered her voice. "It is not my fault that Astril has been allowed to live this long."

Isilian stared at her daughter with shaking hands and fiery eyes. "It is not your place to question the actions of the High Priestess, Daughter."

Wisely shading the hatred in her eyes, Gallian whispered, "Astril is a poison that needs to be drawn out, Mother. I have placed a ransom upon her head that should produce information soon."

"A ransom?"

"All Gernons and Oldens have been informed to kill any Harkonian they see." She smiled, thinking of the net she'd set to trap her traitorous sister. "Once he sees his innocent people being destroyed, Harkan's king will hand her over."

Rage seemed to fly up from every pore of Isilian's body as she forced a terrible windstorm to rush through the open courtyard in front of the temple. "If I could kill you now, I would," she screamed while Gallian bent her body against the force of the gale.

"Idiot! Remove the ransom immediately before we lose any more of our people."

Gallian slowly rose to her feet and raised her arms above her head, stretched her hands out wide and forced her mother's raging wind to a stop.

The features of the older woman slackened before she regained control and continued, "Enormous numbers of our people have been killed because of your foolish action, Gallian. Instead of turning her over, the Harkonian king has retaliated and destroyed untold numbers from the tribes living close to the crossroads. I desired you to quietly search her out and bring her to me."

Isilian turned away from her youngest daughter and stalked into the temple. Turning to face Gallian one last time, she cried, "Call the ransom off and find her yourself."

Gallian watched the High Priestess walk into the temple then stared down at her own hands. *How was I able to stop mother's torrent? Could it have been fear that I saw in her eyes?*

Turning on her heel, she screamed for Cauldon, one of the Seerlings' best spies.

"Yes, Priestess." The man scurried before her.

"My mother wants the attacks on the Harkonians to stop." Then in an afterthought she asked, "How many of our people have we lost to the onslaught of fighting?"

"The Harkonians are determined, Priestess. They know that it was we who called the ransom and thus have narrowed massive attacks on our lands. The crossroads are especially dangerous."

Losing her patience with the nonanswer, Gallian roared, "How many have we lost?"

"At last count, Priestess, we have lost two hundred twelve able-bodied men and women from three different tribes, as well as fifty-seven children. We believe there are less than half that number that have been taken as slaves."

My ransom isn't working. I should have known better than to call for aid from heathens. Hatred for her sister fueled her forward as she ordered Cauldon to gather his best spies for the task at hand.

"Be ready to leave at the darkest hour of the night," she ordered.

Staring at her hands with a new sense of awareness as Cauldon ran to do her bidding, Gallian whispered, "I hope you are ready for me, Sister."

She will destroy you, Isilian's thoughts taunted her. *You should have given her as a Keeper. Instead you killed your own son.*

"I never intended to harm Kellon," Isilian cried out.

You killed him and in your cowardice allowed Gallian to give her own son to me, and now that child is also dead. Your love for your wayward eldest child has blinded you. You should have given Gallian long ago. That sacrifice would have lead Astril into her training, the voice in her head thundered. *You are a disobedient child and deserve what you have been given.*

Shaking violently, Isilian screamed, "I gave you my daughter Elan! I mistakenly killed my own son while sacrificing to you! How much more can you ask of me?"

It is not what you have given, but what you refuse to give that I want.

Isilian shook her head. Terror ripped through her sobs. "I won't give you Astril. I won't do it. You can not ask me to give you the blood of my dearest child, my seed."

Your seed? The voice in her head howled with laughter. *Astril is my seed, and she is failing me. We will put our hope in Gallian now.*

"She frightens me. Her magic is so much stronger than mine was at her age."

Her magic is grown larger by hate! Hate for Astril! Hate for you! The deep voice in her head rumbled as a gust of sour wind blew over her face and through her hair.

Isilian struggled to breathe as she remembered the many times she had shown public favor for her oldest daughter only to receive constant rejection.

"There are so few of us left," Isilian wept. "You have not blessed me with more children. If I cannot win Astril back, then I have only Gallian. She is strong but immature. Her magic is unpredictable."

"Oh, Astril, why have you betrayed me," she whispered to the air.

Betrayed you? the voice questioned. *Astril betrayed me. Why do you hold out hope on that unfaithful child?*

"She is the light of my womb. The destined child to carry on the seed of your name for our people," cried Isilian.

Gallian is now that seed, the voice rumbled. *Astril rejected my ways long before her betrayal.*

"But Gallian will destroy me!"

That is the price you will pay for your mistakes. Astril will pay for her own. The voice thundered, *For her crimes, she will be my sacrifice.*

Isilian shuddered at the idea of taking the life of her beautiful daughter. Then slowly she stood and bowed her head to the gold statue. The cybin she had taken was beginning to wear off, and her mind was her own again.

Raising her arms above her head, Isilian lifted burning eyes toward the idol. "Forgive my weaknesses, Great Goddess. I will do whatever you ask."

Chapter Thirteen

T oren was still working over all that had happened since he rescued Astril from his grandfather's fields. *I really need to get back to Harkan soon.* He paused briefly in the door of Ard's sickroom. His gaze landed on Astril sleeping silently in a chair. *She looks so peaceful,* he thought to himself. A smile flitted briefly over her face while she slept.

It's nice to see her smile even if it's only in sleep, Toren thought as he entered.

He watched her sleeping in the chair and was about to shake her awake when she murmured, "Hurry, Kellon. I'll help you."

"Astril." He nudged her awake.

Stirring, she opened her eyes and smiled, pure delight shining from her face. Her undisguised look of love caught him so off guard that he stumbled backward. In the same instant, her smile faded to a look of recognition.

"Sorry, I was dreaming," she said in a faraway voice filled with sadness.

"I didn't want to wake you, but I thought you might be more comfortable in a bed." Then quietly he added, "Who is Kellon?"

"Kellon?" Astril rubbed her eyes. "Where did you hear that name?"

"You said it just now in your sleep. 'Hurry, Kellon. I'll help you.'"

"Kellon was my brother." Grief crumpled her face. "I thought I saw him when you woke me."

"Oh." He uncomfortably shifted his weight from one foot to the other. "I can sit with Ard for the rest of the night."

Astril walked over to the bed where the sick man slept and laid her hand across his forehead. "The cloths we've placed over his body need to be refreshed. I'm afraid his fever might spike still. Thung is a terrible poison."

"D-do you think he will live?"

The look Astril shot Toren brought no hope as she walked over to stand before him.

"Toren," she whispered. "He... Ard..." Holding her breath, she walked closer and touched his arm with her hand. "I know you love him, but there is much evil that flows in his blood."

Toren stepped back. "You don't know him. He's a good man." He crossed his arms. "He's my cousin."

"He has much evil in him, Toren. It would be better if he died."

Shaking his head in disgust, Toren spit out, "You will do everything you can to heal him."

Crossing the room to the open door, Astril walked with stiff movements. "I will do my best because you wish it, and for no other reason."

She stopped before exiting and turning again to face him said, "There is more kelp in the basket to the side of his bed. Pack the wound with a large handful and wrap it tightly with the cotton. Continue to spoon the honey mixture into his mouth. I will relieve you in the morning."

After completing the task Astril had assigned, Toren sat on a chair to watch his failing friend.

"How can she say such a thing about you, Ard?" he whispered. "Get better soon, my friend."

After saying many prayers for his cousin and rewrapping his wound, Toren soaked more cloths in cool water to help bring the fever down. The night progressed slowly with only the sound of the injured man's labored breathing.

Toren had just closed his eyes as the sun lightly streamed in the east window when he heard a low coughing. He quickly jumped to his feet to attend Ard.

"Where am I?" Ard choked on his words.

Toren knelt down beside the head of the bed and took his cousin's limp hands while he finished coughing. "We are at Priest Augur's."

Ard again choked and gagged. "What happened?"

"You were hit with a poisoned arrow." He offered a slight grin. Ard would not appreciate Astril's involvement in his recovery, but now that he'd survived the night, Toren decided he would benefit from a healthy dose of humility. "If it weren't for Astril, you would be dead right now."

"Astril?" Ard gasped, coughed again, then spit on the floor.

"Yes." Toren leaned back on his heels. "She has healing methods and abilities that go far beyond what we have ever learned. She recognized the poison and knew how to help you."

"Bah! Witchcraft."

Toren held water to his cousin's lips and urged him to drink.

"He's awake?" Astril asked from the open doorway.

Toren turned with a start, spilling the water over Ard's chest. "Yes, come and see." He handed Ard a cloth, and the big man took it with a grunt.

With a guarded look of concern on her face, Astril edged toward the bed. Ignoring Ard's frowning attempt to evade her hand, she reached down to touch his forehead to check for a fever.

"The fever is down. That is very good. He should sleep better now." She then asked, "Do you feel as though ants are crawling over your body?"

Ard's eyes widened. "I think I felt that in the night, but it's gone now."

"You need to stay down for a few days. Then you can get up with assistance for short times only. It will take long months before you are fully recovered." Looking to Toren she added, "You stay with him, and I will find some food. He should eat if he intends to recover."

At her exit, Toren looked to his disgruntled friend. "Now do you believe that she healed me when I was a boy?"

Ard nodded.

"Where's Toren?" Ard spoke with a hint of strength in his voice later that same day.

Astril turned from wringing out a large white cloth. "He was up with you all night and needed to sleep."

"Oh." He lay tense as a wounded boran, watching her every move. *He smells like one too,* she thought, allowing only a slight smile to play at the corner of her lip.

She placed the cool cloth on his forehead then turned and sat down on a chair across the room, throwing him a cautious look.

"Why are you doing this?" He attempted to sit up on the bed.

Getting up, Astril walked back to his bed and pushed him firmly down. "Because Toren wishes it."

Ard let out a slow chuckle. "I suppose on your own power you would have let me die?"

The look she threw him as she turned to leave the room surely left no doubt of the truth of his words.

"I'm sorry. Please don't leave." He reached as though to grab her arm.

Turning back to him, Astril picked up the cloth again and began swabbing his face. "You need to rest."

Ard gave her a grateful smile then turned his face to the wall, his ravaged body falling slack as sleep overtook him.

Finally he's asleep. Astril lightly placed the cool wet cloths across his forehead then turned to sit back down in the chair. *Perhaps he's not as evil as I first believed. Toren loves him, so maybe he isn't that bad.* Astril still couldn't help but remember all the advances and abuse she had put up with in the short time she had known the giant. Her shoulders shuddered involuntarily at the thought of his large, hairy arms holding her down, crushing her.

Many days later, Toren and Ard returned from a short afternoon stroll, Ard with the assistance of a walking stick Toren had made for him.

"I need to get back to Harkan soon." Toren steadied his cousin while he lowered himself back into bed.

"I imagine you are desperately needed to help ward off the attacks of the Gernons." Ard grunted as he lay down.

Toren leaned the stick against the wall where Ard could reach it. "The attacks are becoming less frequent." His shoulders bowed under the weight of the news he'd received. "A messenger arrived yesterday. It seems Astril's sister's plan backfired, and they got the worse of it all."

Ard let out a loud laugh that caused him to grab his shoulder in pain. "Well it serves them right. Who are they to demand anything from us?"

"The Seerlings have suffered great tragedies at our hand."

"Good!" Ard laughed again.

Toren was just about to rebuke Ard for his callousness when a loud scream went up in the hall outside the room. Both men rushed to the door just in time to see Astril race past them.

The girl ran straight into Priest Augur, who had just rounded the bend. The impact of the crash cast them both down to the floor.

Astril worked to untangle herself from the priest's arms as she shrieked at an approaching servant, "Stay away from me, devil woman."

Toren's long strides quickly caught up to the pair entangled on the floor, and helping them up, he had to yell to be heard above Astril's screeching.

"What's going on here?"

Drinna, as fat as she was tall, came running up behind Astril, holding out a Harkonian woman's gown. Toren recognized her as the nurse he had hired earlier that morning. Panting and holding her chest she cried, "Put this on, you heathen."

"No," Astril yelled, writhing and flailing in an attempt to escape Toren's grasp. She slipped free and bolted.

"Astril!" Toren lunged after her and pinioned her arms, protecting his face as best as he could from her violent thrashing. Normal women *liked* new clothes, didn't they? "What's wrong with you? It's only a dress."

Astril stopped her screaming, and he let her go. Panting, she grabbed the garment and threw it in his face. "Then you wear it." By the time he disentangled himself from the dress, she'd rounded the bend in the hall and flung herself down the stairs and then outside.

"I told you, Prince Toren, you can't make a proper lady out of that heathen," Drinna drawled out her words.

"She's not a heathen," he flung behind him as he pursued the fleeing girl. Curse her, if he left to tend business in Harkan, who would protect the fool girl from herself?

"Astril, wait," Toren called after her.

Slowing her steps, Astril turned sideways and motioned to the offending dress. "Keep that thing away from me."

Toren caught up to her and pulled her about to face him. "I'm sorry. But I need you to wear this."

"Why?" She glared at him.

He considered telling her it was for her own good, but decided he'd get better results by trying a different angle.

"The attacks have lessoned, but for the safety of the priests it is still important to disguise your presence here. We need you to look as much like a Harkonian woman as possible." With some difficulty, he managed to convey a kind tone despite panting from the chase she'd led him on. *How could a small woman run so fast?* "Besides, it's not like we're asking you to dye your hair."

Her eyes grew large in astonishment, and he laughed. "We did think about it though."

Astril slumped down on the grass. "Why won't you just send me back?" She pulled up clumps of ground in frustration. "Your people would be safer if you did."

Toren sat down beside her, still holding the dress. "Astril, you were not the reason for the attacks, but only the excuse that your sister used to create them." Then he spread the dress over his lap, held the bodice to his own chest and turned the fabric this way and that. "Besides, I think you'll look really pretty in this."

Again she gave him a disgusted look. She turned her head away and gave a most unladylike snort. "Do you really think my wearing such a stupid outfit will help protect the priests?"

"Yes," he answered. "And it will help protect Drinna."

Astril turned back to him and rolled her eyes. "That devil woman grates on my last nerve. She's known me a few hours and is already nagging me. Do you know what she put in my hair before I got away?" Astril grabbed a handful of her own hair. "Lavender scent. I just got my hair clean from all the traveling and fighting, and she puts that foul-smelling stuff in it."

Laughing, Toren pulled her to her feet. "I thought I smelled something strangely feminine about you."

He smiled at her and motioned to the dress with a nod of his head. She took it and held it out in front of her as if it were something dead.

"Fine," she said. "For the safety of your priests, I will wear this… thing, but the first person who says I look like one of your foolish women is going to get hit hard."

At his sudden outburst of laughter, she straightened her back and marched to the house holding the offending garment as far from her body as possible.

That night before dinner, Toren made a point of telling her how lovely she looked in the new dress. His delight was cut short by a sound punch to the stomach.

"Astril?" he gagged. "What's wrong with you?"

He could tell she struggled to maintain her composure. *Is she laughing at me?* He watched her walk toward the table and decided not to push his luck with any further comments. *Boy does she pack a wallop.* He chuckled while rubbing the spot where her jab had unexpectedly landed.

Dinner was fairly quiet with only Priest Augur interjecting a word or two. They were a small group, only the priest, himself, Astril, and Ard. Although together, each seemed silently alone. At times Toren thought he felt the weight of Astril's stare upon him but found no evidence when he looked up from his plate. He glanced over at his cousin, who sat silently rubbing his injured shoulder. *Now that he is up and about, maybe Ard can keep Astril in line so I can go back and help with the fighting.* He dismissed the thought quickly when he saw the cautious smile his cousin sent her, and Astril's determined scowl back.

After dinner, Ard went back to his room to rest while Toren and Priest Augur sat reading scrolls.

"Ahem," the priest cleared his throat loudly. Toren glanced up from his reading just in time to see Astril, again wearing boy's clothing, disappear down the hall.

"What am I going to do with that girl?" he griped out loud and ran in the direction she had gone. Stealthily he spied on her, watching her look around the large entryway then slowly open the door that led outside.

"And where are you going now?" His voice echoed a little louder than he had intended and caused her to jump around, startled.

With a sheepish look on her face, Astril stared over at him. "I…" She paused, then gave a soft cough. "I was just going out for a walk."

Toren forced his face to keep a stern expression. "Why are you wearing those clothes again?"

Astril looked down at her attire. "Oh, I thought you only wanted me to wear that thing when I was around you."

"You knew that I wanted you to wear it all the time."

"Fine!" she screeched in his direction then turned back toward the door to head outside.

"Where are you going?"

"Argggggghhhh!" She slammed the door and stomped back toward the stairs that led to her room, giving him a hard shove as she passed.

Well, that answers that question. I can't leave until I know Ard's well enough to keep her here. Toren decided to post several guards around the property to keep an eye out for any further attempts at escape.

Chapter Fourteen

Several weeks had passed, and the relationship between Astril and her rotund warden had not improved. Since she was not permitted to hunt or fight or perform any other enjoyable task, Astril had taken to feigning sleep late into the morning. This provided a dual enjoyment for her as it not only made the boring days shorter but also tremendously annoyed her jail keeper, which had become a task that gave Astril great pleasure.

She heard the heavy-footed steps of the oversized woman long before the door to her bedchambers opened. Hiding a mischievous smile while keeping her eyes shut tight, Astril waited for the morning's argument to begin.

The bothersome woman thrust the bedchamber curtains wide opened and in a singsong voice squealed, "Good morning. It's time to wake up."

Astril clamped her pillow tightly over her head and rolled toward the wall away from the light.

"Get up," Drinna demanded with an impertinent swat to Astril's behind. "It's a beautiful morning."

"Ohhhhhh." Astril pulled her pillow over her head and curled up into a tight ball. "Leave me alone."

Drinna pulled the pillow away from her and fluffed it up. She shoved the soft down behind Astril's head, then walked quickly over to the bed-chamber closet and pulled out a light purple dress.

"How many of those foul things do you have?" Astril squeaked. Every morning Drinna produced yet another constraining gown for her to wear. Not once had she been asked to wear the same dress twice. *How wasteful can these people be?* This dress was especially ugly with its untold layers of purple lace and plunging neckline. *Why, that will barely cover my whole chest!*

Drinna held the small, frilly dress up to her own body and twirled around, laughing. "Don't you think this one is divine?"

"No, I don't. Put it back." She tugged the covers over her head. Drinna would have to bind and gag her if she thought she'd get her into that hideous contraption.

"Just like a heathen to not know good quality," Drinna said pulling the covers off and giving her a smile that to Astril's horror beamed with fond-ness. "Now get up and get in the bath water I've drawn. It is good and hot right now, but will quickly get cold. Either way, you're taking a bath."

"If it will get you to shut up, fine." Astril jumped out of bed, making sure to not seem too enthusiastic. Having taken her share of cold baths on hunting trips, she found the luxury of warm water was one she appreci-ated.

Drinna helped her take her nightdress off and clucked her tongue. "I'll need to fatten you up, that's for sure. You're all bones. Don't heathens eat?"

Astril threw her a sour look and stepped into the warm, rose-petal bath. *Drinna has really out done herself,* she admitted silently while easing slowly down into the tub. She couldn't help but let out a happy sigh as she lifted one of the floating buds and breathed in the sweet scent.

"Now, use that soap." Drinna commanded as she turned to leave the room, "And I want to put curls in that short hair of yours, so don't get it wet."

After the woman left, Astril immediately ducked her head underwater and muttered, "Devil woman."

"What have you done?" Drinna screamed a moment later when she reentered the room with a length of toweling. "Your hair is all wet."

Astril smiled sweetly. It did feel good to vex the woman.

"Very well," said the servant. "Now you'll be missing the morning meal so I can dry and curl your hair."

"Ugh," Astril grunted as she stood up then ripped the towel out of Drinna's hands and rubbed dry. She flopped down on the bed, wishing she hadn't gotten her hair wet after all.

After what seemed like an eternity of bickering, Drinna finally stood back to appraise Astril's appearance. She nodded with approval.

"Do all Harkonian women go through this every day?" Astril thought she would rather wrestle a boran to the ground before sitting through another hair-curling session.

"Of course," Drinna responded. "Proper young ladies make sure they look perfect before anyone can see them."

"I'm no proper young lady," Astril scowled at her fiercely, baring her teeth.

"You can say that again." Drinna smiled and then produced a length of purple twine from the pocket of her apron. "Your curls turned out so nice. I think I'll add this to your hair."

"No! Enough. Not one more thing." Astril gave a humiliating scream as she backed out of the room with her hands held high in an attempt to ward off Drinna's inexorable primping. The annoying woman had reduced her to retreating like a coward.

Just outside the room, her back bumped up against a solid object. Whirling, she realized it was Ard.

"You look very pretty today." he smiled down at her in a way that only fueled her anger more.

Throwing him the most evil look she could muster, Astril sneered, "Save your smiles for that devil woman in there."

"I heard that, you little heathen," Drinna huffed, then slammed the door leaving Astril alone in the hall with Ard.

He shuffled his feet, and his face turned bright pink. He smiled then offered her his arm.

Astril ignored his offer, laughed out loud and shook her fist at the closed door, then ran down the hall in search of food.

Finding the dining hall empty except for Toren, she stormed up to him. "Look what that woman did now. I cannot stand another minute of her pestering ways."

Astril ceased her rant as she saw the downcast look on his face.

"What's the matter," she asked in a subdued voice.

Looking up at her with dark eyes, Toren answered, "My father died."

Astril placed her hand on his shoulder and stared down at the sad young man.

"He was a good man," Toren said, "but he was plagued by illnesses all his life. I guess this one was more than he could handle."

Toren took her hand in his own and kissed the tips of her fingers. The action sent shockwaves up her arm. She continued to stare at his face as he stood and looked lovingly down at her. "I have to go home, Astril."

Seeing her slight nod he continued, "This is a difficult time, and I need you to stay here with the priests. Ard will protect you."

Looking away, she sighed and said nothing.

Toren pulled her chin back toward him. "I believe I'm doing the right thing by keeping you hidden, Astril. Please promise me you will stay."

She forced a smile to her lips and nodded. "You have my word that I will not leave until you return."

Smiling despite his sadness, Toren gave her a quick hug then hurried from the room.

"You are very much like your grandmother." Priest Augur's voice startled her.

She turned toward the voice but couldn't see the priest. "I wondered if you remembered her."

Priest Augur stepped from behind a column and looked down at his feet as he slowly approached. "I had a deep respect for her."

Astril let out a long sigh as she sat down in the seat where Toren had been and ran her hand through her curled mass of hair. "I loved her so much even though she was a disgrace to our people."

"It is not a disgrace to care about people as your grandmother did, Astril."

She looked at him, her eyes misting up. "You do not understand the Seerling way. To show concern is to show weakness. My action of saving an enemy boy is considered the highest disgrace in my land. Our way is to kill, not save."

"That doesn't seem to be your way," the priest responded.

Astril's heart was heavy as she leaned forward and placed her face in her hands. "I made a big mistake in coming here."

"Why did you come, then?"

Astril bit the inside of her mouth until she tasted blood then answered, "Because I promised Toren I would come."

Priest Augur shook his head knowingly and sat down beside her. "Why would you make such a promise to a Harkonian prince? Do you owe him something?"

Pondering his words, Astril sighed. "No, I owe him nothing. He is like a brother to me."

"Is that the reason you rescued him from the boran so long ago?" questioned the priest.

Astril nodded her head. "He reminds me very much of Kellon."

After a short silence, Augur asked, "But is that really the reason you have chosen to submit to his wishes?"

"What do you mean?"

"I've seen the two of you together." He bowed his head and reached out to touch her hand, which she pulled quickly away. Sighing he said, "I do not believe you think of him as a brother."

Astril knew the truth of his words. She had also noticed a powerful bond between herself and Toren. On many occasions over the past weeks, he had sought her out for company. It felt as though they could talk on any subject for hours and never tire. She enjoyed their times together as much as he seemed to. The feelings within her heart every time she was with him confused and frustrated her.

Shaking her head, she looked at the priest. "The Great Goddess would forbid any future with him."

"And you do everything this goddess commands," Priest Augur asked quietly.

Astril gave him a quivering smile and shook her head no.

Quiet ruled the room as each of them sat engrossed in their own thoughts.

"You have not asked me how I met your grandmother." The priest broke the silence.

Astril gave him a questioning glance.

He smiled. "Your grandmother was working in the fields of a neighboring Olden when we met."

She laughed. "No Seerling of the line of the high priestess would lower herself to such work."

Priest Augur smiled. "She did not consider hard work lowering herself, Astril. I'm sure you remember that your grandmother was unusual for her line."

Astril nodded her head and looked back down at the table as he continued.

"She was so lovely with her light hair. I had never seen a Seerling before meeting her. We began talking right away and developed a... an unusual friendship."

Priest Augur closed his eyes and fell silent for a moment.

"We had many conversations, and eventually she told me she wanted to know more of the God that I serve."

Astril did not quite believe what he was telling her but still she listened intently.

"Your grandmother taught you to heal, didn't she?" he asked. "She taught you many things."

Astril smiled softly and nodded her answer as he went on.

"Did she teach you of her great love for the One True God?"

"Before her death she made me promise I would seek you out. I suppose that is the real reason I allowed myself to be brought here."

"Prince Toren told me how strange it was that you stopped fighting him."

Again silence dominated the air between them as they sat in thought. Finally, Astril spoke.

"I loved my grandmother very much. She was very wise but lived a life of seclusion." She put her head back down in her hands and fought back tears. "She was the only one who ever really loved me."

The priest reached out and patted her shoulder reassuringly.

Astril swallowed a hiccupping sob and wiped her eyes. "Her mother despised her for not fulfilling her duty to the Great Goddess, so she was banished. She was redeemed when my mother chose to serve under the High Priestess. Still she lived in forced solitude at the hand of her sister. When High Priestess Ruman died of a sudden sickness, my mother was named in her stead. Mother then redeemed my grandmother even further, allowing her some freedoms. If it wasn't for my mother's bravery and sacrifices, my grandmother would have died in complete disgrace," Astril told him.

"Do you believe that your mother's actions were brave?" he asked.

Astril shrugged. "She is a great leader. Our people live in fear of her daily."

"Forcing a person to follow you out of fear does not make you a leader, Astril. It makes you a tyrant. A true leader is a servant like your grandmother."

"But my mother has given so much to the Great Goddess, and the people serve her because of those sacrifices." The sight of Elan, Kellon, and Corin crossed before Astril's mind, and she dropped her head in pain at the memories.

"Some sacrifices are for selfish gain, child. They are destructive and will eventually destroy the one making the sacrifice."

"I don't understand. How can a sacrifice be selfish?"

The priest patiently explained, "Sallian once explained to me that the High Priestess makes the yearly animal sacrifice as a means of acquiring deeper power. She said that the High Priestess claims that the greater power helps her protect her people but is really used to keep the people bound to her by fear."

Astril nodded her head in agreement. "Mother uses her power to force submission. No one comes against her because she is so powerful. Only our line is allowed to learn the real magic and commune with the Great Goddess, but it is our line that is slowly diminishing. Soon there will be no one left to lead the people."

"The yearly sacrifice is for the selfish gain of the High Priestess no matter what she tells herself or others. The sacrifice of life, whether it be from death or neglect, is a selfish sacrifice that many leaders choose to pay to further themselves."

He waited and watched as Astril tried to process the words he had spoken, then he added, "Your grandmother was different. She understood that by sacrificing her own rights and remaining quiet, she could give you the chance of a better life. The sacrifices she made were for you and for her family."

Astril sat shaking her head at the words he spoke. *These ideas are so foreign. Could my grandmother have really known all of this and still followed this priest's god?* Still she couldn't deny the twinge of hope that caused her heart to beat faster. *What he says seems so right, but it goes against everything I have ever been taught.*

"All I have ever known of sacrifice means loss. My mother gave my sister Elan as a Keeper. I always believed that was a high honor, but when my nephew was given to the same fate, I followed and found out the truth. They are slaves, living in horrible conditions, and working hard every day to provide for the priestesses. Corin died because of my sister's sacrifice. He died, but the priestesses benefited from the hard work of the Keepers." She stiffened, and a cold, hard shell encircled her heart, blocking off all emotion. It was a protective measure she had learned very early in life. Staring down at her hands she hissed, "I will never make a sacrifice to any god."

"What your mother and sister did was evil, Astril," he answered slowly. "A child is a precious gift that should be cherished and loved, not discarded for the selfish gain of others. The One True God does not ask that of us."

Astril felt the shell of her heart start to melt away as the priest spoke. *Yes, Corin should have been cherished.* She choked back her emotions, trying hard to cover her heart once again. "What does He ask for?"

The priest smiled down on her. "The only sacrifice He asks for is you."

She stared up at him in astonishment. "How is it possible to sacrifice myself on an altar stone?"

"Astril," the priest softly spoke, "you do not sacrifice yourself with a knife. The One True God wants that your very life be a sacrifice to Him. He asks only that you worship and serve Him. That you give Him your heart and that you put no other god above Him."

"He is an unseen god. You have no idols of Him for me to worship. How can people believe in a God they cannot see?"

Patiently the priest responded, "Through prayer and meditation and seeking His truths in the ancient scrolls."

Looking down again, Astril contemplated his words. "This God of yours is strange." Then quietly she got up and walked out of the room. Her appetite for food had been replaced by something quite different, but it still didn't make any sense to her.

Behind her, Augur's whisper tugged at her heart. "One True God, please help her understand the meaning of the words I speak. Bring her into Your warm embrace. Love her as You loved her grandmother, my Lord."

Chapter Fifteen

Morgan had felt the palace was very quiet since the elder prince's death, and Prince Toren had hidden himself away from everyone while taking care of the arrangements. This dinner was the first time she had seen him since the funeral, and she had hoped it would be pleasant.

"I have to admit, I do find some comfort in my son's death," said King Kortan to his grandson a few days after Prince Verne's funeral rites had ended.

Morgan looked up at the king, bewildered by his sudden speech. In fact, she was surprised to hear anyone speak. But she knew by the king's suddenly chipper tone that something was amiss.

"And what is that?" Toren asked with a strangely guarded expression over his handsome face.

King Kortan looked at his grandson across the dinner table and laughed. "Why, knowing I have something that witch wants—your little Seerling slave." He then roughly grabbed Princess Emile's hand. "Doesn't that give you comfort as well, Daughter?"

Morgan couldn't believe how callous the king was being. Couldn't he tell that Princess Emile's shoulders were shaking? *She's sad.* The princess stood politely and excused herself from the eating table.

King Kortan shrugged his shoulders and let her leave, then addressed his grandson once more. "I know that I placed you in charge of all the slaves this morning, and you can surely do with the heathens as you wish, but I would truly like for you to bring her back here to serve." He then laughed again. "I actually miss that fire in her eyes."

Disgust flickered across Toren's face as though he couldn't quite hide his reaction to the king's cruel words.

"I don't believe that bringing Astril back here is a wise decision, my king." Toren stared down and held his knife in front of his plate as though he couldn't decide if he were full.

The words of the king and Toren's dark look confused Morgan greatly. Why would the prince object to bringing the heathen girl back to the palace and why hadn't he told her that he had been elevated in charge of all the slaves? This was a high honor, and she wanted to be proud of him. She wanted to share in his accomplishments, but he never told her anything.

"Oh, come now," the king replied with a look of disappointment. "We have it on good word that the attacks on our people have been called off. There's no danger in bringing her here to share with the rest of us." Then the king turned to Morgan and laughed. "Perhaps she has grown more hair for my rugs."

Morgan had thought the rumor was a lie until that moment. Could the king really have made a rug out of the slave's hair? She absently touched one of her own dark curls then looked to the prince, who was failing miserably to hide the dark, angry look that spread across his features.

Morgan sat shocked as the prince challenged his grandfather. He stood quickly and turned his chair over behind him. The loud bang caused Morgan to jump even though she knew it was coming. "She will stay where she is, Grandfather."

Smiling at the outburst, King Kortan waved his hand at the young man's anger. "Peace, my son. She's your slave to do with as you wish."

Morgan felt the king staring at her and could hear what he said, even though he lowered his voice and spoke behind his hand to the prince.

"Only take care you keep it hidden from your wife."

Shocked and upset by the whispered words she had heard, Morgan knew her face flamed bright red. She stared at the prince not knowing what to think or how he would react.

She watched him stare daggers into his grandfather, who only shrugged them off, unnoticed. *Why won't Prince Toren defend my honor as his intended?* She cried out to herself while watching him rush out of the room.

"I suppose it is only the two of us for dinner tonight," King Kortan said with a leer at her.

Why did the prince get so angry when King Kortan mentioned bringing the slave back here? Morgan questioned herself. *One would think he cares for the slave; perhaps even loves her.* Refusing to believe her own thoughts, Morgan forced a smile back at the king and attempted to finish her dinner even though everything crumbled like dried oats in her mouth.

I will be happy. It doesn't matter if the prince has a thousand pretty slaves. I will be his wife. I will be queen! She forced herself to dwell on those thoughts. After all, what did it matter if he loved someone else? Hadn't her mother told her to stop dreaming about his love?

"A woman betrothed to a future king can not expect to be adored," her mother had corrected her more than once.

I just have to keep reminding myself that Prince Toren is going to marry me, not some Seerling slave.

⌒

"Mother," Toren called after the running woman before him. He caught up to her in the confined corridor and grabbing her shoulders held her close. "Are you all right?"

A torrent of tears swept over her as she clung to him. He had seen her cling to his father so many times when the king's words upset her, and now it was his turn to provide the needed comfort.

"I miss him so much," she wept into his shoulder. "He was such a good man. Toren, he wanted so much more for you than just a throne."

"I know, Mother." Toren replied, "I hope I can do him honor in all that I do."

The princess slowed her crying and smiled shakily up at her son. "I believe you do that every day."

She cupped her hand to his cheek and her dark eyes grew serious. "I do not believe the gossip I've heard, and neither did your father."

Toren was shocked by her words. "What gossip?"

Shaking her head in disgust, Emile said, "I will not bore you with the idle words of foolish people. I will only tell you that it is about your relationship with the Seerling."

Again shock filled him at what she said. "Mother, I feel a debt to her for the deed she did in saving my life from the boran." He tried to make his mother understand his intentions toward Astril, but knew it was useless if he didn't understand them himself. "I promised her back then that I would not allow anyone to hurt her, and I intend to honor my word." He attempted to give her a comforting look while still trying to convince himself of his own words. "There is nothing between us but friendship. I even believe she thinks of me as a brother." He choked out his final thoughts with what he knew was a pitiful chuckle.

"And do you think of her in that same manner?" she asked tenderly.

"I owe her a debt. That is all," he said. The stiff frustration in his voice surprised them both.

Cupping her hand against his cheek, Emile whispered, "I believe you are doing the right thing where the girl is concerned."

Toren smiled down at his mother and hugged her closely. *She always believes in me, even when I doubt myself.* He gathered strength from her unconditional love and support.

As they turned to walk down the narrow, white hallway, Emile asked, "Will you be leaving to check on her soon?"

"No." He answered. How could he go back to the enjoyment of Astril's company when his people needed him? His father's death, along with the war against the Seerlings, had brought morale on the palace grounds as well as in all Harkan to a terrible low, and his grandfather had done nothing to make the situation any better. "There is much I need to do here. I am also worried about the sudden stop of the Seerling attacks."

"That is a good thing, don't you think?"

"It would seem so, but I feel in my heart there is a greater danger approaching." Toren walked his mother back to her chambers. She did not press him for any more information. How could he explain the dark cloud that hovered over his heart? Everyone believed they had beaten the Seerlings.

None of this makes any sense. Astril's mother wanted her back. King Kortan had told him of her terrifying visit and how she had reacted when told that Astril was gone. He had never before seen fear in his grandfather's eyes, but that woman's visit put it there. Why would she willingly put herself and her people in danger to get the girl back, then call off the attacks and fall into oblivion? *Would she really give up her hold on Astril?* Toren shook his head and went on to the main hall. He needed to consult with the generals.

The prince worked tirelessly for many weeks taking over his father's duties in the palace while at the same time trying to gain knowledge in regard to what the Seerlings might be doing. Finally, word came through the ranks that a large band of Seerlings had been spotted moving across a portion of Harkan.

Toren questioned his generals in detail on what they had learned.

"Yes, my prince, I believe the words of the farmer are true," the first general spoke.

"I don't understand," Toren questioned. "Why would a group of Seerlings be traveling in the night this far north except to attack our people?"

"I do not know, my prince. The farmer said he saw only glimpses of the group as they traveled. He said there looked to be about thirty or forty in all," the general responded. "However, we have not heard of a single attack on our land."

"And they were heading southeast?"

"Yes," said the general. "Also, I must inform you that we interrogated an Olden family we caught traveling that same night. The man of the family refused to say much, but it was evident by the look on his face that he feared something great."

"What did you do with the Oldens?" Toren asked.

The general stammered, "They are being prepared for field work as slaves, my prince."

"Upon whose order?"

"Your grandfather's."

Toren looked fiercely at the general, "I, not the king, am in charge of the slaves and I tell you to release them now."

"Yes, my prince," said the general bowing deeply in respect as he made his leave.

Toren sat down in the main hall, stroking the stubble on his chin while deep in thought. *What could the Seerlings be up to?* The thought baffled him, but he knew he didn't have much time to dwell on it. Soon his grandfather would want an update on all he was doing. Ever since his father's death he had assumed more responsibility at the palace. His grandfather had even given him charge of the troops as well as the slaves. *When the time is right, I will release all of the slaves,* he thought.

Throwing himself into his work, he turned his attention back to the list he was making in preparation for the next day's meeting with the king.

"Miss Morgan to see you, Prince," Holan, the main hall attendant called out.

Why does her mere name cause my skin to crawl? Toren shook off the unpleasant sensation. *She is the last thing I need to be dealing with right now.*

Then forcing a smile, Toren beckoned the girl to him.

"Yes, Morgan, you requested an audience with me?" He worked hard to hide his annoyance at her interruption.

Morgan flashed him a coy smile and batted long, dark lashes in his direction. "My lord," she said. "I have a request to make of you."

"Yes?" He forced himself to show patience.

Pausing and then smiling at him Morgan went on, "It is such a beautiful day. The harvest is in full bloom, and the air is sweet with the smell of abundance. I had hoped you might take your noon meal with me outside in the shade."

Sighing deeply and looking over to her with a forced smile, he thought that was the last thing he wanted to do. "I suppose I could take a short break and eat."

His kindness was rewarded with a warm smile. "Very good. I will send my attendant for you as soon as the meal is prepared."

"That will be fine," Toren answered then turned from her with a dismissal wave.

He could hear her nearly skip from the room. She had never done anything but be kind to him, yet he couldn't stand being in her presence.

He smiled softly to himself, remembering the night he had first seen Astril dressed in a Harkonian gown. The memory caused him to rub his stomach sympathetically where she had once punched him. *I'd rather get punched in the stomach by Astril every day for the rest of my life than sit under a shaded tree even once with Morgan.*

Turning his thoughts back to his list, Toren forced the image of soft, golden hair and large, deep gray eyes from his mind.

"That was a delicious meal, Morgan. Thank you," the prince said after leaning back against a pillow under the shade of the large tree.

"I'm glad you enjoyed it, my prince," she replied demurely while secretly admiring his appearance. *Prince Toren is handsome.* She noticed that his brown hair slightly curled at the ends because it was too long and smiled to herself remembering the kind brown eyes, now closed, that were formed in his strong face. *See! He can be content in my presence,* she congratulated her efforts. *Maybe this will show him that we'll have a good marriage; that I'll be a good wife.* Still staring at him intently, she struggled to come up with a topic to keep him focused on her. She didn't want to lose his attention to sleep, and he did look very peaceful.

Quickly she asked the first thing that popped into her mind, "Has General Ard recovered from his wounds?"

Opening his eyes and casting a warm smile her way, Toren replied, "Yes, with Astril's good care he will be back to his old ways very soon."

"Oh," Morgan sighed. *That's just what I need, Ard back to his old ways.*

Toren sat up straighter and gave her an intense look. "What's the matter?"

Forcing a smile back to her lips and pretending to be jolly, Morgan replied, "Oh, nothing."

"Something is wrong. I saw it on your face just now. What is it?"

"He doesn't miss much," Morgan thought as she idly toyed with a small red flower. She hesitated before trying to explain. *Why did I have to bring this up?* She didn't know the prince well, but she did know that he never let go of a subject once it had sparked his attention. "It's just that… well… the general is very forward."

"What do you mean?" he probed.

She paused for a moment, not willing to look him in the eye. "He… has been very forceful with me. Even while you were here he would… well, he would grab me and…"

She felt as though she were condemning herself by Ard's actions so she quickly added, "I spoke to the princess about all of his advances. That's why she asked you to take him on your trip."

Toren stared hard into her eyes making her wish she had let him sleep. "Are you telling me that Ard…" he cut off his words

Morgan didn't want Toren to think that she had done anything wrong, so she tried to back track her words, softening their implication. "No, he didn't do… he only acted like he…"

Finally she gave up in frustration and admitted everything. "Well, he treated me as though I were his property. Then he said you didn't love me and that you wouldn't have me and that…" She ended her tirade of words with a loud sniff and smothered cry. "I'm sorry. I should never have said so much."

Toren's face held a look of pity as he touched her hand in a way that brought her hope. *Well, I have his attention now,* she gloated within.

"Morgan, do not be sorry for being honest with me. I am the one who should be apologizing. You are under my protection, and I let you down. Please forgive me for not paying enough attention."

There, he admitted it. He just said he needs to pay more attention to me. Morgan leaned in close and puffed out her lips exactly the way she had been taught that men like. She was certain she would receive his kiss. Holding her breath and half closing her eyes, she sighed and waited. *Why hasn't he kissed me yet?* Opening her eyes to slits, she saw him look away from her. He looked so confused. *What's wrong with him? Doesn't he know how much the whole thing with Ard has hurt me?* She pouted.

A dark shadow passed over his face, and he turned back to her and shouted, "Astril!" The sudden mention of the slave's name frightened her, and to make matters worse, he jumped up to his feet and left her sitting there all alone.

"I'm sorry," he called behind him as he ran off toward the castle. "I have to leave."

Embarrassed and confused, Morgan sat under the shade tree watching him run away from her. *Now where's he going?*

Astril, Toren groaned inwardly as he ran through the palace doors. *What have I left you to?*

"Gather my men," he yelled at the first attendant he saw. "Tell them to make haste. We leave for Helgard immediately."

Within one hour Toren and his party were riding at full speed toward the home of the priests.

CHAPTER SIXTEEN

I wish to learn what you taught my grandmother," the girl announced from the doorway of the library.

Priest Augur turned from his scroll reading and smiled at the young seeker then completed reading out loud. "O our God, will you not judge them? For we have no power to face this vast army that is attacking us. We do not know what to do, but our eyes are upon you."

"Did you hear what I said?" Her irritated question rang off the walls. She stood with one hand on her hip, and her face carried a comical expression of annoyance.

He had seen how impatient she could be and how determined once she had her mind set. *Good.* He smiled to himself. *She's almost ready.* Looking up from his reading, he motioned for her to sit across from him. "Patience, child. First tell me what you think of the words I just read."

Astril stood rigidly in the doorway. With one foot placed inside and one lingering slightly toward the hall, she looked like a frightened young doe about to bounce away.

"I just told you that I want to learn about this God of yours. Doesn't that mean anything to you?" she whispered.

"Yes, yes, of course it does," he answered while sweeping his hands toward the chair across from him. "Please sit and listen."

Astril chose a chair far across the room to sit, and she nervously rubbed her hands together. Every time he saw the girl, he remembered the woman who had stolen his own heart long ago.

Sighing, he picked up the scroll and read again, "O our God, will you not judge them? For we have no power to face this vast army that is attacking us. We do not know what to do, but our eyes are upon you." Putting the scroll down, he smiled at her again and asked, "Now, what is your opinion about this?"

Still staring at him, Astril paused, cleared her voice, then answered, "I... I really don't know. What army?"

"Well, this ancient story is talking about an army that was about to attack the people of the One True God. They came up against His people, and He fought the battle for them."

"What?" She laughed, still rubbing her hands together. "How can a God fight for people?"

"He does, Astril!" the priest exclaimed, his hands gesturing wildly in front of him as he visualized his Lord moving mightily on behalf of His people. "The scrolls tell us of many times when He intervened and won the battle for His people. In this scroll, He caused the invading armies to fight up against one another. The fighting ended with the enemy killing each other, and His people never had to lift a sword."

Shaking her head slowly, Astril exhaled then muttered, "This is truly a strange God you serve."

He let out a small laugh and went on, "He did this for His people because their eyes were upon Him, Astril."

"I don't understand that."

"I know, child. You cannot possibly understand this now, but one day its meaning will be clear, and it will bring you help and comfort."

They sat in silence for a few moments, him not knowing how far to push. He could tell by the look of wonder on her face that all he had said was foreign to her. It was hard to keep his excitement at a new disciple from spilling out and frightening her away.

Calming himself down, he asked, "You said that you wish to learn about Him?"

Astril nodded. "I do wish to learn about the God that my grandmother served."

"Then why don't you tell me what you remember about her."

A look of love softened her features as her hands relaxed in her lap. "I remember that she used to sit quietly for long periods of time in her hut, reading. Sometimes she would read aloud when it was only the two of us. But most of the time she read silently. She often cried while reading. She once told me that there was a greater good in the world that I should seek out and find. Do you think she was talking about this God of yours?"

"Yes, I do. Your grandmother and I spent many hours together speaking about the One True God." He smiled at the memory of sitting so closely with Sallian reading over the scrolls and talking. He had never met a woman who could keep up with him in conversation, but Sallian stood toe to toe with him. Her intelligence and passion matched his own. "At one point I realized she had begun to teach me."

Astril stared long and hard at him with her lips parted slightly.

"You are still confused. Aren't you?"

"Yes," she answered. "I just don't understand how my grandmother found you, or why you would help her. I mean, you're a Harkonian. We don't help each other."

"Really?" he asked with a knowing smile. "I suppose it was just an accident that you healed Prince Toren long ago and that you helped Ard even though you hate him so."

She stared down at her hands and shook her head. "I shouldn't have. It's not the Seerling way."

Calmly, he got up from his seat and pulled a small chair over to where she sat. Braving a possible rejection, he reached out his hand and placed it upon hers. Much to his relief, she didn't pull away from his touch, only continued to stare down.

"Child, you are very much like your grandmother. She was not a typical Seerling either."

Astril looked up with tears threatening to spill out of her large eyes. "How did she get this far north? How did she find you?"

"Your grandmother had just had a terrible fight with her mother and was forced to leave Seerling land. She wandered for many years over the country before I found her working in the small village east of here."

A look of understanding crossed her face. "The High Priestess wanted her to give my mother to the Great Goddess as a Keeper so her older sister could bear children, but my grandmother refused and was banished only days after my mother was born. When my great-aunt became the high priestess, she called for my grandmother's return. She wanted to show the people that she could have compassion. It was really an attempt to show them who was really in charge. After that, my grandmother lived in seclusion in her own hut, rarely setting foot outside."

It filled him with grief to think of her sad, solitary days. *If only I could have been there,* he thought ruefully then reminded himself that it was not the will of the One for them to be together. He had accepted his path in life long ago and so had Sallian.

"Yes. I found her working in the fields for an Olden family." The thought of her gathering wheat on that hot first day of their meeting filled him again with sadness. She was so beautiful. All he had wanted was to pick her up in his arms and care for her forever, but it was never to be.

He realized that silence had fallen between them, and the girl was staring intently into his face, waiting. Smiling for her sake, he went on. "I first noticed her because of her unusual hair color. A color not far from your own."

Astril fingered her own hair and smiled. "She was so old and gray when I knew her."

"She must have suffered greatly at the hand of her mother, my dear. But I believe she never gave up her hope in the One True God. Hers was a faith that could last an eternity and fill the deepest gorges."

"Before she died, I vowed to her that I would seek you out." Astril smiled warmly, a look that lit up her face in the glow of the library fire. "I believe my capture and Toren's bringing me here are destiny's way of forcing me to honor that vow."

Taking her hand in his, Priest Augur responded, "No, my dear, not destiny. All of those things are in the will of the One True God. It is His will that you came here. Now it is up to you to decide what you will do with your time."

Tension filled her face, and her voice was broken as she whispered, "I wish to train as you trained my grandmother. I want the faith that she had."

Clapping his hands in front of him, he joyously exclaimed, "This is the will of the One True God and an answer to your grandmother's prayers. She always prayed desperately for her future children to know the truth."

"She prayed for me?" Astril asked quietly.

"It was her greatest desire that your mother and your mother's children live their lives with the great love of the One True God residing in their hearts… in your heart."

Astril again stared down at her hands. He knew her emotions were overtaking her speech so he waited patiently. It was some time before she spoke again. She raised her face toward him, tears rolling freely down her cheeks and asked, "How do I get this love that my grandmother had?"

Priest Augur gently touched her shoulder with his hand. "You have to invite Him to come into your heart."

She shook her head fiercely and again looked as if she might bolt out of the room. "No! I don't want to invite anyone into my heart," she cried. "I saw what happened to my sister when she invited the Great Goddess into her. It… consumed her." She shuddered violently.

He wanted so desperately to relieve her pain but knew that only the One True God could heal all of the evil she had seen in her short life.

Clearing his voice, he decided to move in a different direction. One that might help her understand. "Tell me what differences you saw between your mother and your grandmother."

Her left eyebrow rose to a sharp point as she stared into his face. "What do you mean?"

"As a child, I'm sure you saw many differences between the life of your mother and that of your grandmother. Tell me about them."

Astril thought for a moment. "My mother was always doing her duty for the Great Goddess. She sacrificed her time with her children and her relationship with her own mother to serve that god."

"And your grandmother?"

"My grandmother sacrificed her own comfort to provide love and security for me and my sister. She also loved my mother even though her love was not returned."

Priest Augur smiled. "And did you notice anything else?"

"Yes. My grandmother always seemed to be at peace even when times were dreadful. In every situation, she provided a warm hand of reassurance and kindness." Then looking away she whispered, "My mother was consumed with hate and anger over everything. Her hand carried the weight of abuse, not love."

"Astril, that peace you saw in your grandmother was given to her because she allowed the One True God to reside His love within her every day. There is no room for peace and love with your mother's god."

Astril smiled and wiped the tears off her cheeks, "I think I understand the difference now. What do I need to do to gain His love in my own heart?"

"You only have to pray for Him to pour down His love and reside within you."

She hung her head. "What if I don't know how to pray?"

He smiled and reassured her with a pat to the hand, "All you have to do is repeat the words that I speak. Will you do that?"

Astril sighed slowly then nodded her head in agreement.

He instructed her to bow her head and close her eyes while he laid his hand on her forehead. "One True God, I ask that You bring Your mighty love into my heart…"

Astril repeated his words, then he went on to say, "Reside within me so I may know Your great love and peace…"

"Reside within me so that I may know Your great love and peace…" she echoed.

Finishing, the priest said, "And allow me to grow deeper in Your mercy and grace every day."

She repeated, "And allow me to grow deeper in Your mercy and grace every day."

"And now I will pray a blessing over you, my child," the priest said, squeezing her trembling hands.

"One True God, Your child wishes to learn more of You. We ask that You reveal Yourself to her and help her walk in the direction that You have planned for her. We ask for her protection from an enemy more evil than we know. Thank You for this wonderful young woman, One True God, and for the great blessing she will be to You and to Your people. Bless her, keep her, and bring her into Your knowledge and love."

Maintaining a bowed head, Astril sat completely still.

He couldn't help but chuckle at her. "It's over."

"What?" She raised her eyes to him. "That's it?"

Smiling down at her he answered, "Yes, my child, that's it."

Joy radiated from her eyes. It was the same look that everyone he had led to the One showed. The look never failed to fill him with happiness and peace.

Throwing her arms around his neck in a tight embrace, Astril cried, "Thank you. Thank you so much."

He watched her leave the room as if running on air, the bittersweet moment tugging at his heart. "Oh, Sallian you would be so proud right now. She is truly beginning to grow. Only the One knows what evil the days ahead may bring, and only He can bring her through the fire."

It had been only a few short days since Drinna's young charge had accepted the love of the One True God in her heart. Ever since that day, Drinna had seen a growing change in the girl. Astril's smile came easily now and brightened her face in a lovely way. She worked hard at her daily lessons and at times wearied the priests with her constant questions and insights.

It was an unusually bright day outside, and all the priests were busy at their work. The scent of jasmine and fresh grass hung in the air, tantalizing her senses. Drinna had completed her morning chores much earlier than expected. So with not much to do until the evening meal, she sat under the shade of a large tree, playing with the girl's short hair. Astril lay with her head in Drinna's lap. Dark brown lashes layered her closed eyes. A soft smile played at her lips as she rested.

"So, you're going to behave yourself now, huh?" Drinna asked while curling a light-colored hair softly around her finger.

Astril lazily opened her eyes and smiled up at her. "Oh, Drinna, I feel as though my heart might burst with happiness."

Drinna laughed, and swatting a fly away from the girl's forehead, said, "That's what happens when you fall in love with the One True God. He has a way of making the most difficult situations easier."

Astril sat up quickly. "Now I understand why Toren tried to save me and why he is so kind to everyone."

Drinna gave the girl a knowing look. "Yes, the One True God certainly made a gem out of that young man. To think, he could have taken after his grandfather."

"I'm sorry I've been so mean to you, Drinna," Astril said with a teasing smile playing at her lips.

"Oh, you make it fun, you little heathen," Drinna said while fanning herself with the hem of her apron. "Now get on with you, or Priest Augur will wonder why you aren't pestering him."

Astril gave Drinna a big hug and then jumped to her feet and ran off toward the temple.

"She's going to have to learn to run in that getup," Drinna laughed as she watched the girl trip slightly over the hem of the heavy gown. Then looking around she saw General Ard and realized that he was also watching Astril. The unguarded lust on his face as he watched the girl climb the steps to the main building filled Drinna with dread. *That one has a dark look about him that Astril better watch out for,* she thought to herself then vowed to keep a closer watch on her young charge.

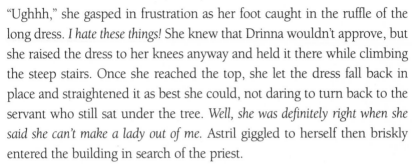

"Ughhh," she gasped in frustration as her foot caught in the ruffle of the long dress. *I hate these things!* She knew that Drinna wouldn't approve, but she raised the dress to her knees anyway and held it there while climbing the steep stairs. Once she reached the top, she let the dress fall back in place and straightened it as best she could, not daring to turn back to the servant who still sat under the tree. *Well, she was definitely right when she said she can't make a lady out of me.* Astril giggled to herself then briskly entered the building in search of the priest.

He almost lived in the study area of the building, so Astril went there to find him. Her latest memorization had confused her greatly, and she wondered what his thoughts might be.

Opening the door, Astril stepped forward to enter then tripped over the ruffled edge of the gown again. This time she was sure it ripped. *Great! Drinna's not going to be happy about having to fix this.*

"There you are, Astril," Priest Augur said with a laugh after seeing her trip over the gown. "I don't think you've quit gotten the hang of wearing that thing, have you?"

Looking down with disgust at her dress, Astril sighed, "It is frustrating, that's for sure." Then smiling said, "I've memorized another line from the old scrolls."

"You are one of my brightest students," answered the priest. "Let me hear what you've learned."

Astril couldn't help but be proud of her efforts. She was so on fire for learning. Never in her life had she been given such an opportunity to study, and she found that she liked it.

She stood before him and recited, "The One True God will deliver them to you. Be strong and courageous. Do not be afraid or terrified because of them, for the One True God goes with you; He will never leave you nor forsake you."

"Do you understand what that line means for your life, Astril," he asked.

Wringing her hands before her, she bit the side of her lip then answered, "I think it means that when times get very dark, and I'm afraid of what lies ahead, I need to push through with what I know is right, and He will be with me. He will not forsake me."

Priest Augur nodded his head then said softly, "There may be things that happen, Astril; things that are yet to come that you do not understand. You may find yourself alone and afraid. Do not lose faith during those times. Hold on to what you are learning. The words of the One True God bring life and not death, my dear. Hold tight to them, and He will direct your path."

Her mind was reeling over everything he had said. She sat down in a huff in the cushioned arm chair across from him, sending a heavy wisp of dust into the air. She waved the dust out of her face before asking, "What if I can't do it? What if I lose faith?

Priest Augur smiled and blew some of the dust particles away from the scroll that was in his lap. "Child, all you can do is believe that He means only good for you and that your life is in His hands."

"That's easy to believe while I'm here with you." She shook her head and leaned back against the chair, closing her eyes. "I just don't think it will be so easy when I stand before my mother."

"No, Astril. It won't be easy, but that's why you are here. The One is preparing you for a greater task, and you are using your time wisely."

Astril continued her lessons for the day with the priest, but her heart was heavy in anticipation of what might come. Was the One really preparing her for something greater than what she now knew or was it simply her destiny to die at her mother's hands? *What does He want from me?*

That night Astril had trouble getting to sleep as thoughts of her people, of her mother and her sister ran wildly through her mind.

"One True God, please help me be strong in whatever path You lead me," she whispered to the air then fell into a fitful sleep.

"Astril." A deep voice grated through her room in the darkness of the early morning, jolting her awake.

"Who's there," she cried, jumping out of bed. "Show yourself."

"You know it's me, Astril." Ard's bold chuckle sent her heart thudding madly. What did he want? "Now calm down. I'm not going to hurt you. I just want to talk."

His voice was getting closer.

Astril felt with her hands along the wall, trying to get to the farthest corner of the room, away from the approaching voice of the large man.

"What are you doing in here?" she hissed through clenched teeth.

He chuckled again, even nearer in the darkness. "I told you, I just want to talk to you."

The air in front of her whispered across her cheek. A shadow darted her way. His hand? Astril avoided Ard's touch by slinking closer to the wall and moving slightly to her left.

"Be still so we can talk." His whisper was taut with tension.

"Get out and talk to me tomorrow." She swiftly slid away, and his shadowy form lunged toward her.

This time his hand brushed across her chest. She jumped backward, and the long skirt of her nightdress clung to her legs, causing her to stumble. She knocked into a chair. Grabbing hold of the chair's back, she braced her arms and using it to support her weight, kicked her feet out into the darkness. Satisfied by his grunt that her kick did some damage, Astril raced for the door.

Turning the handle, she was able to get it opened only a crack before Ard's large arms crushed around her waist. *Why can I never get away from this man?* she thought wildly.

She attempted to scream, but it was cut off as he clamped a silencing paw over her mouth and slammed her close up against him.

He held her body tightly against his own, pressing her arms to her sides. Air became precious as his hand pressed hard against her mouth. She felt his hot breath on her ear and cringed to think of his intentions.

"Astril, I have seen how you long to be in my arms," he whispered. "We can slip away tonight. No one will miss us. I will protect you." He smeared a slimy kiss across her ear and still holding a hand over her mouth, continued, "You will not be burdened with Toren's puny attempts at playing hero any longer. I can protect you far better than he can."

Astril stared out into the blackness of the room as the giant continued to whisper in her ear from behind. Her entire body shook as she stood unable to move in his grip.

"I need you more than he does. Please say that you'll leave with me." Ard lowered his head over her shoulder and nipped his teeth along her cheek, an action that caused him to loosen his grip on her mouth.

She recognized her opportunity and sank her teeth deep into the firm, salty flesh of his hand. Ard bellowed a curse and flung her across the room, and she scrambled toward the door. She had only enough time to grab the handle and pull before he crossed in front of her and caught her in his grip again. This time he forced her to face him. She struggled desperately against his giant hands that crushed her upper arms.

"Why can't you stop fighting and accept that we're meant to be together," he screamed, shaking her so violently that her head flopped like one of the dead animals her mother sacrificed.

Ard stopped shaking her and stood with his back to the open door. The stream of light revealed the determination on his face as he stared at her, panting. He was going to take her no matter what. *There isn't anything I can do to fight him,* she cried to herself. She had never felt so helpless and weak in her life.

Just as she had given up the thought of escaping, a loud *pop* echoed in the room, and Ard's head jerked forward. His eyes rolled back, and he groaned her name while holding tightly to her for support. Another *pop* exploded in the air as he again lurched forward. His body went slack and crashed into her. She teetered under his weight but maintained her balance as he fell to the floor in an unconscious heap.

Shaken and standing in her torn, rumpled nightdress, Astril stared straight into Toren's eyes. His face was contorted with rage as he raised his sword over his cousin's crumpled form, its bloodied hilt glistening in the first rays of dawn.

Chapter Seventeen

Toren stared down at the disheveled young woman before him. Her nightdress was torn immodestly at the shoulder, and a bright red handprint smeared across her mouth and cheeks. With every tear that streamed down her face, Toren thought he felt his heart rip more.

"Get him out of here and tie him up in his own room," he roared at the quickly approaching soldiers.

"Toren, you came." Astril breathed heavily as she fell into his arms, her body limp with exhaustion from the fight.

"I am so sorry," he said as he picked her up and set her gently on the bed. "I should have listened to your warning about Ard. I was so blind."

Astril leaned against the shoulder he offered and quietly cried.

Toren placed a protective arm around her shoulders. Holding her close, he could smell Ard's sweat emanating from her, further proof of the battle. *I'm going to kill him.*

"Astril," he said after a moment. "Did he… hurt you?"

She looked up at him with a tearstained face. It was the final urging his heart needed before it ripped in two. "No. He said he just wanted to talk, but I didn't believe him."

Toren watched her shudder and again silently vowed to deal with his cousin's offense.

"Has he attacked you before?"

Her body racked with sobs, Astril nodded her head. "The other times were not this violent. Except when he punched me in the forest, but then he didn't do anything else."

"He punched you?" Toren questioned incredulously. "Why didn't you tell me?"

"I didn't think I could."

He knew the truth of her words. She had tried, but he had cut her off, refusing to believe anything bad about his cousin. Staring deeply into her eyes, he felt shame at not being there to protect her and guilt for not listening in the first place. He shook his head, deeply burdened by his own failure.

The exchange between them was interrupted as Astril's servant ran into the room, screaming.

"Astril, are you hurt?" Drinna cried, casting a suspicious look at him.

Astril smiled weakly at the protectiveness of the advancing woman. "It was Ard, Drinna. He came in my room and…" She cut her words off with a shudder then looked at Toren who withdrew his gaze when he thought he saw admiration in her eyes. "Toren saved me," she added with a proud tone.

Drinna kept a distrustful eye on him as she pulled him to his feet and thanked him for his help then quickly ushered him out of the room. "I'm sure that you understand the poor thing needs her rest right now," she said in her determination to get rid of him quickly. "Such a giant of a man to fight off. What a girl!" Drinna emphasized the final words as she slammed the door shut in Toren's face.

He stared at the closed door with a shame-filled heart. *How could everything go so terribly wrong so fast? All I've ever wanted to do is protect her, and I can't even do that right!* His heart cried out when he heard the sound of a chair being dragged across the floor and pushed under the door handle. Touching the door lightly, he realized that he could never have her if he couldn't provide even basic protection.

Wrath boiling through him, he turned on his heel and sped through the hallways to Ard's room.

He found his cousin passed out on a chair, his arms and legs bound with coarse rope. Toren grabbed the unconscious man and shook him violently awake.

"Wha…" Ard said in a groggy voice. Realization at his situation flashed across his face, and he began to struggle against the ties that bound him to the chair. He blinked up at Toren. "Where's Astril?"

At the sound of her name, all of the rage Toren had within him coursed down his arm and into his fist, and he punched his cousin full in the face. His knuckles split open with a meaty *crack* from the impact of Ard's teeth, but he didn't care. The pain felt deserved.

"How dare you touch her!" he roared. "You had no right."

"I love her," Ard pleaded, and Toren let his rage out again with another hard punch to the mouth. This time he broke open his cousin's mouth as well as his own knuckles.

Ard made a gurgling sound in his throat.

"Shut up!" It gave Toren a strange sense of satisfaction to stare at the dark blood that coursed down the corner of his cousin's mouth.

Silence covered the room as the two men stared one another down.

After a few moments, Toren's anger subsided, replaced by exhaustion from his own rage and defeat by the events that had taken place. He turned to sit on the bed. "What has changed you, Ard?"

"Changed me?" His cousin choked and then spit, spraying a mouthful of blood onto the floor. "I haven't changed. I'm still the man I've always been. I'm still the man who has to stand by in his younger cousin's shadow. I don't have anything, and I never have. Everything is yours. You are the rightful heir to the throne; you have Morgan; you have your grandfather's love; and now you have Astril."

Then turning pleading eyes toward him, Ard said, "Give her to me. I will protect her from her people so you can go home and marry Morgan. You will make a good king, and she will be your beautiful queen." Toren sat still, not believing any of what he heard. Ard's voice turned desperate as he shouted, "I will give you command of all my men and all my possessions are yours if you give Astril to me."

Toren jumped up from the bed. "You can't barter for a human life like you would an animal, Ard."

Ard ducked his head at the intensity of Toren's voice. When another blow did not come, he raised dark, hate-filled eyes back up and sneered, "What are you going to do with her, little cousin? Are you going to marry her over Morgan?"

He laughed aloud. "What would our people think of having a Seerling queen on the throne?" he taunted.

Toren shook his head in disbelief at the torrent of words Ard threw out at him.

Ard seized the opportunity of Toren's silence. "Or will you hide her away, and keep her for your own use? Honestly, cousin, you're no better than me."

The accusation sent Toren's fist shooting out with a massive punch to the side of Ard's head. The larger man's chair fell backward onto the floor. Grabbing his cousin by the shirt, Toren screamed down at him, "You will go back to Harkan and stand trial for your crime."

Ard spit blood in his face. "What crime? She's a slave. There was no crime." Still bound hand and foot, he sneered his contempt.

Toren struck the man in the face again then stormed out of the room, wiping the foul stench of Ard's blood off his face with the collar of his shirt.

You know he's right, he thought. *There is no punishment on the judgment books for attacking a slave, and Astril is still listed as my slave.*

"Once I'm king, those laws will change."

Sleep eluded Toren that night. Early in the morning he left his chambers and sat down at a large table in the study room. It was not long before he was joined by his mentor and priest. The two men sat in silence for a long period of time both contemplating the evil that had taken place the night before. While Priest Augur stared in front of him at nothing in particular, Toren sat with his face in his hands as though he were a beaten man.

"I thought I knew him. How could he do something so vile?"

"Lust can drive a man to commit many crimes," the priest answered quietly. "When you combine that with jealousy, well, it was only a matter of time before something evil happened."

"What can I do with him? He can't stand trial, since the law says there was no crime because she's a slave."

Priest Augur sat for a moment, rubbing his white beard. "He could stand trial for his crime against Morgan. I believe the king would find that an insult, since she is your intended."

Toren let out a sigh. "Yes, that's all I can do. I'll send him back to Harkan and have him stand trial for his crime against her."

"Will you be leaving soon then?"

Toren sat for a long time before answering. "No, I will stay here. Once my grandfather finds out what Ard did to her, he will try to force me to marry Morgan immediately." Staring down at the table for a long moment, Toren went on, "I'm not ready to marry her. I'll stay here and let Ard stand trial based on the word of my soldiers and Morgan."

Smiling, Priest Augur shrugged. "I think you need to get some sleep now."

Toren knew that his face showed the exhaustion he felt, but he insisted on staying awake. He felt that he needed to perform some sort of penance for his failure but just couldn't figure out what to do to absolve himself.

He knew the priest was staring at him, but he didn't want to look up and expose the pain that filled him to his core.

"Punishing yourself will not change what happened to Astril."

"I know," Toren said still not willing to look at the priest. "I only hope she will forgive me for not believing what she said about him. If I had believed her, she wouldn't have been attacked. I should have been here to protect her."

"You will find that she has changed much since you were here last," Priest Augur said quietly. "Do not take more blame on yourself than you ought. She has already forgiven you."

Toren sat back in the chair and watched as his longtime friend and mentor walked out of the room.

It had been a long night and an even longer morning for Astril since Drinna had decided to camp out in the bed with her. The large woman took up so much room that Astril was relegated to a small corner of the bed. She had lain awake most of the dark morning, her mind still running over Ard's attack, and Toren's valiant efforts to defend her.

After picking at her meal, she left the dining area then entered the study where she found Toren. She noted with concern the dark, sour look that brooded over his features.

"Hi," she said, forcing a smile. "I missed you at the morning meal."

Toren cast a tired look in her direction. "Did you get any sleep last night?"

She laughed softly in an attempt to lighten his mood. "Not really. Drinna insisted on sleeping with me. Her snores could wake the dead."

Realizing that he was in no mood for humor, she commented, "You look terrible."

"Thanks," he muttered in return while slinking farther down in his chair.

Losing patience with his sulkiness, Astril demanded, "Toren, what's wrong with you?"

She sat still waiting for a reply. *Does he think this is all my fault?* The thought made her angry. "Fine. You obviously don't want to talk to me so I'll leave you to sulk." Crossing her arms, she stood and stalked away from him.

"I'm sorry," he whispered.

She stopped.

"Sorry for what?" Her words were still laced with impatience. Why could the fool man not come out and say what he had to say? Still she turned back to him.

Toren looked up at her, his eyes filled with sadness. "For not keeping my promise."

Confused, she walked closer to where he sat and stood in front of him. "What promise?"

Toren closed his eyes and folded his arms across his broad chest. "To not let anyone hurt you."

"Oh, Toren," she whispered, bending over and touching his hand. "You were only a little boy when you made that promise." She moved her hands to his shoulders and forced him to look at her. "Only the One True God can keep a promise like that."

She could tell that he was overcome by all that had taken place as he leaned forward and closed his eyes tightly. Slowly he reached his hands around her waist, pulled her close, and buried his face into the front of her gown.

Astril allowed herself the pleasure of stroking his soft brown hair as he held her tightly and cried.

He is so much like Kellon, her mind insisted as she held him close.

But he's not your brother, her thoughts betrayed her. *You love him.*

Shaking her head softly, still holding the crying man in her arms, she thought, *Yes, I do love him. I love him like I loved my brother.*

No you don't.

"Toren," Astril said in a husky voice as she disentangled his arms from around her waist. "Let me… get you something to eat."

"I'm sorry." He wiped the tears from his cheeks with a slap of his hand and stared down at the floor. "I shouldn't have done that."

Standing a little farther away from him than before, Astril pasted a fake smile on her lips. She knew she was failing terribly at hiding the distraction that had now entered her heart. "I—I'll go and get you some food."

He lowered his eyes, and as she raced out of the room, she puzzled at the shame she'd seen flicker across his face.

CHAPTER EIGHTEEN

Throughout his trial, Ard had alternately dozed and trimmed his fingernails with his hunting knife. The whole thing was ludicrous, nothing more than Toren's petty attempt to get back at him for taking what should have been Ard's all along. Still, he tensed as he waited for the king to deliver his verdict.

"Ard, for your crimes against Prince Toren's intended wife, I revoke your rank of general and banish you from the palace until such time as the prince chooses to bring you home," said King Kortan at the end of the trial.

Bowing his head, Ard hid the deep look of rage that crossed his face. Nothing mattered anymore except getting Astril for himself. *Toren has no idea what he holds in the palm of his hand.* He seethed inside, working through the details of his newly formed plan. He barely heard anything his uncle said.

King Kortan sighed out loud and went on, "Ard, you must be more careful in the future." Ard knew that the king possessed a similar personality to his own. But even with their similarities, Kortan favored his grandson over his nephew. *Toren is weak, always relying on the One to guide him. He won't take her, but I will. And when I do, he will know who's stronger.*

Ard heard reassurance in the king's voice but didn't care for any of his soothing words. His mind was fixed on what he wanted, and it didn't include anything that the king offered. Still he wisely stood his ground and listened to the king say, "It will not be so horrible. I will give you a nice country estate and plenty of servants to attend your needs. Perhaps you may even take a wife. I am sure that Prince Toren will not remain angry for long."

Ard nodded his head and thanked the king for his kindness and was dismissed from the court.

"I'll make him pay," he uttered under his breath as he stormed down the hall. "I'll make them all pay."

"Ard," Morgan simpered behind him, trying to catch up to his long strides. It was funny how only a few months ago the sight of her beauty sent his emotions in a whirlwind. Now he was annoyed just looking at her. Her simpering disgusted him. *How could I have ever been attracted to such a selfish girl?*

"I'm so sorry," she squeaked. "I didn't mean to tell. I never thought they would take away your rank."

Ard continued his pace, ignoring her apologies and the hand she had laid on his arm.

"What are you going to do now," she asked breathlessly, still racing to catch up.

Ard stopped suddenly and turned to her. He had had enough of her pestering and wanted to get her away from him. Darkly he stared into her eyes. "I am going to barter."

Morgan panted for breath, her hand raised to her chest as though she might faint from the exertion of their walk. Every movement she made annoyed him further. *Astril would never act like that.* Everything about Morgan screamed pampered selfishness, and it made him angry.

"What are you bartering for, Ard?"

With as much anger as he felt in his heart, he answered, "An animal more precious than you could ever imagine." His intentionally harsh words caused her face to crumple in confusion. Then understanding filled her eyes, and they welled with tears, as he'd known they would. Stupid, manipulative female—crushing her was so easy it wasn't even fun. Disgusted, he rounded the corner and left her blubbering in the hall.

His conversation with Morgan left Ard feeling angrier than ever. He needed information, and he needed it now! Holan, the king's main hall attendant was the perfect target to vent his rage upon. The sniveling man knew everything that went on in the palace and had the king's trust. Sweat dripped from Ard's brow down onto the face of the smaller man he held firmly against the cool stone wall.

"All I know is that they were traveling by night," the frightened attendant said. "The last time anyone reported spotting them was two nights ago. The farmer who saw them said they were east of the crossroads, heading west."

Finally, word on where the Seerlings are. This is all going perfectly. Ard smiled and let go of the man's shirt, leaving it wrinkled from his firm grasp. An action that he could tell relieved the smaller man before him. It had always pleased him to have others show fear in his presence, but now he relished the impact his size and strength held. "That was two days ago?"

"Yes, my lord."

"Ready my steed and prepare food enough for four days' journey," he commanded.

The attendant paused. "But my lord. I was told that you were banished from the palace. Wouldn't you want more than four days worth of food?"

The servant's question pleased him greatly. *Good. Everyone knows my fate. It will make it that much sweeter when Astril is lying in my arms and not Toren's.* Ard responded, "I only need four days' worth. Now go"—he balled up his impressive fist and shook it in the servant's face—"or I'll give you a reason to be late for your duties."

The servant scurried away to do his bidding.

I shall easily find this traveling party in that amount of time. After that I will be richly rewarded.

That same evening, Ard set out on his trek headed west. It was not long before he recognized the shallow tracks made by Seerling steeds. He smiled to himself. The Seerlings would never find their prey if they continued heading west.

"That many traveling together can not hide well," he said while continuing on his journey.

The night of the third day of travel he laid down on his pallet knowing that he was closer to the Seerlings than was safe. Lying still for so long and staying awake was difficult, but he wanted to make sure he heard everything and was ready in the event of an attack. At the darkest hour of the night he was able to make out the faintest rustling sound of leaves just behind him. *Those aren't animal rustlings.* He grinned.

He lay completely still on his pallet. Too often he had underestimated Astril's ability to fight. If she was any indicator as to the unusual strength and abilities Seerlings held, he was going to be ready for anything. Ard forced himself to stay in place even after hearing the soft padding of approaching footsteps. *It will happen fast. Be ready.*

He continued to hold himself in check as the approaching footsteps came closer and halted. A bright flash of light went off just to his right but didn't damage him as he kept his eyes closed tight. *Predictable heathens.*

"He didn't move." The whispered words came from his right. "Is he dead?" a second voice questioned. Something hard and sharp prodded at his back.

Slowly moving his hands over his head and rolling to his back, Ard spoke, "Do not harm me. I have information about Astril that you need."

The Seerling to his right jumped high in the air at the sound of Ard's voice and bludgeoned him in the head with a staff.

"No!" he screamed into the night, but darkness overcame him.

Slowly the world came back to life. As if in a fog that was slowly clearing, Ard made out the sound of soft humming above him. A sour scent filled his nostrils, one he could not recognize. Opening his eyes and looking around slowly, he realized that he was lying on the floor of a boran-hide tent. Gaining mental clarity, Ard pulled himself up on his elbow to survey his surroundings. The action brought a shooting pain to his head, reminding him of what had happened earlier that night.

"You told my soldiers that you have information about Astril." A soft, feminine voice murmured in his ear. "Tell me, and I will let you live."

Ard's head was reeling from the pain of the blow he had endured. He tried to turn to face the woman but wasn't quick enough as the voice moved to speak on his left.

"Tell me now what you know," she commanded.

Shaking his head to clear the fog that persisted, Ard groaned at the new shards of pain while he looked around the room, searching for the owner of the voice.

A blur passed before his eyes as he turned again back to the right. Spinning back around to face the front, Ard was confronted by a familiar face. She was kneeling in front of him and staring intently within inches of his face.

"Astril?" he questioned. *No this isn't Astril. It can't be.*

Reaching his hand out and touching the long, dark blonde hair that waved freely about her soft face, Ard realized he was looking at Gallian, the sister Astril had told him and Toren about on the way to Augur's. *So young. She can't be more than sixteen harvests old.*

Gallian smiled at him and allowed him to stroke her soft hair gently, something Astril never would have endured. She laughed sweetly and batted luxurious black lashes, drawing him in with her voice. "We look a little alike, don't you think?"

She left him dazed and disappointed when she stood in a motion quicker than his eyes could make out and was immediately standing on the other side of the tent. *How did she… ?*

Still staring down on him, she added, "Even though she is much smaller and weaker than I am."

How did you… ?" He pointed to where she stood. Realizing how stupid he looked with his jaw opened wide, he quickly shut his mouth.

Gallian's hair took on a life of its own as it began to wave freely in a soft breeze. The sour air again filled the tent, making him gag. "I am only going to ask you this one time more." She glared at him. "What do you know of my sister?"

Ard forced away his sudden fear and tried to ignore the unusual power of the girl. He remembered why he had sought to find the Seerlings. As he stood to tower over her, a look of humor cross her face. He realized his size meant nothing to her, and it frightened him.

Shaken, he said, "I want to barter."

"Barter?" her questioning voice rang sweet in the quiet night air as the sour wind whipped through his hair and around his face.

Realizing that he was becoming intoxicated by the smells in the tent and the sound of her voice, Ard shook the cloud from his head. "I want you to give me something in exchange for the information I have."

Ard watched fearfully as the girl's thin body shook with rage, and she lifted her arms over her head. Her hair flew in waves about her face, and the terrible wind tore violently through the tent. Her eyes sparked with what he thought to be fire. And the soft beauty of her face turned rock hard.

"How dare you come to me asking for anything," Gallian screamed. She grabbed him around the neck and lifted his body off the ground.

Ard struggled against the unnatural strength of the thin girl who held him in a death grip. *No! This is impossible!* Her chokehold threatened the very breath from his lungs.

"Now you will tell me what you know of my sister, or you will die!" she screamed. He clawed at her arm, legs flailing while staring down into her evil eyes. A quick look of pain crossed her features and small scream escaped her lips as she abruptly dropped him to the ground.

He fell, clutching his throat and gulping in precious air. Gallian's face cringed in pain as she grabbed hold of her left arm and cradled it. *So she isn't as powerful as she thinks.*

Still holding his aching throat, Ard stood again and attempted to show a bravery that he didn't have. "I know where your sister is, and I will take you there if you grant me one gift."

The terrible look the girl gave him left Ard feeling like a large piece of meat about to be attacked by a hungry wolf. Never had he felt so exposed.

She smiled, and rubbing her arm, nodded. "Tell me what you want, and I'll decide if you deserve it."

Ard chose his words with care. "First I want you to know that I am second in line to be king of Harkan. After me there are no others. I am in a position to give you valuable information that will help in bringing your people safely home from slavery. I also have the power to bring you to your sister."

Gallian stood with unblinking eyes. "And what prize do you want in return for such valuable information?"

"Astril." He braved the name out.

The evil look of hate that passed over her eyes made him shudder, but he held his ground.

Gallian looked him over very slowly. Again he imagined himself as her prey. She then walked toward him and placed her hand across his chin, drawing it down over his chest as she circled his body. He held his position firm even though his knees threatened to buckle.

"First you will tell me where my sister is. Once I have her, you will give me the information you have on Harkan." She stood on her toes to kiss his neck, sending cold shivers down his spine, and whispered, "Then you will have your prize."

Ard could feel the fog of her seductive spell filling his head but was powerless to stop the effects. He knew he had just made a pact with evil but was willing to do anything it took to get what he wanted. Gallian crossed to stand in front of him, waving her hands in his face. The foul wind filled his nostrils as she whispered words he could not understand. The wolf had returned to her face and was ready to pounce. Why couldn't he gain clarity over his mind? Gradually his world became a fog. He was trapped in her magic.

CHAPTER NINETEEN

"Well, Miss Astril, you are very dull these last few days," Drinna said, "What's got your spirit so downcast?"

Astril forced a smile for the sake of the large woman who sat on the chair across from her in their chamber. Ever since the night of Ard's attack, Drinna had insisted on sharing the room with her. Astril knew the woman's concern came from a place of pure love, but the coddling was so foreign to her that she struggled with frustration every time the attendant drew close.

"I'm okay," Astril lied. *Just please leave me alone. I can't take all this attention. It's too much.* For a girl who had grown up in the shadow of evil, the love and care she was receiving on a daily basis were overwhelming and hard to swallow.

Drinna stood and laid her hand upon Astril's forehead. Astril forced herself to remain calm at the touch. She silently reminded herself that she couldn't flinch every time someone reached out to her. *Not everyone wants to hurt me.*

"You don't have a fever. So it must be something ailing in your stomach."

"I told you I'm fine, Drinna. Please don't pester me."

Looking Astril over from the top of her head to the bottom of her feet,

Drinna sat in silence for a short time then began to laugh.

"And what's so funny?" Astril asked in an irritated voice not expecting such a response from the larger woman. Here she was feeling poorly, and this woman was laughing.

Still laughing loudly and holding her stomach as if in pain, Drinna responded, "Now I recognize your symptoms. You're in love."

"What!" Astril rose in her chair, turning it over behind her. "How dare you. I am not. Toren is like a brother to me, and that's all!" She then stamped her foot hard on the ground to prove her point.

Drinna covered her mouth with her hand, presumably to keep any further laughter from bursting over at the sight of Astril's childish action. All Drinna's efforts were wasted, much to Astril's frustration, as her guffaws spilled over anyway.

Astril grabbed up the chair and sat back down in a huff then allowed the foul mood inside her to fill her face in as ugly a way as possible.

The expression only made Drinna laugh harder. Standing up, the rotund woman went to the closet, and picked out a light green dress. She presented it to Astril for approval, all the while wiping tears from her cheeks.

"You know I don't care," Astril said with an exaggerated role of her eyes.

Drinna hiccupped back a laugh and walked over to help her step into the gown.

Astril groaned at the pushing and shoving that Drinna had to do to pour her already thin body into the dress. *Drinna altered all of these dresses to fit me, but she made them too tight.*

"I'll be so glad when I never have to wear another one of these uncomfortable gowns again," she muttered.

"If you don't like being shoved in and up at your small size, what do you think I feel like," Drinna answered. Then to emphasize her point, she puffed out her cheeks, grabbed her own waist, pushed up her breasts, and allowed her eyes to bug out while falling to the bed in a pretend faint.

Astril forced herself to not laugh at the spectacle the attendant made of herself and instead sat down in the chair, buttoning the sleeves that fell to just above her elbows.

"Astril, why don't you tell me what has depressed you so," Drinna said in a more serious tone while struggling to her feet. "Perhaps I can help."

"I'm just worried about Toren. He took the situation with Ard very badly, and I'm sure it was even harder given the sudden death of his father." Astril stopped for a moment and then added, "Also, I think I might have hurt his feelings."

"What did you do?" Drinna asked calmly, kneeling in front of Astril and lacing up the bodice of the gown.

"A while ago I found him in the dining hall. He was sitting there depressed, and I think angry about everything. Well, he was very upset and was hugging me and I..."

Drinna's hands stopped moving the laces as she sat back on her heels and listened intently to the story, nodding her head for Astril to continue.

"Well... I got uncomfortable with his hug and left the room really fast," Astril explained. "Now I think he's angry with me. He hasn't spoken a word to me since."

Silence held the room in check as Drinna concentrated on lacing the front of the gown. As soon as she finished, she sat back down on the bed and slyly raised her eyebrow. "Why would you be uncomfortable with his hug? After all, didn't you just say that you think of him as a brother?"

Astril glared daggers through her attendant. "Ugghhh!" she cried then jumped up and huffed out the room to find Priest Augur and begin her daily lessons. Closing the door behind her, she could just make out the last sounds of Drinna's loud laughter.

"Infuriating woman!" Astril hissed as she stalked in the direction of the study.

There he is. Priest Augur breathed out in relief. He had been praying long and hard for the young man and was afraid that in his current state, Toren might do something drastic. He had never seen the prince so depressed.

It was a beautiful day, but the storm that hovered over Toren threatened to fill the garden he sat in. All around him were flowers of every hue. Even the tree that he leaned against blossomed with honey flower vines. But the prince sat silent, brooding, lost in his own thoughts. *Does he even see the beauty that surrounds him? The gifts of the One meant only for him?*

"Prince Toren, my boy, there you are. I've looked everywhere for you."

Toren didn't look up. He sat concentrating on his folded hands placed loosely in his lap. Even though his gaze was downward, Augur could see the frustration that played havoc over his face.

Sitting down under the tree beside the young man, he asked, "What has become of you this past few weeks? You have hardly eaten, and you're constantly hiding out somewhere."

"I'm fine," Toren answered in a quiet tone.

The two sat together in silence for a long time before Augur spoke again. "Toren, you need to forgive Ard and move on with your life."

That did it. This time Toren did look up at him, his face filled with disappointment and anger.

"Forgive him? I trusted him to take care of her, and you saw how he repaid my trust." Shaking his head, Toren stared at the priest. "No, you can not ask me to forgive such a vile person."

Priest Augur patted his hand reassuringly. "Toren, you know this will consume you if you don't let it go. Astril has already forgiven Ard's actions, and it was she who he offended."

"How can you call that an offense?" Toren pleaded with the priest. "Don't you understand what he could have done—what he would have done if I hadn't gotten there to save her?"

Shaking his head, Priest Augur looked at the defeated man beside him. "Toren, you take too much on your own shoulders. Astril is now a child of the One True God. You have to release this possessive hold you have over her and allow Him to do His job. He is the only one who can truly protect any of us."

Toren sat in silence, still shaking his head, then said quietly, "No, she's mine to protect, and I failed."

Priest Augur sat beside him, not believing the words he had heard. *How often have we discussed giving everything to the One? Why doesn't he understand that this hold he has over the girl will be the very thing that causes him to lose her?*

As he sat silently contemplating what to say, he caught site of Astril coming through the garden gate. She was a vision of beauty and perfection with her hair pulled back high upon her head. Soft, light-colored curls played across her forehead and ears. Her elegant neck was exposed as were her shoulders. The green dress became her very well.

He knew that Toren had purchased scores of gems for her to wear, but he had never seen her in any. *A simple girl with simple tastes. No wonder he can't let go of her.* Augur smiled at her where she stopped just inside the gate with a troubled look over her countenance.

"I think I will leave you now." He patted the prince's arm and got up to greet Astril.

Walking over to her, he placed his hand on her shoulder and smiled down. "He is much troubled. Perhaps you can help ward off his bad mood."

⁂

Astril watched Priest Augur walk away. He looked much older than his years, and the strain of worry that etched his face made his appearance even more aged. She turned back to Toren, who sat under a tall elm, then she braved herself up as best she could and walked over to sit beside him. He didn't even look up at her. She ignored the stab of pain in her heart and set out to make amends.

She took his hand in her own, holding it tight. "I'm sorry I left you alone the other day."

When he didn't answer and didn't look up she went on, "I got very confused and… well… I promise to be a better listener today."

Toren looked at her with a forced smile. "I'm sorry I cried on you like that. I should never have done something so shameful." He turned his face away, refusing to look at her again.

"Toren, crying isn't shameful." She smiled, relief washing over her that he wasn't angry at her actions. "It shows me that you are human and that you care."

He hung his head even further and stared at his hands.

Astril turned her body around so that they sat knee to knee. "Toren, please look at me."

Her breath caught in her chest as he looked up, and they locked eyes.

Steadying her breathing, she forced herself to speak past the sudden lump in her throat. "I've been thinking about what you said to me."

"What did I say?"

"When you told me you were sorry for breaking your promise," she explained. "I want you to know that I have never held you to that promise, and I never will."

Toren's eyes filled with anger, and he let go of her hand then stood up and shouted down at her, "It's not your decision to make."

He started to walk away, but she grabbed his arm and he stopped. She pleaded, "Toren, don't be angry. I just wanted you to know that I want you to be free from that promise."

He turned back to her and gently took her hand from his arm and covered it with both of his own. "Astril, don't you understand?" His eyes begged her to know what he felt. "I want to protect you."

"I know," she said with a small smile, "but you don't have to."

They stood there for many minutes looking into each other's eyes and not speaking. She knew that she was very much in danger of falling deeply in love with him, but she couldn't tear her gaze away.

"Astril, I would give up my own life if it was the only way I could protect you." The conviction in his voice pierced deeply to her soul. No one had ever cared so much for her. Could he love her? *No! He can't. I won't let him!* Her heart beat so loudly she was sure he could hear it.

"Why?" she asked, her eyes tearing up. "Why would you say something like that? You don't even know me."

Toren took her arms in his hands and smiled for the first time in days. It was love that she saw. *No! Please don't love me. Please don't.*

"Yes, I do. I know you better than anyone." His eyes misted as he held her close. The warmth of his arms felt so good. How could she feel security that she knew was false?

"Astril, you are like the very sun to me. I never knew that the earth could be filled with so much light until I met you. I... love you."

She stared up at him. *No. This can't be happening. He can't love me. No!*

"I don't care if you love me as only a brother." He went on. His eyes were begging her to love him. *Oh, how easy it would be to let go, to give him my love.*

Astril snapped back to the reality of the moment as he was saying, "I just need for you to know that I have always loved you. From the very day that you dragged me back to the crossroads after saving me, I have loved you."

Crying, Astril tried to pull away from his firm grip. "Toren, I... we... we can never have a future."

"Why?" he pleaded, pulling her closer into his embrace.

Astril fought against his hug. "Don't you see what is going to happen, Toren," she cried. "Gallian will find me. I told you from the beginning that my life is forfeit. You can't love me because I don't have a future."

Shaking her head, she went on, "I came here because I made a promise to my grandmother that I would seek out the One True God before I died. I found that opportunity with you. I am so sorry that I have endangered everyone with my selfishness." With the last words she turned away from him, intending to run back to her room.

He grabbed her arm and pulled her close again, allowing her to cry into his shirt. "Astril, you are the only person I have ever met that isn't selfish. What you did was the right thing. Please don't worry. I'll protect you from your mother and sister."

Astril shook her head violently and screamed into his chest, "No! I won't allow you to be harmed because of me. I've been so foolish to wish for a life that cannot be mine. It's time I leave this place." Breaking free from him, she ran to her chambers.

Once back inside, she forced Drinna out of the room despite her objections. The older woman's face was stricken, but Astril had to do it. She couldn't stay here pretending any longer. The sooner she left, the better they would all be. Working it all through her mind, she sat down to devise a plan. She knew that there was no way Toren would allow her to leave, especially now. She had to find a way to get around his watchful gaze. Reaching under the mattress, she pulled out the boys' clothing that he had given her to wear for their trip to Helgard.

These will have to work again. She ran her hand over the bodice of the light green gown. *The only good thing is that I won't have to wear another one of these.*

It wasn't long after she had entered the room that she heard a soft knock at the door.

"Astril." She heard Toren's husky voice. "Please let me in."

She walked over and spoke through the closed door, "I want to be alone."

With her face pressed to the hard wood she heard him sigh deeply and listened as his footsteps receded down the hall. It broke her heart, and she allowed the tears to fall unchecked down her cheeks.

She stared around the room, searching for wood that would suffice for a staff. Looking over the four posts that held the frame together, she nodded. *This will have to do.* She went over and pushed and pulled with all her might. A loud *crack,* and the post released its hold of the frame. She measured it against her own height, and judging that to be good, balanced it in her hand. Then she picked up the dagger that Drinna had insisted they keep after Ard's attack, and began carving.

Chapter Twenty

For the next two days, Astril stayed away from everyone. She even gave up her lessons with Priest Augur to prepare for her trip. No one knew what she was up to since she refused any visitors and ate only small amounts of the food Drinna brought. She ate enough to keep her strength up and kept the non-perishables in a piece of fabric. She knew her time there was quickly coming to an end. Within her heart she felt a brooding sense of danger approaching and wanted to be clear of Helgard before it found her.

She had completed her preparations and planned to leave that particular night, as a heavy mist had fallen and would shroud her from curious eyes. Now she stood at the window in her chambers, staring down into the darkened courtyard. Through the mist, she could make out dim shadows slinking over the stone wall. Stealing a glance at the courtyard every few seconds, she changed out of her nightdress and into the boys' clothing. She tucked her freshly copied scrolls into the back of her shirt and secured them by the small belt she wore about her waist.

"So it begins," she whispered to the darkness. "If only I could have left earlier perhaps this would have been avoided. It's too late now."

Astril finished buttoning her tunic and reached to put on her boots when Toren burst into the dark room. "One of the guards has disappeared. I think we might be under attack."

Astril whispered back and pointed out the window. "Yes, I know. It's my sister."

"You don't know that for sure, Astril." He crossed the room to stare out the window at the thickening mist below them.

They stood in silence for only a short time before Astril turned toward him. "Toren, it's time. You see that mist down there? It's not natural. My sister created it. A full-scale attack will occur soon, and we need to be ready."

She watched his jaw clench tightly as he nodded his head, still staring down at the courtyard.

"Toren," she whispered turning him around to face her in the darkness. "I need you to make me a promise."

"Astril, we don't have time for this," he said turning to leave the room.

Resting both her hands on his shoulders, she persisted. "Promise me that no matter what happens down there tonight, you will not try to protect me."

Again Toren tried to turn away from her. "Astril, we can talk about this later."

If he went down to fight, Gallian would slaughter him. Astril could think of only one way to distract him so that she could keep him safe.

She reached up and held his face in her hands then stepped up on her toes. Catching her breath at the knowledge of what she was about to do, she leaned in and allowed herself to kiss him with all the passion she felt in her heart. Her unexpected embrace caught him off guard. She felt him tense and then soften to her kiss. Even the evil that threatened below could not keep her from enjoying the taste of his lips, the warmth of his arms. She was losing herself in her own plan. *Stop it!* Begrudgingly she forced her mind back to the present and still kissing him, reached for the water vase that sat on the table beside them. It was an improvised plan, but one that had to work.

Holding the vase behind her back, she pulled away from his embrace. "We have a big job ahead of us." Her voice sounded foreign after the kiss they had shared. She couldn't look at him. He cleared his voice but didn't speak. She could feel his breath on the top of her head but still refused to look up. "You'd better go and get your men."

He released his hold of her and cleared his throat again before saying, "I want you to stay up here until the fighting is over."

Still looking down, she nodded her head in reassurance, and he turned to leave the room.

Lifting the vase high over her head, she took a step toward him and whispered, "Please forgive me."

Her heart broke in two at the cry from his lips when the vase cracked over his head. The weight of his body slammed against the bed as he blacked out and crumpled to the floor in an unconscious heap.

"What have you done?" Drinna gasped in the doorway.

Looking up at the attendant, she responded in a husky voice, still overcome by the kiss. "It had to be done for his own good. My sister has come for me, and you know he would never let me go. They'll kill him if he goes down there. This is the only way I could think of to keep him safe." Huffing under his weight, she tried desperately to lift him up then turned back to the attendant. "Please help me get him on the bed."

With the two of them working they were able to lift his heavy body up and lay him out in a comfortable position.

"Drinna," Astril breathed hard. "Please check to make sure there isn't any real damage to his head, and don't leave this room for any reason."

"But Astril..." the older woman began.

Astril turned back to her before leaving the room. "Thank you for loving me, Drinna. You have taught me so much more than you will ever know. Please tell Toren that..." She choked on the raw emotions that had crept into her throat. "Tell him that I really do love him, and I always will." Astril picked up the dagger and sheathed it in her belt. She then grabbed her newly made staff and raced from the room.

Astril quickly maneuvered through the familiar hallway and down the stairs, exiting the building to enter the courtyard. She recognized the sour, sulfuric smell of the mist and knew she had been correct. Somewhere down there Gallian stood watching her and using her powers to create the cloudy air. Placing her staff solidly upon a plank in the wooden floor of the outdoor porch, she launched her body through the mist, over the steep stairs, and landed on the ground in a fighting stance. With slightly bent knees, Astril threw out her left hand while holding her staff tucked easily in the crook of her right arm.

She immediately ducked out of the way of a soft whizzing sound just off to her left. Again using her staff as a weight, she raised her body through the air, landing a solid kick to the head of a Seerling soldier. Astril jumped into the air to avoid the second whizzing sound of a Seerling staff just at her feet. Thus she fought hard, landing her blows on more of her countrymen than she could count.

Astril knew she was gaining ground as the strikes she endured upon her own body became fewer.

I imagine that I taught most of these fighters how to use their staffs to begin with, she thought viciously while slicing her dagger through the air, making contact with flesh. *What a way to repay me.*

With the dagger still in her hand, she whirled the staff around above her head and struck down another soldier. She jumped up on the back of the male and catapulted herself, while cutting the air with her staff. Two soldiers cried out just before Astril made out the sound of applause.

"I must say," uttered a low, feminine voice. "Your fighting hasn't changed as much as your appearance has."

Astril stood in fighting stance, staring blindly into the heavy mist. All of a sudden the fog pulled back, leaving a clear corridor between the two women, and she could see her sister waving her slender white arms. Gallian held a delighted smile upon her lips as she walked through the clear passage to stand in front of Astril.

"Gallian," Astril spit.

"Honestly, sister, you look terrible, and what have you done to your hair?" Gallian laughed then faked seriousness, "Won't mother be surprised."

Astril watched closely, aware of her sister's unpredictable nature. The smile on the priestess's face spread even larger as she nodded her head to the side. Astril's eyes followed the direction her sister had indicated and was able to make out the large, dark form of a man walking through the mist to stand at Gallian's side.

"Ard?" she questioned incredulously. "What have you done?"

Gallian looked to the man at her side and planted her hand on his shoulder in a way that showed ownership. Looking back at her sister, she practically glowed with joy. "So you do know this man."

Ard stood transfixed at Gallian's side. She knew that he was under the magic of her sister and nothing could shake that. Where his face had once held a hunger and thirst for life, it now lay flat.

Shaking her head and maintaining her stance, Astril ignored the feelings of pity that sprang up for Ard and addressed her sister. "All right, Gallian. You have me. Let's not make this any more difficult than it has to be."

Evil gleamed from Gallian's eyes, and she stepped a few paces closer, then waved her hand slowly around the courtyard. The motion pushed back the eerie walls of mist, allowing moonlight to brighten the grounds. Astril looked around the circle and took in a sharp breath. All around her were the priests of the One True God kneeling and being held by her countrymen with staffs at their throats. Astril knew even the least skilled Seerling could snap the neck of an enemy in that position.

"You know that I love difficult situations, dear sister," Gallian sneered.

Astril knew that the stakes had changed. She knew Gallian delighted in discourse and would intentionally enjoy the massacre if only out of spite. Calm needed to rule, or Gallian would unleash her evil power at the expense of the priests.

"Do not hurt them, and you will have what you came for."

Gallian's face showed a look of fake shock and disappointment as she walked over and laid her hand on the head of one of the priests.

"Me, hurt them," she simpered with a pouting lower lip. "You are the one who has hurt them. You have hurt us all, my dear sister. What I do tonight will lie on your head, not mine." Gallian dug her fingers through the priest's hair and shook his head to prove her point.

"Yes," she screeched. "Whatever happens tonight will lie on your conscience."

Astril remained guarded, standing and staring at her younger sister who took obvious delight in the pain she caused the poor priest. She dug her long nails deeper into the man's scalp and smiled as he yelped. Her pleasure in the man's pain was cut short by a Seerling who quickly approached from her right. Although she scowled at the interruption, she stood still while the female soldier whispered in her ear. Ard stood close by Gallian's side through the entire exchange, still dwelling in his magical trance.

"Good, good," the young priestess replied while shaking her hand in dismissal.

Losing interest in causing the priest more pain, Gallian turned back to her sister. "You have always been a deceiver. Haven't you, Sister?"

It felt as though her lungs were being squeezed of their very life as Astril watched her sister hold out her hand to the outdoor porch.

"Why would you try to hide something from me, sweet Astril?"

A string of grunts and squeals punctuated the sounds of hand-to-hand combat on the porch.

She's found Toren! Astril's heart cried out.

At that moment two Seerlings dragged Toren outside by the shoulders. By the look of him, he had not yet fully recovered from Astril's blow. It took two others to subdue Drinna's fighting before they were able to bring her out to kneel next to him.

Gallian took the stairs in fours as she advanced toward the captives. She lifted the prince's head upward and glared down at Astril. "This is a fine-looking Harkonian. Wouldn't you agree, Sister?"

Rage filled Astril, and she tried to keep it from showing. But Gallian laughed and went on, "Yes, I think you do know that. In fact, I think this is the prince that you rescued. Why were you trying to hide him away from me?"

Astril knew that her sister loved to watch her get angry, but she couldn't stop the bitterness that filled her face. Gallian laughed down at her, yet Astril remained silent.

In a mocking voice, Gallian added, "Oh, Sister, don't be so surprised. You knew we would find out."

Her voice filled with sadness that carried a sharp edge. "You know, Sister dear, it really is unfair of Mother to ask me to bring you home without any reward for myself." Gallian paused to run a lascivious gaze over the semiconscious Toren. "I believe I deserve some reward for my actions. Don't you?"

Astril refused to respond even when Gallian produced an evil smile and knelt in front of Toren, running her hands boldly over his broad chest. "Well then, it's decided. I will take your prince for my mate."

Astril screamed in rage and rushing toward her sister, propelled herself up the stairs. Gallian stood upright and in a quick motion of her hands created such a terrible windstorm that Astril was knocked off the stairs and against a tree. Her breath was gone, but still she struggled to get up. She had to save Toren from Ard's fate, but how. What could she possibly offer on his behalf?

"Astril!" Toren screamed struggling to stand up against his captors.

Every inch of Astril's body ached at the impact of being hurled into the tree and then falling to the ground. She forced herself to stand and confront her sister. Augur's words came to her again, and his talk of the true meaning of sacrifice. And she knew what she must do.

"Gallian," she said while gasping for precious air. "I will do whatever you wish if you will allow Toren his freedom."

Her younger sister only laughed. "I don't think you are in a position to make deals with me, Sister."

Walking toward the steps of the porch with her staff held out submissively in her hands, Astril bowed her head and replied, "You forget, Sister, Mother cannot offer a dead sacrifice to the Great Goddess. If you refuse to allow him his freedom, then my body will suffer greatly under the fight." She then stopped and glared up at Gallian. "And you know I will never stop fighting until I am dead. Then what will you have to offer?"

Gallian hurled one last sweep of wind, throwing Astril back into the tree, before calming herself. "Fine! I'll let your precious prince have his freedom." Then turning to the soldiers she screamed, "Shackle her with chains so she can not harm herself. I'm taking her home to be sacrificed."

"No!" Ard screamed, shaking his head as though to clear the poison from his mind. He rushed toward the stairs. "You promised her to me. She's my prize. Honor your word!"

Gallian smiled seductively at the man then slowly strolled down the stairs to stand in front of him. Standing on the bottom stair, Gallian looked up into his eyes. "I never promised you could have her, you big beast. I promised you would receive a prize."

Ard reached his hands to his head and tried desperately to shake the magical fog that held him spellbound to her. "I want no more of your witching words. You promised her to me."

The girl held out her hand for him to take and when he refused, she took his.

Bringing it to her lips, she gingerly kissed his palm. "My love, do not worry yourself over that powerless girl. I am taking you back to Seerling. A man of your size and strength will produce many powerful priestess daughters for me."

Ard turned his head away in disgust. The look on his face made it clear that he finally realized the evil he had gotten entangled in.

"I will never submit to being your mate, witch."

Lightning fast, Gallian grabbed his sword from its sheath at his side and plunged it deep into his heart.

"Then you will die," she hissed.

Astril knew he was dying, and the thought filled her with sadness as the large man fell to the ground, his own sword buried in his chest. Toren broke free of his captors and ran to his cousin's side.

"Ard," he whispered, taking the dying man's hand.

Ard looked at Toren and choked on his own breath. He then reached up and gently touched the prince's face. "I... am so... sorry, my friend." His head drooped to one side.

Blood coursed out of Ard's mouth and nose. With his hand, Toren slowly closed the eyes of his childhood friend.

"I forgive you, brother," he whispered as the dying man inhaled his last. Astril watched Toren in awe. Even though the man had wronged him, Toren still forgave.

"What a waste," Gallian sneered then turned back to her soldiers as if dismissing any thought of the man she had intended to take as a mate. "Set Astril's prince free and kill all the others."

Astril and Toren jerked their heads toward Gallian and in unison screamed, "No!" Astril fiercely fought against her captors while Toren sprinted toward Gallian only to be cut off by three Seerling men. Gallian's face was filled with the foul mood she had obtained, and she walked over to Astril and slapped her hard. The impact threw Astril's head backward, cracking her neck.

"Oh shut up, Astril. You've grown so soft you forget the Seerling way. Just be glad your precious prince is going to live."

Astril stared defiantly at her sister and was about to speak when Toren said, "Please, let them live."

Gallian turned to him and growled, "Why should I give anything to you when no one here cares what I want?"

Toren stood and tried to walk toward her. Gallian raised her hand against the tight hold of the soldiers and allowed him closer.

"Toren, don't talk to her," Astril cried only to be ignored by them both. She knew that Gallian could easily mystify him with her words and magical wind.

The prince stopped just in front of her sister. "If you will allow all of these captives to live in peace, I will go with you to your land."

Gallian walked toward him, and reaching her hand out, touched his stubbled cheek softly. Lust filled her face, and Astril turned away, sickened.

In a seductively low voice, her sister said, "And you will be my prize for this trek across the world?"

Astril looked over to them just in time to see that the magic Gallian used through her voice was beginning to take its effect on the prince.

She stood helplessly by as he sluggishly spilled out the words, "I will accompany you to your land and stand before your mother if you will allow them all their freedom." Toren shook his head, and his eyes cleared for a moment as he added, "After I stand before your mother, you can do with me as you wish."

Gallian produced an almost childlike smile and in a quick moment transported herself across the courtyard to stand in front of Astril. "Did you hear that, Sister?" She giggled. "I think it will bring me great pleasure to know I have something you want."

She then turned back to Toren and added for all to hear, "I like this bartering system you Harkonians have. I accept the terms."

She turned to her soldiers and ordered, "Release these men to their homes. We leave for Seerling now."

Chapter Twenty-one

Your Majesty." An attendant ran into the main hall, breathlessly shouting. King Kortan sat engrossed in a game of tafl with Holan. "A messenger has just come in from Helgard."

Kortan looked up at the man and waved his hand in dismissal. "Tell him I'm busy." He then looked the board over with a critical eye and smiled. Holan's attempt to trap his king was pitiful. To win, the servant had to surround Kortan's king on all four sides or on three sides against the board edge with his table men.

"I've got you now, Holan." Kortan roared with laughter as he moved his king closer to the edge, very near to winning.

"Majesty," the attendant interrupted again. "It is a matter of great importance."

Kortan was furious at being disturbed during his favorite game and growled in the direction of the man, "Well, what did he say?"

He knew he was frightening the attendant but didn't care. "M-Majesty, h-he said that General Ard has been killed and… and Prince Toren has been taken captive by the Seerlings."

"What!" bellowed the king. His wild hand gesture toppled the game board over, sending the wooden pieces flying. "Bring the messenger in immediately."

King Kortan felt the blood drain from his face as he listened to the messenger's report of all that had taken place in Helgard.

He questioned the young man, wanting every detail of the events. "And you are sure that Prince Toren bartered himself for the lives of the priests?" he asked incredulously. *Doesn't Toren know that his life is worth a thousand of those priests? Why would he risk his future for them?* The thought of Toren giving himself to save the priests infuriated him.

"Yes, Majesty," replied the messenger. "First Miss Astril bartered her life to save him, then Prince Toren bartered his life to save the priests."

King Kortan jumped to his feet at the name of the Seerling slave and screamed, "Never mention that heathen's name in this court again." His mind had not found a moment of rest since he had encountered the High Priestess in his own court. He was certainly not in any mood to have her slave daughter's name drawn in the same breath as his grandson's.

The frightened messenger backed away from the throne and bowed his head low in respect. Kortan knew the man was weary from his long journey but he had not quite finished with him. He forced the man to stand in the main hall and endure the same questions over and over until he was satisfied he had every detail.

He finally sent a dismissal wave to the man. Standing, he then began to pace back and forth in the large, empty room. Holan, his favorite attendant, entered from some hiding place and asked if he would care to retire for the evening. The king only shook his head no. He was too overcome with what had taken place to even think of resting.

He then called the attendant to himself and asked, "What am I to do, Holan? My son, the heir to my throne, is dead. His son is missing and the only other one who has any blood right to inherit has also died." He stopped and paused for breath, then rubbing his head with his hands, said, "I don't even know where to begin looking for Toren and if I did, would it be the right thing to bring him home? His decision to go with the heathens instead of sacrificing the priests shows poor leadership. If only I knew for certain what direction I should take."

Holan stood still for a short time then cleared his throat. In a hushed tone he said, "I have heard of an Olden mystic who lives near here who could read your future, my king."

Kortan looked at his servant with narrowed eyes. Holan had always been a true friend to him and a good advisor despite his young age. Still, the king didn't completely trust him. Even though every appearance screamed loyalty, there was a seething ambition just under the surface that crept up at times.

Instead of reprimanding the servant, the king chose to quietly remind him, "Holan, you know that the priests have forbidden everyone in Harkan from having any encounter with mystics. They believe their power comes from an evil source."

Holan smiled deviously and whispered back to him, "Surely the great King of Harkan does not bow his knee to simple priests."

Kortan looked his servant over carefully. Holan's words held truth. *Why should I bow my knee to them? I am king, and I make the rules around here.* He smiled conspiratorially. "Perhaps this mystic can help me. I don't know if I should try to recover Toren or leave him to his ill choices. Even if I did try to get him back, who would know where to find them?"

He paused, rubbed his thumb to his beard, and sighed. "Yes, send for this mystic."

Holan bowed obsequiously before turning to walk out of the room and do the king's bidding.

"No!" cried Princess Emile after hearing the news of her son's disappearance. She grabbed hold of the male servant's shirt, clutching it tightly in her fists. "What is being done to rescue him?"

The servant offered her a gentle hand. "I have heard no news as to what method of recovery the king will use."

Emile covered her face with her hands and ran out of her chambers and through the hall, heading for the gardens in the back of the palace courtyard. The back gardens were famous for their rare flowers, some of which bore vicious thorns. Running through the tight lanes of the garden, she ignored the painful cuts she received on her upper arms as the harsh thorns bit her. Finding a small, dirt patch in the middle of the garden, she threw herself down upon the soft earth and bitterly wept.

"One True God," she cried into the air. "Please protect my Toren from harm. He is so brave but often forgets to rely on You and Your power. Oh, Lord, please keep him in the safety of Your great and mighty arm…"

Emile lay down on her stomach and rested her weary head on the soft ground. She continued her vigil for her son's safety throughout the rest of the day and far into the night. It was late in the evening when she awoke to a servant's gentle shaking. She stared down at her dirt-covered hands and dress, then back up to the servant, and began crying again. Despite her grief, she allowed herself to be led back indoors and to her bedchamber, where her maidservant undressed her and put her to bed.

The next morning, Princess Emile was exhausted from her late-night prayer vigil and depressed not to have heard any word of rescuing her beloved son. With puffy eyes and a pounding head, she was in no mood to exchange information with the tall young woman that approached her in the hall.

"Princess, is the news of Prince Toren and General Ard true?" Morgan asked with trembling lips.

Emile turned with a downcast face, wishing she could find a secure place to hide and continue her prayerful pleading for her son's safety.

Instead she wearily looked at the young beauty, "Yes, Morgan it's all true."

Morgan's hand flew up to cover her mouth, and she began to weep. "I am so very sorry." At those words she ran off.

Emile watched her rush away and was surprised to find that she felt no great pity at the girl's grief. Turning back to her own chambers, she decided that the morning meal was not something she wanted after all.

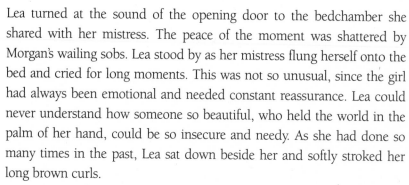

Lea turned at the sound of the opening door to the bedchamber she shared with her mistress. The peace of the moment was shattered by Morgan's wailing sobs. Lea stood by as her mistress flung herself onto the bed and cried for long moments. This was not so unusual, since the girl had always been emotional and needed constant reassurance. Lea could never understand how someone so beautiful, who held the world in the palm of her hand, could be so insecure and needy. As she had done so many times in the past, Lea sat down beside her and softly stroked her long brown curls.

She patiently listened as the young woman relayed the horrible tale.

"I am so sorry," she whispered after hearing the terrible news. "I never wished death upon the general." Lea couldn't help but remember all of the times the giant had accosted her as well as Morgan. Still, the knowledge of his demise was difficult to hear. *He had so much to look forward to in life.*

Morgan looked up at her with a puffy face. "I never did either." She confided, "To think, if I had not told on him then Toren would never have sent him away and then… he never would have died." She ended her statement by flopping back down on the bed and burying her head in the pillows.

Lea shook her head and tried to comfort her young mistress. "There is no way that you could have saved that man, Miss Morgan. He allowed his jealousy of the prince to destroy him. This is not your fault."

Morgan refused to be comforted and continued to wail. "And now Toren is lost to me as well. Oh, Lea, what is to become of me?"

Lea couldn't hide the small smile that tugged at her lips as the true nature of the young woman was revealed. Luckily, Morgan was so caught up in herself that she didn't see the mocking smile.

Selfish to the core, she thought ruefully, then said aloud in as comforting a voice as possible, "They will find Prince Toren. Just you wait and see. He will be back here soon, and then you will be married."

"He's with that Seerling now and will never return to me," Morgan screeched. "How can I marry a man who loves someone else?"

Why should he return to you? Lea thought, then remembered her duty and tried to comfort her mistress again. "You don't know that he does not love you or that he might love this slave. Don't fret over things that you cannot control. Just wait and trust in the One True God to make it all work out."

Morgan gave her a pathetic look that showed she really didn't understand what Lea meant. She then rolled over on her side, facing the wall, and began weeping for herself again. Lea stood, knowing she could not help, and quietly walked out of the room, shutting the door behind her.

CHAPTER TWENTY-TWO

It took several weeks of hard travel for the party to move from Helgard to Seerling. Gallian divided the group into three traveling parties so they would not attract as much attention. Astril had heard her sister say they had brought too much attention to themselves searching for so long for her, and they needed to be more guarded on the trip home. The group that accompanied Astril and Toren across the land was small but strong.

In traditional Seerling fashion, Gallian forced the party to travel while the sun slept and to rest when it peeked out for morning. The Seerlings had adapted their boran tents to hide among the brush and trees of the landscape. Their steeds were set loose during the daylight hours to graze and rest as if wild, then called back again at evening. Taking barely traveled roads and bypasses, the group traveled each night in near silence.

Near the end of the second week of traveling, Astril began to recognize landmarks that showed they were nearing their destination. Her legs ached considerably since Gallian had ordered that she walk with a few of the other soldiers the entire way to Seerling. Great bruises blackened her arms under the heavy weight of the chains that bound her during the day. At night she was given a tent to herself where she was chained at both the arms and feet.

"She doesn't want to make any of this easy for me. Does she?" Astril commented to herself one night while walking alongside an extremely young Seerling soldier.

"Astril," the girl riding the horse said, "Please, Priestess Gallian will be very angry if she hears you talking."

Looking up at the young woman, Astril forced a small smile. "I'm sorry, Neopani. I wouldn't want to endanger you." *I trained this girl myself. I wonder what she thinks of her old teacher now,* she thought ruefully.

Two nights later, Astril, exhausted and sore, was actually looking forward to the shelter of the tent that morning where she could sit and read from her hidden scrolls. The sun was just beginning to show in the eastern sky when she heard the orders given by Gallian to move on through the day.

What is she doing now, she thought wearily. *Doesn't she even care about the welfare of her own soldiers?*

Looking up ahead, she saw Toren riding behind one of the male soldiers. She was still frustrated that all of her attempts to keep him safe had failed. *At least Gallian's lust causes her to take better care of him than I've received.* He rode with his shoulders slumped forward, staring straight into the backs of those ahead of him. *Gallian has him in her trance,* Astril thought in disgust. She forced the mental images from her mind of what her sister was doing as the group continued their trek.

It had been a hard day, and Astril knew that more than one of the soldiers was close to dropping over due to exhaustion. Finally, her sister made the motion to stop for a rest just as the moon was peeking over the top of the highest trees.

Several Seerling soldiers made quick time of pitching the boran tents while Neopani escorted Astril into a tent and helped her wash up for the evening.

She smiled at Astril as though she held a great secret and whispered, "Priestess Gallian wants you to look especially nice tonight."

Astril ignored the girl's remark and allowed herself to be cleaned. Her energy was spent from the day of travel, and she didn't even attempt a fight for escape when her chains were temporarily removed so her clothing could be changed. She barely noticed the weight of the chains being placed back on her hands and then on her feet as she enjoyed the refreshing feeling of the clean gown that was placed upon her body. *Has it been so long since I felt the cloth of my own land? I never noticed how soft the evening gowns of Seerling women are.* The white, sleeveless dress was open at the neck to the shoulders and hung slightly loose in the bodice and waist. She knew by the way it fit that it came from her sister's belongings. The hem pooled at her feet when she stood and smelled of the green grasses of Seerling.

Lost in the luxury of the moment, Astril didn't notice Neopani pick up her dirty clothes.

"What are these?" the girl asked while flipping through the pages of the handwritten, bound scrolls.

"Those are mine. Give them back now!" Astril lunged at the girl but was cut short by the chains at her hands.

Shaking her head, Neopani backed out of the tent and closed the flap securely.

Astril sat in the still silence of the tent, dreading what her sister would do once she saw the scrolls. The nice feeling of being clean and wearing such a soft, comfortable dress gave her no pleasure anymore. Astril was exhausted and barely touched her meal before drifting into a restless sleep. Her mind took her to the image of a beautiful dark-haired boy staring at her with large gray eyes. He held a mischievous grin on his face, resembling Toren. In the dream the laughing boy was running up a hill. Astril watched from below as Toren raced past her, laughing and chasing the small boy. As she watched, darkness began to envelop the hill, casting a shadow upon them. Toren and the boy slowly vanished before her eyes. In the dream, Astril began to scream for them to return. *No, don't go. Please come back.*

Her heart raced and sweat poured from her face as a gentle shaking of her hip brought her mind back to the reality of the tent where she was held captive. Looking up with half-closed eyes she saw the face of her sister bent closely over her.

Astril was startled to see Gallian so close but refused to give her any satisfaction of knowing it. Gallian had always relished any attention she could get, and Astril knew that an action on her part would only play into her sister's game. "What do you want?" She yawned for emphasis then rubbed her eyes with the palms of her hands.

Her sister showed obvious annoyance at Astril's apathetic response still she crouched very close, watching Astril intently. "You were dreaming of your prince and our lost brother."

"No, I was not."

Gallian smiled and cocked her head to the left. It was the same way she'd looked when she couldn't quite figure out a problem as a child. "Yes, you were. As I entered the tent I heard you scream, 'Toren, protect Kellon.'" Gallian's smile turned into a sneer as she added, "How can you dream of him protecting our brother when you couldn't do it yourself?"

Astril wearily rubbed her face and in an exhausted voice again asked, "What do you want, Gallian?"

Still squatting before her, Gallian pulled her arm from behind her back to reveal the scrolls that had been taken by Neopani. "You have fallen into the same trap as our grandmother."

"I serve the One True God now, Gallian."

Gallian's head cocked even further to the left, and her brow furrowed tightly. "So you have rejected the ways of our people completely. You have rejected your calling and the Great Goddess."

Astril stood slowly to her feet despite the chains that bound her to the tent. Gallian stood as well, still holding the scrolls. Strength Astril never knew she could have coursed through her veins, reviving her weary body. "I have found my way into the real light, Sister. I can show you the path to the One True God."

"You can not be serious. What makes you think I would ever leave the power of the Great Goddess?" Gallian's words were laced with skepticism. "Mark my words, Astril. You will pay for rejecting her. Mother will make sure of it."

"Gallian, it doesn't have to be this way. I can help you."

"Help me?" Gallian paused and attempted to look genuine, but Astril knew her manipulative ways too well. "Yes, Sister, that is exactly what I want you to do, but not with these." With those words, Gallian lifted the scrolls above her head. With her left arm she created a sour gust of wind that carried them up. Astril watched silently as the words of the One True God flew from the tent out the opening at the top.

After watching the paper scrolls exit the tent, Gallian turned her gaze back to her sister with a look that Astril could not interpret. She sighed and wiped her hands on the front of her mauklan shirt. "I have tried in vain to bring your prince into my power, Sister. It seems he is maddeningly loyal to you." She looked down at her hands with a scowl then back up at Astril. "He is too stubborn to submit to what I want from him. However…"

Astril stood her ground not allowing her sister to see the relief that washed over her entire body at the admission.

Gallian snapped her fingers together, producing a small gust that blew through Astril's hair. "At first I was very upset by his stubbornness, but then I realized that this is all going to work out for my benefit."

Despite all her attempts to appear as though she didn't care, Astril felt her eyebrows draw upward slightly. The small action brought a gale of laughter from her sister before Gallian continued, "If I know you as well as I think I do, Sister, then I believe you are still keeping yourself pure. Aren't you?"

Gallian laughed again as Astril felt her face flush red. "If you have indeed kept yourself pure, then Mother will receive an extraordinary portion of the real magic at your sacrifice."

Astril stared at her and waited. Sometimes, Gallian could be so hard to read.

"Yes, my dear sister. For the first time ever, a human will be deliberately sacrificed on the altar."

Her heart sank deep into her chest, knowing what Gallian's words meant. *So, mother would kill me after all.* Her mind raced, seeking a way to save Toren as she stood her ground and waited for her sister to continue. She knew her life was forfeit, but she had to find a way to save his.

"The Great Goddess will indeed be greatly pleased with the offering of a pure priestess daughter and reward Mother generously. If Mother receives such a large portion of the magic, she will become far greater than I can even imagine. She will be given longer life, and I will probably never take her position."

Gallian pouted with false innocence, still staring at her older sister. "I know you hate Mother as much as I do, Astril. Is it fair to allow her to live on with tremendous magic, torturing our people with her heavy demands? Is it fair to let the woman who killed our brother and sent my son to his death have a long life?"

Gallian walked closer to Astril and placed her hands on her older sister's shoulders. "You say that you want to help me, Sister. Well… there is only one way."

Astril turned away from the evil glint in Gallian's eyes. Everything her sister had said filled Astril with dread at what might come out of her mouth next.

Gallian drew closer, bending her head to whisper in her ear, "I have a present for you, dear sister. Something that I am sure will benefit us both."

She then stepped back and called for her soldiers. Immediately the tent flap opened, and Toren was pushed inside.

He fell to the ground and slumped on his knees. Gallian walked over and lifted his chin so Astril could see his glazed eyes and drooping mouth. Astril watched in horrified silence as Gallian waved her hands before his face, producing a foul wind that blew over him. "Since you will not succumb to me, I will give you what you desire most." She smiled down at him then turned back to her sister and with a look of contempt said, "Though I do not understand why you want her." She turned back, walked past Toren, and made to leave the tent.

Astril stared past Toren and screamed at her sister's retreating form, "Gallian, get back here. What do you think you're doing?"

Turning around as she reached the tent door, Gallian gave her a mocking smile. "Enjoy your last evening alive, Sister." She quickly exited the tent.

The realization of what Gallian expected sent a chill up her spine. She looked down at Toren, who knelt staring at her. His eyes had brightened, and he smiled. Upon his face he wore a look of desire she had never seen on him before. *He looks like Ard!* Shaking her head, she stood in horror watching every move he made. Toren was completely taken over by Gallian's seducing spell.

She stepped backward as far as the chains would allow as he stood to his feet; a towering giant in the small confines of the tent. Her eyes widened as she watched him unbutton his black shirt with slow, deliberate movements.

"Toren, you don't know what you're doing. You're under her spell." She cried out at him with her hands raised defensively before her. He continued his approach, unmoved by her words.

"Toren, please fight it. Fight off her magic." Astril's words resounded in the quickly closing gap between them. The look he gave her clearly showed that she was the only thing he planned on fighting.

He stood in front of her with his chest bare and eyes hungry. Taking her by the upper arms, he licked his lips as if desirous of a drink then bent his head to take a kiss. His lips were greedy and full of passion, far different from the kiss they had shared the night they were captured in Helgard.

Frustration rose up, clouding her mind. After all, it was Toren's kiss and not some monster. It would be so easy to give in to what Gallian wanted. To give in to all the desire she felt for him. *Mother shouldn't be allowed to gain so much power! Besides, I love him. I really love him, and he loves me.* She pulled away from him and stared up into his handsome face. All thoughts of her mother and sister melted as she fell into the power of Toren's dark brown eyes. His adoring gaze made her realize how deeply her love for him ran. For a moment she felt powerless against it and melted in his strong embrace.

She felt safety in his muscular arms but knew deep within that it was false. *There is no real safety except in the One True God.*

Pulling away from him again, she slowly repeated the words of the ancient scroll, "O our God, will You not judge them? For we have no power to face this vast army that is attacking us. We do not know what to do, but our eyes are upon You."

"What did you say?" Toren's whispered words tickled her ear. *I have to stay strong,* she reminded herself.

Looking up at him, she repeated the words of the scroll, "We have no power to face this vast army that is attacking us. We do not know what to do, but our eyes are upon You."

"I know that. It's from the ancient scrolls." Astril saw the cloud over his eyes begin to push slightly away. "The One True God fought that battle for His people."

"Yes, that's the one. I didn't understand it until now." She was excited to see him coming to himself again and placed her hand on his stubbled cheek. "We have to keep our eyes on Him, Toren."

He smiled and nodded as if he understood then began to softly nuzzle her neck.

"No, you don't understand what I'm saying," she persisted, pulling away from his embrace again. "We have to keep our focus on Him, Toren and only on Him."

The cloud had formed over his eyes again, and his face took on a wolfish grin as he forcefully pulled her against him and kissed her neck. *No, I had him back for a moment.* She shook her head and fought off his roving hands. *It was the words of the One that brought him back! Only His words can bring Toren back.* Immediately, Astril remembered the last scroll she had memorized with Priest Augur. It was an ancient song, written by a long ago king.

Softly she began to sing.

In You, O Lord, I have taken refuge;
Let me never be put to shame;
Deliver me in your righteousness.
Turn your ear to me
Come quickly to my rescue
Be my rock of refuge
A strong fortress to save me.

Her voice gained strength as she continued singing the ancient psalm.

A sweet scent of incense swept through the tent, and Toren released his hold of her. He stepped backward, watching her closely. His breathing steadied, and he knelt to the floor. Toren's eyes began to clear as he sat staring up at her. Astril knew Gallian's hold on him was breaking, and she continued to sing.

Since You are my rock and my fortress,
For the sake of Your name
Lead and guide me.
Free me from the trap that is set for me,
For You are my refuge.
Into Your hands I commit my spirit
Redeem me, O Lord, the One True God of truth.

She knelt down before him and placed her hand on his forehead then whispered a prayer, "One True God, please deliver Toren from this evil spell and break down the strongholds that have lead him into the enemy's power." His features softened as he closed his eyes and seemed to be at peace. With her right hand still placed on his forehead, she moved her free hand behind his head and gently guided him to lie down on the pallet. Peace and contentment filled the small tent as the man she loved rested quietly beneath the touch of her hand.

But I trust in You, O Lord;
I say, "You are my God."
My times are in Your hands;
Deliver me from my enemies
And from those who pursue me.
Let Your face shine on Your servant;
Save me in Your unfailing love.

Toren was in a deep sleep. The words of the One had brought him out of the evil of Gallian's spell. Astril stared down at him, watching his chest rise and fall with every breath. Even after all of this, her love for him knew no bounds. She could no longer deny that he was everything she had ever wanted in life, and nothing she believed she could ever have.

Astril choked back the tears that threatened to spill over and laid her head down on his chest. The danger had passed so she allowed herself to delight in the warmth of his body so close to her own. Never in her life had she felt such love as Toren gave when he was in his right mind. The storm in her heart of what was to come still battered, but its impact wasn't as harsh with Toren lying beside her.

She lay awake for a long time, listening to his breathing and wishing she could be content in the silence of the moment. *Whatever happens, I have to find a way to get him away from Seerling and back to his own people.*

"I want to keep my eyes upon You, but I have to save Toren from himself," she whispered into the darkness of the tent. "One True God, please let Mother accept my sacrifice."

Chapter Twenty-Three

Y our Majesty," whispered the attendant. "That person you requested to see is here."

King Kortan looked at Holan and quickly glanced around the main hall. He quietly turned back to his attendant and whispered, "Have her sent to my private chambers." Why did he feel like a naughty little boy about to be caught? *I am the king, and I can do anything I want!*

"Your chambers?" Holan questioned in a hushed tone. "I don't think it is wise to allow a... person like that in your private chambers, my lord."

Kortan hissed his reply, "Do you have any other private place where we can meet?"

Holan shook his head and exited the main hall. Within the hour Kortan was finished with the business of the day and trudging toward his own rooms. There was once a time that he would have respected the word of the priests and kept clear of evil. Things had changed so much since his son's death, and he blamed the Seerling High Priestess witch. He stopped just outside his chambers, feeling as though a heavy cloud had descended upon him. Garnering his courage, he opened the large wooden doors and entered.

The light of the room was very dim as the king tried to make out the large stooped shape that sat in front of the fire. The musty odor of the old hag overwhelmed the room. Once he was inside, and the door was completely closed, he waited as Holan introduced him to the mystic Thauma. Upon hearing her name, the Olden woman turned and stared at the king. He shuddered at her shriveled, dark features. As a young man he had seen many Olden people, but the image was still hard to take in person. Their squared shoulders held long thin arms that reached down nearly to their knees. These, combined with short, stumpy legs, caused an Olden to have an off-balance look. Despite their appearance, King Kortan knew they could be vicious in a fight and was glad for the years of peace between their peoples. The ancient mystic had a wildness to her withered face, but there was wisdom and truth in her eyes.

Thauma pointed a long, crooked finger at the king and in a gravely voice asked, "I have your word that I will be allowed to leave this place unharmed?"

Kortan nodded his head and sat down in the chair that she waved toward.

The mystic walked over to him and with much difficulty, knelt at his feet while pulling a pouch from a belt at her waist. She opened the pouch and withdrew a lumpy bundle of leather. She unrolled the leather and laid it on the floor at the king's feet, revealing an arrangement of tiny, delicate bones. Next she moved the bones around into a circle and reached for a large knife she had tied to her waist belt.

"Give me your hand," she ordered. When he resisted she grabbed it and sliced through the meaty portion of his palm. He cried out more in shock than pain.

Thauma gave him a quick glance that silenced any further noise and squeezed his hand, allowing his blood to drain down over the bones. He cringed at the sight of his own blood sprinkling the yellow bones. Taking up the leather on each of its four sides, she closed her eyes and shook the contents together. Then dropping it back down at his feet, she opened it again and leaned down to review the hidden messages.

"Tell me of my heir," said the king quietly.

The old mystic let out a snort. "The heir to your throne will be the one you have trained."

"Toren?"

Nodding her head, the mystic let out another snort, still staring down at the messages hidden in the bones.

Kortan exhaled and smiled. Relief flooded over him. "And will he be a good leader?"

Again a snort came out of the old woman, and she nodded yes.

"That is what I wanted to know. You are free to leave."

Thauma looked up at him and smiled broadly, exposing brown, crooked teeth. "Are you sure that is all you want to know?" she croaked.

"Is there more?"

She let out a gravely laugh and snorted her answer.

"What?"

Looking only at the bones, she told him, "The bones tell me that your grandson will take for himself the Seed of Seerling."

Kortan stared down at the bones and shook his head, trying to comprehend what her words meant.

Giving him a misshapen grin, Thauma went on to explain, "Your grandson will marry the High Priestess's daughter and thus take for himself the Seed of Seerling. They will rule on your throne."

"No!" screamed the king as he jumped out of the chair and began to pace the room.

Thauma's gravelly laughter showed her obvious enjoyment of the king's anger. "Do you want to know the rest?" she croaked.

The king stared back at her and threw his hands out wildly. He was completely undone. "What more could there be?"

She stood to her feet, and gathering the bones together said, "Under your grandson's rule, your kingdom will be joined to that of the Seerlings. Together they will be more powerful and far more loved than any before you." She smiled in her crooked way again. "Including you, King Kortan."

Thauma held out her hand for payment. The king pulled at his white hair and thrashed his head back and forth as Holan paid the old hag.

After the two left, the king fell to his knees and hissed, "Toren will never betray me!"

He picked up the light-colored rug that sat on the floor below his bed and stared down at its glistening yellow strands. He remembered how Holan had retrieved the heathen's braid of hair and had it woven into the rug. The memory of how much it pleased him to step on it every morning filled him with fire. No slave would rule on his throne. *The only thing that heathen is good for is wiping my feet!*

Holan watched with a catch in his throat as the young, dark-haired beauty approached. Her brown eyes filled her soft face, and her straight nose gave an air of regality. *She is so beautiful. If I were ever to have such a woman, I would know how to treat her right.* Intoxicated, he reached out his hand to assist her down the staircase, catching the soft scent of lavender.

"Holan," Morgan whispered. "Who was that old crow I saw you with earlier?"

He smiled, filled with himself at the attentions of the young beauty. "You know that I can't tell you the matters of the king, Miss Morgan," he teased.

"She was here to see the king?" Morgan's surprised reaction warmed his stomach.

He just smiled and walked on with her hand lightly on his arm.

"What people is she from?"

Holan could never ignore good gossip, and if it kept Morgan's attention, he was willing to tell everything. He stopped walking, looked around the room, and then ushered her quickly to a dark corner.

"She's a mystic of the Olden people," he said in a whispered tone. "One of the last. King Kortan wanted her to read his future and the future of Prince Toren."

"What?" Morgan said, the word carrying to echo from the stone walls.

Holan shushed her words with a tap of his finger to his lips. "She told the king that the prince is going to marry his Seerling slave. King Kortan was so angry I think he might even try to kill him before letting that happen."

He watched as Morgan's face went blank of expression and grabbed hold of her arm as she appeared to black out. She teetered slightly, then straightened herself and pushed his hand away.

"Miss Morgan?"

"I'm fine," she said. "Do you think it is possible that he would marry a slave?"

Holan realized he had made a huge mistake in confiding in the girl. "I'm sorry. I think I've said too much all ready."

Morgan took his hand in hers and reassured, "Please do not be distressed. I pressed the issue, and I won't tell anyone what you've said." Then shaking her head slowly she turned and walked away.

Prince Toren doesn't deserve a woman like that, Holan seethed. She is so graceful and patient, waiting for him while he goes gallivanting all across the world with a slave. She should be flattered and given every attention possible. He turned back to his duties with a determination in his heart that he would show Morgan what it was like to really be loved.

CHAPTER TWENTY-FOUR

stril opened her eyes the next morning, wishing she could stay in Toren's arms forever. Pulling herself up and staring down at him, she smiled at how young he looked. She couldn't resist the urge to touch his soft, brown hair with her hand. The jingling of her arm chains woke him. He opened his eyes to slits and gave her a small smile before becoming fully awake. She tried in vain to suppress a giggle as he groaned and sat straight up, almost knocking into her.

"How did I get in here?" His voice was deep and gravelly. He grabbed his head with both hands and groaned again. "My head is spinning."

Astril touched him lightly on the forehead. "I'm afraid you were under a very heavy spell last night."

Toren's eyebrows scrunched together as though he couldn't quite understand what she was saying. Still holding his hands on either side of his head, he stared into the dim lighting of the tent before letting his mouth drop open. Turning back to her, his dark eyes were troubled. "Did I... do... anything to you?"

She smiled and shook her head no.

Relief washed over his face. "I can't figure out how I got in here. Everything from the past few days is a blur. I think your sister poisoned me or something."

Astril knew it wouldn't do any good to try and explain that he had been placed under a seducing spell or that the strong power of protection he felt for her had actually been the reason he had fallen. One day perhaps the One True God would reveal it all to him, but today she needed him to concentrate on what lay ahead of them.

"Toren, we're going to have a very difficult day ahead of us." He nodded his agreement while still holding his head in his hands. "My mother is dedicated to the Great Goddess, and there may be things that take place today that you aren't going to understand…" She cut off her words. How could she explain something that she didn't even understand herself? How could she tell him that she was going to offer herself for his safety?

"I need you to promise me that no matter what takes place today, you will find a way to get back to Harkan." She finished her words in a quick rush, praying he would agree.

He held up his hand to stop her from saying anything more. "I'm not going to leave you in Seerling, Astril." His attempt at a smile was pathetic, and she could tell by his pained expression that his head hurt.

"Okay," she gave in, knowing it would not do any good to argue with him. "Would you at least promise me that you will do everything in your power to release my people from slavery?"

He nodded then leaned over and brushed her hair behind one ear. His gentle touch warmed her heart. She could not stop the tear that fell from her eye and trailed down her cheek. Oh, how she wished they could have a life together.

"Toren," she whispered huskily. She was about to admit her love for him when the tent flap opened, bringing with it a soft breeze.

She jerked her head up in time to see Gallian appear inside.

"Did you have a nice night, Sister?" the younger woman asked, smiling broadly at the pair as if she knew a great secret.

"Not the kind you think," Astril responded with intended spite. Standing up despite the chains that bound her, she looked back toward Toren just in time to see a bright red flush pass over his face.

The gloat on her sister's face disappeared into a wall of hate. "Will you ever do anything right?"

Astril placed her hands on her hips and smiled sweetly at her. "I guess I am doomed to be a failure in everything, Sister."

Gallian's full lips tightened into a barely visible line. Astril could see her hands shaking at her sides before the girl turned and exited the tent.

"What was that all about?" Toren whispered.

Turning back to him, Astril shrugged her shoulders. If he didn't remember everything that had taken place between them the night before, she certainly wasn't going to be the one to remind him.

A moment later, two soldiers entered and removed Toren from her presence. Sighing out loud, Astril accepted the assistance of a female soldier and changed into the clean mauklan outfit that was left at her feet. The soldier stared uncomfortably at the ground as Astril voiced her thanks to the One True God for giving her strength through the night and safety during the day.

For the final day's journey, Gallian allowed her to ride behind the male soldier Keanu. Astril noted with an impending sense of dread all of the familiar landmarks leading to her homeland. *It won't be long before I'm standing before Mother,* she thought ruefully to herself. *I only hope she honors my sacrifice.*

Astril could only believe that Gallian's statements about a pure, human sacrifice were true. *If Mother will really receive more power from a willing pure, human sacrifice, then maybe I can still save Toren.*

She was so caught up in her own thoughts that she did not realize her sister rode along beside her until Gallian asked, "Are you scared?"

Astril started at her sister's voice and turned toward her. She thought she saw a softness in her sister's eyes that had not been there before, but then Gallian laughed and her facial features tightened. Astril looked away, ignoring her.

"Finally, Mother will be pleased with me."

"Gallian, you would do all of this to gain Mother's approval?" Astril asked, turning back to her little sister who stared over her steed's head at the soldiers in front of them. Her expression was hard, giving her the appearance of a much older woman.

"Gallian," Astril cried out from her heart. "I've always loved you. You know who I am. Is this really what you want?"

Still looking ahead, the priestess turned her head only slightly toward Astril. The same hate-filled smile spread across her countenance. "You love me?" Her sister drew out the question as if savoring it on her tongue. Darkness flashed over her face as she kept her eyes forward. "What have you ever done to show me love?"

"Oh, Gallian, what has changed between us? What have I done to cause you to hate me so much, Sister?"

Without hesitation, Gallian turned flashing dark blue eyes upon her. Hate seethed from every pore of her young body. "If you had done your duty, my son would be alive and in my arms today." She then turned and galloped away.

Astril felt the muscles in Keanu's chest tighten as she held on to him. He had heard their conversation. *What must my soldiers think of me now?*

There was once a time when she had been close to every soldier. All of the battles they had fought and the long hours together had formed a bond between them that she had never felt in her own family. Now, they were taking her to her death, and there wasn't anything any of them could do about it.

It was a long hard trip, and Toren was consumed with fear for Astril's safety. Often he tried to get a glimpse of her riding behind a well-muscled, male Seerling. Only once did the young priestess stop the group to eat. Gallian pressed them hard.

Dusk had fallen on the sky and again Toren was trying to locate Astril. The woods were becoming dangerously tangled by heavy brush and tall weeds. The soldiers slashed their way through with their daggers. The man he rode behind came within an inch of slicing Toren's ear as he drew his knife back to cut through the heavy foliage.

They passed through unscathed to an open field with small huts scattered about. Passing the huts, Toren watched a few Seerling children at play as their mothers chatted nearby. Every action of the bystanders froze when their party passed. He saw one young mother's eyes grow wide in terror before she turned her face away.

The number of huts grew larger as they delved farther into Seerling land. Village life seemed to stop instantly as the inhabitants they passed turned their heads away, refusing to look at them. Silence reigned supreme. It wasn't long after passing the homes that the travelers reached an area devoid of huts. Instead the earth was dredged up in a wide circular trench. In the center of the circle was a giant iron statue of a woman. A black granite slab lay at the statue's feet. Toren shuddered to think of the evils this area had witnessed. Beyond the statue stood a round whitewashed building, surrounded by gleaming columns. No Seerling stood anywhere near this area.

Gallian's hair flew about her in a torrent of her own magical wind as she dismounted her steed, shrieking, "I have brought a mighty gift for the High Priestess!" Restrained by her guards, Toren watched helplessly as the young woman rushed to the muscled man's horse, and grabbing Astril by the arm, jerked her to the ground.

Shaking his head, he couldn't believe his eyes. Astril didn't put up a fight. She just allowed her body to fall to the ground.

Gallian dragged her sister by the arm toward the temple, still screaming, "I have brought a great gift for the High Priestess who serves the Great Goddess."

Just as the young priestess completed her scream, the white doors of the round building opened to allow an older woman to walk through. *Why, she's almost as tall as Morgan is,* Toren thought while staring at her. She was everything his grandfather had described and more. Power emanated all around her in a frightening way. There was a great evil at work in this place, and Toren was sure most of it came from the woman he now looked upon.

Gallian held her breath as her mother, the High Priestess, bounded down the stairs toward them. Hope sprang full in her heart as she waited for her mother's embrace; the embrace she had always desired.

She had to face disappointment once again when she realized that her mother's love-filled gaze fell on her traitorous sister and not herself.

"Astril!" Isilian ignored her youngest daughter and picked Astril up from the ground, holding her close to her own bosom.

Gallian felt the stares of her soldiers all over her at the High Priestess's unusual actions. Embarrassed and enraged by being passed over once again, Gallian dropped her sister's arm with a fallen face.

"Mother, she's a traitor!"

Gallian flinched when her mother's gaze finally landed on her. "That will be all from you!" The spiteful words flew out of her harsh lips, stinging Gallian.

She watched in horror as the older woman turned back to her oldest child and tenderly stroked Astril's short hair. After reviewing the bruises on her arms and legs, she turned back to Gallian, accusing, "Who did this to her?"

Gallian turned her face away, refusing to look her mother in the face.

She glanced back in time to see her mother lovingly place her hand across Astril's face. Astril pulled away from their mother's touch just as she had always done. The typical response almost made Gallian laugh out loud. *When will Mother learn who it is that really loves her?*

Hurt flickered across Isilian's eyes briefly due to Astril's rejection of her love. Their mother dropped her hand to her side then stood up and screamed out orders to two of the soldiers. "Bring her into the temple."

Gallian saw the anger that quickly spread over her mother's face as she noticed Astril's prince for the first time. The man had been forced to the ground on his knees and was now the recipient of Isilian's full attention.

"Who is that?" Isilian roared, pointing a long finger in his direction. Gallian shrank away from the harshness of her mother's voice.

Even though her face was turned away from her mother's wrath she was determined to keep him for herself. She would have preferred the larger Harkonian, but he'd been fixated on Astril and had to be destroyed. However, she had liked the intensity of his desires. It brought her great displeasure to kill him. Her only choice now was the prince, and she wasn't about to give up a perfectly adequate mate. *He's still pretty big and healthy. Mother won't refuse me. She can't, not after everything I've done for her.* "He is my reward for such a long travel in search of your traitorous daughter."

Isilian's footsteps were inaudible as she hastened toward the young man, grabbing him by the jaw and lifting him in the air to look closely at him. A dark cloud burst forth on her face as she let him drop to the ground. Twisting her hands in front of her and waving her arms, Isilian let out a giant burst of wind that struck Gallian and several of her soldiers to the ground.

The intensity of Isilian's windstorm raged heavier as she screamed toward Gallian, who lay on the earth in front of the iron statue, "What have you done?"

"He's only a Harkonian, Mother." Gallian defended herself with her arms in front of her face in an attempt to ward of the vicious wind that threatened to tear her apart.

"Only a Harkonian!" Isilian sent out another terrible wind that picked Gallian off the ground and threw her against the base of the statue.

Falling to the ground, Gallian cried out and grabbed her lower back in pain.

Her mother's eyes flared with red sparks. "Do not think me stupid, Gallian? I know who he is. He has the look of his grandfather all over him."

She knew she should have killed the man as well as the priests. Gallian's selfish actions had again resulted in her mother's hatred. *When will I ever be good enough for you?*

Isilian turned toward the temple, ordering the soldiers to bring the prince into the temple along with Astril.

"I will deal with your disobedience when I am finished with your sister!" her mother threatened as she shut the temple doors tight.

Gallian's eyes burned with tears. She was frightened by her mother's intense anger. *It's not fair! I've done everything to gain her love, and Astril has not done anything.*

All of the years of trying to please the High Priestess and always falling short, the countless times her mother had chosen Astril over her, had made their mark on her heart. A cold new determination grew within Gallian. She was not going to lose her prize. She knew a way into the temple from behind, a secret way. As a child she had often used the small door to enter and watch her mother's rituals. Slowly, she rose to her feet and looked around her. The soldiers who had not accompanied her mother were milling away, no doubt going to their own homes. She wiped her tearstained cheeks and crept to the back of the building.

CHAPTER TWENTY-FIVE

silian walked through the dark, narrow labyrinth that snaked toward the inner worship room with deliberate steps. *This is my last chance to convince her to submit to her training. Even if I have to destroy Gallian, Elan, and this Harkonian, Astril will begin her service.*

She stared into the back of the Harkonian prince's head as she walked silently behind. He was large. Of that there was no doubt, but why wasn't he fighting? It took only two small soldiers to subdue his arms. Isilian knew how strong Harkonian men could be. After all, hadn't the Great Goddess forced her to kill Astril's father? Images of the farmer she had once loved raced over her memories. Manipulating her mind away from heartache to that of worship of the Great Goddess, she pushed her heart pain back to a dull aching.

The circular path narrowed even further until the Harkonian's shoulders brushed both walls. The soldiers who held him in place had to walk before and behind him until they reached the opening into the inner worship room. The dark beauty of the room always took her breath away. It was humbling to realize everything that the Great Goddess had awarded her. *One day this will all be Astril's.*

With reverence, she approached the golden statue and lit a few candles. She placed her hands before her face and bowed low.

Then standing and turning around, she observed without emotion the soldiers who were chaining the Harkonian prince to the wall. Her eyes scanned the candlelit room in search of her daughter. *Why are they touching Astril?* Fire filled her body until every muscle shook.

"Take your filthy hands off of her!" The fury inside Isilian at seeing her daughter being chained exploded from her fingertips into a wild torrent that sent the soldiers flailing into the wall. Astril was also sent flying with the fierceness of her wind. Regret at what she had done to the girl filled her as she ran toward her daughter.

Gently she took her daughter's arm and lifted her to her feet. Astril's balance shifted, giving her the appearance of being intoxicated. *She hit her head!* Isilian cried within while holding tightly to make sure she didn't fall.

Astril raised her hand to her head and gave it a slight shake. She looked up at her mother in astonishment then pulled her arm away quickly. Isilian was used to the girl's rejection, but it still stabbed her heart every time.

"Why would you do this, Astril?" she asked in a quiet voice that was laced with the fire that still dwelt within her. She turned her eyes away from her daughter and waved her hand for the soldiers to leave them, then asked more harshly, "Why would you betray me?"

Astril kept her head bowed before her mother.

Isilian knew she wouldn't get an answer so she turned to stare at the golden statue of the Great Goddess, seeking instruction. When nothing came, she bowed her head for a moment. Turning back to her daughter, she gestured toward the Harkonian. "So this is the boy you saved nine sacrifices ago."

Astril's nod was almost imperceptible as she stared down at the worship room floor.

Isilian looked at the young man with contempt. "This is the prince of my enemy." Still staring at the young man, Isilian stated, "Your sister has done a very foolish thing. We have already lost many of our people to death and slavery at the hands of the Harkonians. Stealing him will no doubt cost many more lives."

She walked over to where the man stood. The chains that bound him were positioned low on the wall, designed for much smaller people. They barely came to the young man's elbows, which caused his arms to hang in an awkward way.

Behind her, she heard Astril's voice break slightly. "Mother, this man is not important to us. We should send him back to his home for the safety of our people."

Isilian stopped before the Harkonian and ran a long fingernail softly down his cheek. He was very handsome; strong like his grandfather, but his eyes were soft like those of his sickly father. What was that look that crossed over his face as Astril spoke? *Could that be pain?* She smiled, beginning to realize.

"So, Daughter, this man means nothing to us?"

"Yes, Mother. He's not important at all, just one of their princes." Her daughter's words came out too quickly saturated with relief. "Gallian took him out of lust. Let's send him away from here quickly so our people will be free."

That is pain, deep pain on his face. Hope began to grow inside her heart. *He's in love with her.*

She smiled at him. *He shall be the conduit that brings the seed forth.* Clucking her tongue and caressing his chin with her forefinger nail, she whispered, "Don't worry, young man. She's lying." She let her long nail linger in place under his chin, perfectly positioned in the soft flesh. "You're in love with her, aren't you?" She almost laughed when the boy's eyes turned downward, avoiding her gaze.

"Mother, he's not important to us. Please send him back to his home." Astril's voice became strained behind her.

Still concentrating on the young man before her, Isilian ignored her daughter's pleas. "Would you give up your life to save my daughter?" This time the young man's gaze jerked forward. There was strength in his jaw and intensity in his stare. "Yes," she chuckled. "I believe you would."

"Mother!" Astril screamed.

The deep pain of her daughter's voice interrupted Isilian's thoughts briefly. She chose to ignore the nagging of her own heart at what could be between the two young people. Her duty and position had wrenched the sweetness of love from her, and now the only desire of her soul was to attain the power of the Great Goddess for herself and her daughter. The need for it burned inside her, excluding any emotion her beloved child might feel. "Unfortunately, it does not matter whether you love her." She then turned her attention back to her daughter, "Does it, Astril?"

Her daughter's face was stricken with grief and misery. Sadness spilled out of every pore as Astril shook before her. "No, Mother, please don't do this," the girl cried, falling to her knees. "Please let Toren go."

She's in love with him. She really is in love with him. Isilian felt a distant melting of her heart at the girl's pleas, but she ignored the tugging and forced her mind back to what lay ahead.

Lost in her own thoughts of what needed to take place, Isilian barely heard Astril say, "Mother, I have kept myself pure."

She could not understand what the girl meant. How could this have anything to do with sacrificing the man and taking her rightful place next to her mother?

"I am untouched, Mother." Astril persisted standing to her feet in front of the statue. "Gallian says that if I go to the sacrificial altar of my own will, you will receive a larger amount of magic from the Great Goddess."

The Harkonian screamed, "No!"

Astril flinched.

Isilian turned to look at the Harkonian who fought against his arm chains, begging for her daughter's attention. She stood transfixed, trying to understand the pure love the two had for one another. Both were willing to die so the other could live.

Astril quickly finished her speech, "If you allow Toren to go freely home, I will go to the altar on my own power and be your sacrifice. Surely you will be rewarded with more priestess daughters."

Isilian was greatly confused. "You would do that for this man of Harkan?"

Astril nodded and stared into her mother's eyes. They both ignored the young man as he pleaded with Astril to not give her life for his sake.

Isilian continued to stare at her daughter. It was evident that Astril loved the man, but why would she offer herself in his place? This idea baffled the High Priestess so she made up her mind to follow her original intent. "You do in fact love this man?"

Astril's face fell, and she turned away without responding. Isilian had to know the truth from the girl's lips. If she truly loved him, everything would be right. The Great Goddess would honor Astril's sacrifice of her love on the altar. Astril's power would be great in deed. *My daughter will be the first to take a human life for the Great Goddess.*

The thought of Astril's future sitting so close at hand made Isilian giddy, but she still needed to know. "Do you love him, Astril?"

"Mother—" the girl cut off her words. Fear fell on her fine features.

"I asked you if you love this man, child," Isilian impatiently questioned again. When Astril did not respond she thrust her long nails into the soft flesh beneath the Harkonian's chin and hissed, "Tell me now, Daughter. Do you love him?"

The Harkonian grunted and writhed against the pain.

Astril rushed to her mother, grabbed her arm, begging for his release. Isilian threw her off with one hand, knocking her to the ground.

"Answer me now, or he dies right here."

Astril jumped to her feet and screamed, "Yes, I love him. I love him with every fiber of my being."

That's it! Isilian smiled brightly and released her hold on the young man, who slumped in his shackles. After smoothing her hair back, she walked over to her pleading daughter and took her hand. Isilian dragged Astril in front of the statue then knelt down, forcing her daughter with her.

"Great Goddess," she prayed in a loud voice. "Give my daughter wisdom. Help her to honor her duty as the Seed of Seerling." Isilian then turned toward Astril and explained, "Don't you see that this is the answer to my prayers?"

Astril stared with an open mouth and slowly shook her head no.

Isilian prodded her to stand up and face her. She cupped her daughter's face lovingly in her hands. "You have been disobedient for too long. You have forsaken your training and chased after your own heart, refusing to take up your birthright. Now the Great Goddess has given you one last chance. If you sacrifice your human love on the altar, the Great Goddess will come to you more powerfully than she has ever come to any of our line. She will make you great, and the prophecy will be fulfilled."

Her daughter stood staring at her, shaking her head.

Taking Astril's shoulders with both hands, Isilian began to laugh out loud. "Yes. This is the answer."

She then turned away and clasped her hands together decidedly. "You will sacrifice him tonight. It does not matter that it is not the proper time or season. The Great Goddess will come to you, and through you our people will be guided into her great light. You will take them into places we have never been able to go. The Great Goddess will guide your every step. You will be great, and all that I have done will be remembered forever."

Isilian was consumed with her thoughts of power for herself and her child. *This is the answer. This is the reason Astril was born. All of my sacrifices have been for this moment.*

Toren silently wept. *She loves me!* Under different conditions her admission would have brought joyous tears to his eyes. Now in the presence of such evil, he could only try to hide his grief. When he had contained his emotions, he raised his head to stare at the tall, blonde woman. He couldn't help but shudder at her power. *No wonder Astril tried to get me to leave. Her mother is evil.*

He had allowed himself to be chained to the wall by the soldiers without a fuss so that Astril might be free. He had convinced himself that he would do anything to keep her from being harmed. Now it seemed he must face a dark path. Would Astril give him to this goddess? The thought filled him with dread but still he loved her deeply. *I told her I would willingly die for her.* He gulped in deep breaths. *One True God, please give me* strength to endure whatever the future holds. *If I must die, please keep her in Your safety.*

"Mother, this is my decision to make," Astril stared up into her mother's evil face. Her small body looked so ill equipped compared to the magic that flew from every muscle of the older woman.

From Toren's position on the wall it appeared that the High Priestess barely even noticed that Astril had spoken. She seemed consumed by her own thoughts as she answered with a small wave. "Yes, of course it's your decision. He's your sacrifice, child." The High Priestess's face was filled with delight as she turned again to her golden statue and raised her hands in worship, chanting words he could not understand.

Clearing her throat, Astril ignored her mother and walked toward him. Despite the many bruises and disheveled hair, she was beautiful. The intensity in her eyes filled him with dread. She would never give him up. He knew it. Love poured out of her, and its power overwhelmed him. He knew his eyes had to be as big as the wrist bracelets her mother wore.

He sank into her touch as she wiped the blood from under his chin. The tenderness of her kiss, mingled with the salt of her tears, coursed through his body, strengthening his resolve.

"Astril," his voice came out in a husky whisper. He would do anything for her, even die. "Give me to her."

The shake of her head was barely visible. He knew she had made up her mind. Before he could say more, she turned around and leaned into him with arms spread out as protective wings.

He could almost feel power release from her body as she tensed up and screamed, "I will not be your seed!"

The High Priestess's hair swept up on an evil wind and whipped about wildly. She turned from her worship and raised her hands toward them. The magical gusts tore around the room, blowing out the candles. The only light left came from the fire pit underneath the statue.

Astril leaned heavily into him, shying away from the raging wind. She calmed her voice down to almost a whisper and begged, "Mother, release Toren. I will be your sacrifice, and you can lead the people with your new magic. You can be the seed of the Great Goddess."

The fury ended in a startling rush, and the High Priestess fell to the floor. Covering her face with her hands, the woman cried, "What good would so much magic be if I can not save my one child?"

Could she truly love her daughter? Toren didn't have time to contemplate the strange actions of the woman, as a low laugh burst out of a darkened corner.

Gallian stepped out of the darkness of her hiding place and into the fire lit room. "You seem to have forgotten something, Mother."

Still kneeling, Isilian turned to face the priestess. Her face filled with rage, and she screamed for the girl to leave the temple.

In slow, deliberate steps, Gallian walked toward her mother. The evil smile pasted in place could not hide the horror in her eyes. Her voice was barely audible as she squeaked, "You have other children, but you seem to never remember."

"Gallian, you have disappointed me with everything you have done." Isilian stood to her feet and turned toward the girl. "Leave my sight or I will be forced to destroy you."

The girl's eyes were filled with pain but her lips still held a smile. "I have done everything in my life to try and please you. Astril has done everything to bring down your anger. She has defied you, lied to you, betrayed you—yet you seek to reward her?" The young woman stared toward them with evil eyes. "I finally understand."

Isilian raised her hand and unleashed a fury of wind. "Get out of my sight!"

Gallian ignored her mother as she moved with lightning speed toward Toren and Astril. He saw the fury in her eyes and thrust his arms forward to protect Astril, only to be cut short by the chains.

"No!"

It was too late. Gallian grabbed Astril's arm with superior strength and slammed her against the wall. Her head hit hard. He watched as her eyes rolled backward, and she fell to the floor.

Gallian held tight to her sister's arm. "I know now that you will never love me as long as this one is alive." With those words she gave out a thunderous war cry, waving her free hand in a circular motion above her head. The gust of wind her gesture excited brought a tremendous roaring into the temple. Toren could not do a thing as she flung Astril around three times then let her go into the air. Astril's limp body flew past the High Priestess and slammed headfirst into the statue.

"No!" Isilian screamed, running to pick the girl up. She lifted Astril's head to her knee, and Toren stared in anguish as dark blood poured from a wound at the hairline of her forehead.

"What have you done?" Isilian cried.

Gallian's laughter echoed off the temple walls as her arms gyrated above her head, creating an evil storm. Flashes of red fire exploded from her fingertips, lapping up the air between them.

With obvious fear in her eyes, Isilian jumped to her feet leaving Astril to lay pooled in her own blood. She held her hands up defensively and stumbled backward, bumping her head on the base of the statue. The unexpected jolt seemed to bring her out of her fear. She raised her own powerful hands and lifted Gallian's body with a quick rush of wind.

The young priestess used the gust to propel her body into the air. She flipped twice around then landed directly in front of her mother. With a power and strength that defied her size, Gallian seized her mother's neck and thrust her into the air. Isilian flailed desperately as her daughter's hands began to crush her throat.

With an evil power, Gallian held her mother by the neck above Astril's unconscious body. The Seerling soldiers who had rushed into the temple after the furious windstorm watched in horror along with Toren as the young priestess strangled the life force from her mother. They stood motionless as a cloud of death consumed their High Priestess. Gallian held her in place well after Isilian's life breath had escaped from her body. Then smiling wickedly, she dropped the body to the ground where it landed on the motionless form of her sister.

Gallian slapped her hands to her sides and in a loud voice declared, "I am now the High Priestess."

She raised her face up with a proud look, then sneered at their astonished gasps and quickly bowed heads. "Take my mother's body to be prepared for funeral rites."

She then addressed Toren's presence for the first time. "Bring him to the sacrifice altar. He will want to enjoy the spectacle."

Toren stood unable to think as the men stripped the chains from the walls and cuffed his hands behind his back. Then somberly they all walked behind Gallian, who dragged Astril's limp body by the arm through the labyrinth halls and out into the bright moonlight.

CHAPTER TWENTY-SIX

Toren could not believe what his eyes had seen. The powerful battle between mother and daughter had raged on while Astril lay unconscious, and now his love was being led unaware to her death. He struggled against the chains that held his arms bound behind him while his mind turned over everything that had happened. What could he do against such evil power? How could he save her?

He stared around the circle at the empty faces of the Seerling soldiers. The men who held him in place stood with blank expressions. They were in shock. It was then that he realized they were as much captives as he, powerless to do anything.

A soft rain began to fall as Toren helplessly watched Gallian drag her sister's body toward the granite altar.

"Wake up, Astril!" He screamed into the still night air. One of the soldiers clubbed him in the head to silence him. Despite the pounding, he could see Astril's free hand flutter. *She's alive!*

Gallian obviously didn't see her sister's movement when she bent down and hefted her body to the altar. Toren's watchful eye noticed that the strength she had displayed earlier appeared to be gone as she struggled under Astril's weight.

She's out of her power. He surveyed the soldiers who held him. *If I can break free, maybe I can…*

Astril's body suddenly came alive as she grabbed her sister's long hair and yanked her facedown on the altar. She pulled herself up and around then propelled her body off of the stone, flying over the younger woman's head and still holding tight to her hair. He watched in awe as she yanked hard causing Gallian's head to jerk to the side, smashing her face into the granite. Astril whirled around, placed her knee square in the middle of Gallian's shoulders, and stared down at her sister with her full body weight pushing down on the girl's head.

Holding her sister's face into the stone, Astril screamed wildly, "The One True God will deliver them to me. Be strong and courageous. Do not be afraid or terrified because of them, for the One True God goes with me; he will never leave me nor forsake me."

Toren watched the entire display and quickly checked the gathering crowd of Seerlings for any sign of danger to Astril. Looking around, he realized that not only were they standing passively by, but few even seemed to care what the outcome of the fight would be.

Gallian struggled facedown on the altar, desperately trying to regain her hold on her older sister. Her efforts were futile as Astril's strength was superior in the moment. Gallian was able to raise her head up only an inch, but Toren noticed that it was all she needed to find where the sacrificial knife had fallen. She reached out her hand to grab it, but Astril blocked her movement with a thrust of her left foot, successfully kicking the knife to the ground.

The quick movement of her feet temporarily knocked Astril off balance, giving Gallian time to break free and rush for the weapon. Astril jumped on the sacrifice altar then flipped over her sister's head. She landed in front of the large iron statue, confronting her sister.

Gallian raised her hands, but her magic was exhausted from her fight with Isilian, and she was only able to force out a small, ineffective puff of air that barely stirred Astril's hair. A look of surprise passed over the younger woman's face at her own weakness. The look quickly changed into one of fury as Gallian rushed toward Astril, holding the knife above her head in an attempt to stab her. Astril quickly jumped out of the way of the attack just as the young woman thrust the knife forward, slicing through the air. Having missed her target, Gallian's knife delved deeply into a small crevice in the stomach of the timeworn statue.

The young priestess grabbed hold of the hilt and pulled, but the knife would not budge from its position. Her body shook with fury, and she screamed unintelligible words to the sky, continuing to pull.

Astril stood by with her knees bent and hands up in fighting stance, watching her sister fight to free the knife from the belly of the statue.

Immediately a loud *boom* went off in the heavens above them and a blinding light burned down from the sky. The flash of white fire struck the head of the statue, changing its dark color to brilliant red. The fire ran quickly down the body and into the knife, which Gallian still had a hold of. The blaze burned through the knife and into the girl's arm. Gallian's body convulsed as the flames flowed through her, licking the moisture from her flesh. A deep red burning devoured her hand, moving quickly toward her shoulder. Toren's lungs choked on the stench of burning flesh, and wisps of smoke rose upward as soft rain fell on Gallian's blazing face.

"No!" Astril screamed, running toward her dying sister.

A male soldier grabbed her around the waist, stopping her from getting close to the danger. "Don't touch her! This is the punishment of the Great Goddess," he cried, holding her tight.

"No!" Astril cried, fighting against the Seerling's muscular arms. "This is the judgment of the One True God."

Breaking free from his hold, she walked slowly to the side of her sister and knelt just out of reach of the flames. Fire consumed Gallian's body until the only things recognizable were dark blue eyes that steamed as she stared at Astril.

"Traitor!" she croaked out with her last breath.

Astril fell to the ground with a bowed head, doubled over, and cried. Toren longed to go to her but his arms were still chained tightly behind his back. Turning to the soldier at his right, he commanded, "Release me!"

The Seerling male nodded his head and unlocked the cuffs. As soon as the chains fell, Toren ran to Astril and took her in his arms, cradling her. "The One True God has saved us, Astril."

Her body convulsed, but he was still able to hear her garbled words, "Only He could have."

He ignored the stares of those who were gathered and held her tight. She clung to him fiercely and released a flood of anguish.

"Why couldn't she change?" Astril cried into Toren's shirt. "Why did they both have to die?" She held him, hoping he would never let go. He was the only thing she had left now. No family and no home, she had nothing. Grief overwhelmed her again, and she clung to him even tighter seeking reassurance in his embrace.

It took a long time, but Astril was finally able to compose herself and look around at her surroundings. She saw the astonished faces of those gathered and realized they too were afraid of what had taken place. She smiled weakly up at Toren then stood shakily to her feet. With an unsteady hand she took hold of Toren's as he rose beside her.

One of the Seerling elders slowly walked toward the pair. Her face was ashen as she spoke, "What are we to do now, Astril?"

"I don't know," she admitted. She continued to hold Toren's hand as one by one the thirteen Seerling elders approached to stand before her.

"You are the only one left to rule us. You will have to be our High Priestess."

Fear gripped her heart as she wondered what the people might do. She looked around at the thirteen old women who were nodding their heads in unison. "You all know that I have fought my training and refused to worship the Great Goddess. I am not equipped to be your ruler, and I will not become your priestess."

The first elder reached out and touched her arm. Out of reflex Astril pulled away and stood slightly behind Toren. She knew it was childish to try and hide, but she couldn't face what they wanted of her. Toren's back straightened at her reaction, and he placed his hand protectively in front of her, holding on to her side.

Still she listened as the woman said, "Our tribes have always been ruled by a woman of your line. You are the only one left. You are the Seed that was meant to take us into the light."

"I am no seed." Astril shook her head. She moved even closer to Toren, burying her head into the back of his shoulder in an attempt to distance herself from what they wanted.

It was then that Toren interrupted the exchange. He moved to stand completely in front of her and faced the crowd. "We can discuss these things tomorrow. Astril is hurt and needs attention, as well as a good night of rest." His voice was commanding and strong. "Once it is safe, take the body of her sister to where her mother's lies."

He then turned his back to the crowd and smiled down at her. Gratefully, she smiled back. Weakness overcame her, and her knees began to buckle. Her eyes blurred, and she felt herself being lifted lightly into his strong arms.

As soon as Toren gathered Astril's unconscious form into his arms, the Seerlings went to work, busying themselves with the cleanup. Several women hovered around them. One of the old women who had first spoken led him toward a nearby hut. Toren felt strength flow through him as he carried the woman he loved inside. *She's mine now, and no one can ever take her from me again!*

With his mind resolved, Toren stepped inside the small house where his head bumped against the door frame. Ignoring the pain, he bent over Astril and walked on. The old woman opened a small door off to the right, and he entered. She instructed him to lay Astril down on the cushioned bed that lay in a corner of the room, and he did so. They were followed by four other women, all carrying bundles of herbs or clay bowls in their hands. Stepping out of the way, he let the women take over.

The door was open to the main portion of the hut, and Toren could see two male soldiers standing at full attention. He knelt down, easing his exhausted body, and watched the careful actions of the women who attended his love.

"Ow!" Astril woke up and grabbed her head. He lunged forward at her cry but was pushed back by one of the women. He saw Astril's searching eyes looking for him and pushed past the Seerling who was blocking his path. Kneeling down at her bedside, he took her hand, keeping a guarded look on his face.

Astril's soft sigh at his touch invigorated him.

She accepted the small cup of drink that one of the women gave her and gulped. She then leaned back and patiently endured the stitching of her head wound. She held on to his hand flinching only twice from the pain.

Once the sewing had been completed, the women stepped back against the walls of the room. Astril's gaze moved to the soldiers in the other room and beckoned them closer with a wave of her hand.

She addressed the men while pointing to Toren with her free hand. "Toren is a friend of Seerling. Give him whatever he desires." She then smiled at him and added, "Give him his own hut and have the women clean him and dress his wounds."

She covered her mouth to hide her yawn before stressing that he was free to go wherever he wanted.

He didn't want to leave. *Too much has kept us apart already.* He complained silently, then stroked her hand and asked, "Wouldn't you rather I stay here with you?"

She sent him a sleepy half smile and closed her eyes peacefully. One of the women took hold of his arm and gently but forcefully led him from the room.

"Her head injury makes her tired," she said. "You will do best to abide by her wishes for now. Perhaps later she will want you with her."

Toren was confused and frustrated at being sent away from Astril, but he decided to do as the servant suggested.

The tiny woman smiled up at him and in a reassuring voice said, "Do not worry. We know how to care for our own." Then looking back at the sleeping girl she softly added, "She's our leader now. We will take good care of her."

The Seerling's words troubled his heart, but he knew how Astril felt. She was frightened of what her people wanted, and he knew she would never serve anyone but the One. After everything that had happened, he knew she would be better off going home with him. After all, hadn't they all stood complacently by and watched her almost die?

Toren allowed himself to be led by the soldiers to a small house far from Astril's. It was frustrating, but he made up his mind to cooperate. He reminded himself that he would soon have Astril safe with him again and all would be right.

The men left him alone in the hut. He had just reached down to take off his boots when two very young women entered without knocking. He stared up at them in surprise. Both blushed and stared down at the floor. One of the Seerlings carried a basket filled with all different types of food. His stomach grumbled, making both of the women smile.

The one set the basket down on the table then they both turned and shuffled outside. It was only a few moments before they reentered with a heavy iron tub. He stood to help but was quickly dismissed by the shaking of their heads.

He sat back down at the table and watched them come in and out of the hut, filling the tub with hot water. He couldn't help but notice how small each of the Seerlings were in comparison to Astril and her family members.

"I didn't realize Seerlings were so small," he said to himself then took a large bite of bread.

One of the young women smiled as she dumped the final pail of water in the tub. "Only the line of the priestess is allowed to take outside mates."

Toren blushed at her words.

His blush brought forth a torrent of giggles from the two young women, and the one who had first spoken added, "The priestesses mate with outside races to grow large offspring. That's why Astril's so big. I believe her father was of your people."

"What!"

His scream sent the two women scurrying from the room in fear. A short time later, one of the elder women that he had seen outside entered to speak with him.

"You frightened Raina," she said while sitting down at the table before him.

Toren looked the elder over and noted the intensity of her gaze.

"I'm sorry." He studied the old woman who was still intensely staring at him and asked, "Does Astril know who her father is?"

The elder shook her head slowly still looking him over carefully. "It is the custom of each priestess to leave the confines of the temple after the yearly sacrifice. She goes deep into the world and finds a strong man she believes will give her strong priestess daughters. She then seduces him and often kills him. It is rare for priestess children to have the same father."

"And Astril's father was a Harkonian?" he asked, shaking his head in disbelief.

The elder reviewed his face before continuing, "It is widely believed that he was. It is also believed that Isilian's second child, a girl, was from that same man. She was given as a Keeper. Isilian also had a son whom everyone says had the same father, but he came to a terrible end. We were never told if Isilian killed Astril's father after the conception of the boy, but we do know that she killed Gallian's. I believe he was a Gernon."

Toren let his breath out in a quick whoosh and reached for a grape, still trying to comprehend what he had been told.

"You are tired and must be in want of a hot bath." The elder gave him a tight-lipped smile. "I will inform Raina that you are not dangerous, and she will warm the water."

He nodded his head and apologized again for scaring the young women. The elder stood to her feet, and folding her hands together in front of her face, nodded her good-bye before leaving him alone with his thoughts.

The skittish girl reentered the room with two other women. Timidly they went about the task of preparing a hot bath and making a comfortable bed for him. He felt terrible that they would not speak even after he apologized profusely.

Once they had finished, the trio left the hut without looking at him.

He checked to make sure the door was completely closed, then undressed and stepped into the warm bath. He smiled as he leaned back in the tub and remembered the happenings of the day. *Everything has changed so quickly.*

"Since Astril is half Harkonian there should be little fight from government in making her my wife," he whispered into the lonely room. "I will take her home with me as soon as she is recovered enough to travel."

Chapter Twenty-seven

stril was startled awake by the sound of voices in her room. Her automatic thought was to grab for her staff. She searched the bed but couldn't find it. Instead, she tensed her body and braced her arms, readying herself for a possible fight. With her eyes straining to see in the dim lighting in the room, she was able to make out the faces of Seerling women she knew to be the thirteen elders. Each managed her own tribe of Seerlings and came to the village of the High Priestess only on rare occasions. Astril's return home must have warranted a visit from them all. She relaxed and leaned against the wall for support.

"We are sorry to awaken you at this late hour, Astril," said the oldest woman. "However, it is a matter of great importance."

Astril sat up fully in the bed before grabbing her head in pain. Memories of what had taken place only a few short hours before flooded her, but she forced herself to stand. Ignoring her physical and emotional pain, she grabbed the clean mauklan from the edge of the bed and quickly dressed.

"We are here to compel you to stay and lead the Seerling tribes," the old woman pleaded while watching her every move.

Astril tied the two sides of the top together behind her neck and shook her head. "I don't see how that's possible...."

The elder held her hand up, silencing Astril's words. "We have served your mother and others from your line for longer than any of us can remember. It is your line that has kept the Seerling tribes united. Our mothers worshipped the Great Goddess and served the line of priestesses because they didn't know better."

The elder looked around the room at each of the others and went on, "Today you broke the old ways, but you can not leave us alone. We need a leader to keep the tribes united. The people know service to only your line. You must fulfill the prophecy and become the Seed to lead us into a great light."

No, I won't do that. I won't serve the Great Goddess. Still shaking her head, Astril sat down on the bed and looked at them thoughtfully. "I serve the One True God. I will never serve another. Therefore I can not be the Seed that leads you."

Each of the elders smiled at her words then looked around at one another nodding their heads in unison.

The chosen speaker addressed her again. "I remember your birth. The mystic did prophecy over you, but what she said was not what your mother believed."

A small gasp escaped from Astril's mouth and her eyes widened, "What did she say?"

"The mystic said that you would be the Seed to bring the Seerling tribes into a great light." Astril did not miss the emphasis on a as the elder spoke. "Your mother believed that light was of the Great Goddess. Your grandmother believed it was the light of the One True God."

At Astril's sharp intact of breath, the woman smiled and went on, "We learned much under your grandmother. Now we will learn under you."

They want to learn about the One True God! Astril's thoughts screamed inside her. She had been so sure that she could no longer stay with her people; that she had no home left.

The elder touched her head gently and sighed. "There are many things you have yet to learn about your people, Astril. Not everyone serves the Great Goddess as your family line insisted."

But how, when... Astril's mind whirled in every direction possible. "You already know about the One True God?"

Nodding their heads, the elders smiled back at her while the eldest of the group responded, "Each of us spent private time with your grandmother before her death. We never spoke of it to anyone, nor did we speak of it among ourselves."

Astril sat staring at them all, shaking her head. *This is all so strange. What will Toren think?* She made up her mind to seek his advice as soon as the sun came up. "I need to speak with Toren about what needs to be done. This is all so difficult for me to fully comprehend alone."

She noticed that the group of elders began to stir uncomfortably, each turning to another and whispering.

The eldest turned a grave face back to Astril. She shifted her weight from one foot to another. "We believe your young prince is planning to ask you to go with him back to Harkan. We believe he will try to force you to become his mate. If you do this, the Seerling tribes will fall."

"No!" *He isn't like that.* "Toren loves me. He would not ask me to choose between my people and our life together."

"He will try to force you to go with him, Astril." Taking her hand, the elder whispered, "You will have to sacrifice your love for him or sacrifice your destiny. And who knows but that your God has brought you through all of this so that you can teach us to follow Him."

Astril stared down at the woman's wrinkled hand on her own. She had never once thought the One would make her choose between her people and Toren's love. *This can't really happen. He's not like that. He will be happy for me and will want to help.* She shook her head fiercely. They were wrong about Toren.

Another of the elders, who had been silent through the entire meeting, stepped forward. "Astril, a seed begins as the tiniest thing. Birds come and eat it. People trample it, but if it finds good soil, it will have a chance. Once that seed dies to itself, it begins to grow. It fights and tears its way through every obstacle to find light. You have walked a long path, and you are now at the place of branching out into a great light; one greater than what any of us can imagine. If you do not reach out to the light, you cannot grow and become all that you are meant to be. This Harkonian will not mean to do it, but he will try to steal that light from you."

Astril bowed her head and wept. In her mind she knew that Toren was young and had made poor choices because of her, but her heart cried out for their love. *Will I have to sacrifice my love for him? Would you ask that much of me, Lord?* She stared at the faces before her. *Is this what Priest Augur was trying to prepare me for?*

"No. You don't know Toren as I do. He will accept my calling." She heard the weakness in her voice and hung her head. In an attempt to convince herself she added, "He loves me."

"Yes," the older woman answered. "He does love you, but he is still young and selfish. He has been sheltered and guarded all his life and does not understand what true sacrifice is. He will force you to choose."

The elders turned from her as she bent over in tears. One held back and paused at her side. "Please, consider what the future of Seerling will be if you allow your heart to make this decision."

After everything she had been through, now she must choose between her own heart and duty to her people. Could the One truly have brought her through all of this so that she could lead the Seerlings to know Him? What higher calling could there be than to win the lost for Him? She had given her heart to Him and though it pained her greatly, she knew she would not choose Toren. *But why can't I have you both?*

Grief for what she knew she would lose overwhelmed her, and she closed her eyes. *How can I endure losing him?*

Toren had been sitting beside her bed for a long time, waiting for her to awaken. The events of the night before still wore on his mind, but they couldn't distract him from the plan he had formed. He wanted to assess the situation and how quickly she could heal before asking. His stomach filled with jitters as one of the Seerling women quietly entered the room with a metal plate of fresh bread and crushed berries.

The sweet smell of the berries filled the room, causing Astril to stir. After opening her eyes, she looked around the room. Her gaze fell on Toren.

"Good morning." She smiled at him while shaking her head in an attempt to clear the fog of sleep.

It always amazed him how her smile could turn his heart into mush. "It isn't morning any longer, sleepyhead, and do you always fall asleep in your clothes?"

She looked down at her rumpled clothing and let out a small sigh. Sitting up, she tried to smooth out the wrinkles in her leather shirt then stood and took a few steps to sit at the table across from him.

"Did you make me breakfast?"

"No," he admitted, wishing he had. "One of the women brought it in. You slept so long I was beginning to worry about you."

She gave a soft laugh that warmed his toes. Reaching for some food she said, "Don't worry. I feel better than I have in years." He couldn't help but notice her flinch as she raised her arm. She saw his look of concern. "Well, maybe not completely better," she laughed.

His heart skipped about a thousand beats as she once again sent a smile his way. He started to speak but decided not to when she averted her eyes back to the table and stood, walking toward the window. *What's the matter?* He couldn't understand why sadness had suddenly filled her face. So he walked over toward her, laying his arm around her shoulders.

"I learned something very interesting last night," he said while watching several children play outside.

"You did," she answered still staring out the window.

"Yes, I learned that you are half Harkonian."

Astril turned her face slightly toward him, then stepped out from under his arm and with an impassive look, yawned. "Is that all?"

Shocked by her lack of emotion, Toren placed his hands on his hips and demanded, "Don't you know what that means?"

Shaking her head, Astril walked back over to the table, eased into the chair, and took another bite of bread.

"It means we aren't as different as we once thought." His passion for her to understand what he wanted filled him to the very core. How could she sit there and not understand how important this was?

"Toren…" she started then stopped. She shrugged her shoulders and took another bite of bread, staring at it as though it were the most important thing in her world. "The man who sired me isn't important. It's just a ritual that the priestesses do." Her face went dark as she looked up at him. "Priestess children do not have fathers. We have the High Priestess and the Great Goddess."

How awful. "Astril," he said with an unsteady voice. "I am so sorry."

She gulped down the last bite of berry-covered bread and shrugged her shoulders in response.

A few moments of uneasy silence passed with her sitting and staring at her hands and Toren looking out the window, frustrated at the way the conversation had turned.

Letting out a small sigh, he turned back to her. "We don't have to worry over the past any longer. We can make our own way, with our own memories, and I'll make sure they are all happy."

Astril started to respond but was cut off when he passionately took her by the arms and deftly pulled her up to face him. "We don't have to follow traditions or even care what others think. Together we can do anything."

"Oh…" she hesitated.

He gave her a shaky smile and slowly released his hold on her arms. "I'm sorry. I guess I just got caught up in the moment."

Astril looked up at him thoughtfully. There was wisdom and knowing in her face. He felt as though she could read the deepest parts of who he was, and it didn't make what he was about to ask any easier.

"It's just that… well… I was just wondering if…" He felt sick to his stomach. "I just want you to… or would you submit to… I mean would you allow…"

She wasn't making his struggle any easier by the way she just stared at him with her mouth partly opened. He felt like a stumbling bear about to be snared in the hunter's trap.

"Would I allow what, Toren?" she slowly asked.

He laughed nervously then cleared his throat. This really wasn't easy. "Would you allow me to… or rather, Astril, would you submit to…" he shook his head, furious with his lack of ability to speak, then rushed out the last few words, "Would you submit to being my wife?" Relief spilled out, and his shoulders went slack. It was done.

His congratulations to himself were cut short when he saw her eyes close, and her mouth tighten. Why wasn't she speaking? Wasn't this what they both wanted? She just stood there for a long time with her eyes closed, not speaking. He could feel the anger about to explode from within but kept silent, waiting.

Finally she opened her tear-filled eyes and looked up at him. Her voice was a mere whisper as she asked, "Would you choose to stay here in Seerling with me?"

Is that what this is about? She's going to miss her people. He couldn't help but chuckle at her typical nature. She was always thinking of others, but this time they didn't deserve her loyalty.

"What's so funny?" She turned her back to him and straightened her shoulders.

He could tell this wasn't going the way he had wanted, so he softened his voice. "Astril, last night you said yourself that you can't stay here. Besides, now that we know you're half Harkonian, won't you want to find your father?"

She turned back abruptly. He ignored the startled look she gave him. "I'll take you with me to Harkan. There you will be safe and one day help me rule the kingdom."

"Toren, I…"

His patience was gone. How could she question him when all he wanted was to love and protect her? He cut off her words with a quick jerk of his body. "You admitted to your mother that you love me. Why is this a problem?"

He could see her jaw tense then relax as a struggle to remain calm swept across her face. Was that pity in her eyes? "I do love you, Toren."

Her sympathy-filled words resounded in his head. "I think that somehow I've always loved you, but..."

"But what!" His fist landed hard on the table, and his scream sent the children outside the window scrambling off. He didn't care. Astril scurried across to the other side of the room. Her look of fear stabbed his heart, but he couldn't get his anger under control.

"I can't leave my people, Toren. They need me to teach them about the One True God."

He looked at her incredulously. "They aren't your people any more, Astril. You're only half Seerling, and besides these heathens don't care about the truth."

"I'm a Seerling and a heathen, and I care," she screamed back at him, and he cringed at the familiar look of battle readiness in her eyes. "The One True God loves us all, Toren." Then she flopped down to sit on the bed and pleaded in an anguished voice, "I thought you believed that too."

He couldn't stand to hear another word. That she was refusing him was all he needed to know. He walked to the closed door of the room and turned slightly toward her. "I can't stay here. My mother needs to be reassured of my safety. I have responsibilities to my family and to my own people." He wanted her to know how important he was in his country, how much she would miss with him gone.

She approached him and touched his arm softly. "It's a three-night journey to the crossroads. If you stay until tomorrow, I will take you myself."

There it was, exactly what he wanted to hear! She had chosen him. Toren quickly pulled her close and kissed her lips, savoring the sweet taste of berries. His chest was filled with hope as his lips brushed lightly over her ear. "It will be all right. I promise. You will go with me. We can send the priests back to teach your people."

"Toren, I meant that I would take you to the crossroads, not go with you to Harkan." Her tears didn't lessen the impact of her words. She had rejected him.

Cold fury made him untangle her arms from his neck and leave the hut. He slammed the door hard behind him. When the flimsy walls rattled, he gave a harsh bark of satisfaction.

That evening, Astril stood over the dead bodies of her mother and sister. She touched each face softly and then lit their grass beds on fire. All of the Seerlings were present for the funeral rites, but no one said traditional words of remembrance.

Everyone stood in silence watching the flames eat away the flesh of each priestess. Dark clouds billowed above the pyres as the air filled with the stench of seared skin and hair. Astril couldn't help but think how different each of their lives could have been had they never committed themselves to the torturous rule of an evil goddess. All of the sacrifices they had made were lost to the earth. The age of the Great Goddess was dying with each flame. It was time to begin teaching the truth to a people who had lived under tyranny and lies for far too long.

Once the bodies were engulfed, Astril turned to look at the empty faces of her people. Had they ever known hope? She knew she was making the right decision in not leaving with Toren. Still the pain shot through her, and she watched his proud back as he walked away from the gathered group. Her heart ached as she prayerfully whispered into the cool night air, "Help him understand why I won't leave here."

Chapter Twenty-eight

T oren stayed the night only because Seerling lay far south of Harkan and a lone traveler risked attack by boran, or equally dangerous, wild men. Besides, he still wanted to be in Astril's presence for as long as possible even though they would never be together as husband and wife. The next morning he and Astril, accompanied by four male Seerling soldiers, began the journey toward Harkan.

Why would she choose them over me? They tried to kill her, and all I've done is love her. He sulked to himself. The steed he rode was smaller than those of his land, with a jolting gait and a tendency to lag behind the other horses so that his calves ached from urging it forward, whereupon it would lurch into yet another bone-jarring trot.

For the first long day of traveling, he forced himself to not look at Astril even once. During their evening meal he sat by and seethed as he watched her joke with a male soldier while making dinner. *How dare she flaunt herself in front of me like that. She knows I'm in pain, and she's making jokes.*

Toren refused his food and turned his back as she came over to speak with him. *Let her suffer like I am,* he thought, feeling justified when he stole a glance and saw the look of sadness that crossed her face. He lay down for the night earlier than the rest but was not able to sleep. His tortured thoughts ruled over him.

He found it even harder the next day to keep his resolve. He refused all of her attentions and would not look at her even when she spoke. *You're acting like a child,* a voice whispered in his thoughts. Toren shook his head to remove the thought and flopped down on his pallet. For a second night, he found he was unable to sleep.

After two sleepless nights and long days of traveling on the ridge-like spine of his alternately balking and jouncing mount, he was in fouler spirits than ever the next morning. He did eat some fruit in the midday, but would not take any of the meat or bread Astril offered him. His back was sore and his posterior sorer, but he was going to suffer in silence if it killed him. That evening the group ate a meal of burnt boran flesh and lay down just inside the edge of the woods. Toren's stomach was as sour as his mood at the little food he had ingested, and he turned over on his mat to get more comfortable. He moved in time to see Astril sneak away from the campsite, heading farther into the forest.

He slowly got up and checked to make sure the others slept soundly, then followed in the direction she had gone. Toren walked quietly, haunting her steps. It was not long before the densely wooded area opened into a quiet field. She had stopped at the edge of the meadow and stood in front of him, watching several small animals graze in the moonlight. Her hair glistened with the rays of the moon, and he could see the soft outline of her chin. A light breeze lifted his spirits as it passed through her hair then over his face. The scent was intoxicating.

He walked up close behind her and was only slightly surprised when she whispered, "I've missed your smile."

How does she know it's me? "I haven't had much to smile about these last few days."

His breath caught when she moved to stand close to him. She raised her mouth, inviting his kiss. She had a look of love all over her face that built his courage. All of the anger he had felt from the last few days vanished as he lost himself in their love. Placing his finger along her jawline, he caressed her cheek softly. "Astril…"

A powerful sense of ownership flooded over Toren as he wrapped his arm around her back and pulled her close. He enjoyed kissing her and feeling her loving response. She did love him that much he knew. The passion of the moment encouraged him in such a way that he unthinkingly allowed himself to become more aggressive and pull her closer, holding her tighter than ever before. The warmth of her soft body so close to him lit a fire in his stomach that he couldn't control.

"Stop!" she cried, struggling against the strength of his arms.

He couldn't take her rejection, not again. "I still own you, Astril. I can force you to be with me."

He was shocked and shamed by his own words and thoughts even before she pushed him away.

"Is that what I am to you, a slave?" Her question beat like a drum against his heart. How could he have said that?

He watched in shame as she turned away from him and ran back to the security of the camp. All of a sudden the memories of what he had tried to do the night when they were held captive in the tent flooded back to him. And now he had attempted the exact same thing even without Gallian's spell working hard over him.

He could hear the breaking of branches and her racking sobs as Astril ran back to her soldiers. She was safer with her own murderous people than she had ever been with him. The realization filled him with despair. *Is this why You won't give her to me?* His heart screamed upward to the One.

Conflicted by his own actions, Toren knelt down on the soft earth and stared up to the heavens. "Why can't I just love her?"

It was a very long time before he quietly returned to the camp, his questions unanswered. Looking over to where Astril lay, he shook his head and lowered himself to his bedroll for another restless night.

In the morning, the group ate their meal in silence, cleared away the campsite, and mounted their steeds. Astril explained to him in a terse voice that it would be an easier day of travel, but he was too ashamed to look at her while she spoke.

The traveling party arrived on the west side of the crossroads just as the sun was rising high.

Astril crossed her spotted steed in front of Toren's, blocking his path. She wiped a tear from her cheek, and her eyes silently pleaded for his understanding. It was something he could not give her. "I will never stop loving you, Toren."

He looked down at his horse and shrugged his shoulders. "It feels as though you all ready have."

It gave him a strange feeling of satisfaction to know she watched as he crossed in front of her and raced over the bridge toward home without looking back.

Morgan awoke to her servant screaming and bouncing on the bed. "Prince Toren's home! Wake up. He's home."

Morgan sat up straight and smiled.

Lea, still jumping, laughed, "He's home, Miss Morgan."

"I heard you," Morgan laughed, not quit sure how she felt about it. She had been having such a great time with Holan recently. He was so attentive, but with the prince's return, she knew she'd have to give up that friendship.

"I think everyone heard you." She then put on a straight face and ordered Lea to stop bouncing on the bed. "You better pick out a green dress. You know it's his favorite color."

After several hours of dressing and primping, Morgan felt she was presentable enough to go and find her prince. But was he ready for her?

Toren stood before his grandfather's throne. King Kortan smiled at him. "Tell us what you know of the Seerlings, my son."

Toren kept his face emotionless as he relayed the message of all he had experienced. He purposefully left his interactions with Astril out of the story as well as any details on how to return to Seerling. Once he knew he had sufficiently appeased his grandfather's curiosity, he exited the main hall.

"Prince Toren, it is so good to see you again," he heard the breathless voice of Morgan say behind him. Forcing himself to remain impassive, he turned to face the smiling girl.

"Hello, Morgan," he said kindly. "I see you are doing well." Toren noticed that the girl had indeed grown far more beautiful and looked quite lovely in the green dress that clung to her every curve. *Would Astril ever wear a dress like that again?* he thought then berated himself in anger.

His kind words brought forth a surge of chatter from the dark-haired beauty as she spoke about all she had done in his absence. Toren half listened to her prattling, trying hard to keep his mind from wandering off to Astril.

Morgan must have sensed his frustration because it wasn't long before she excused herself from his presence. Waving good-bye, she left him to his tortured thoughts.

Toren struggled against himself for many hours before he finally decided on a course of action. *I made a promise. Even if she doesn't want me, I intend to keep it.* He made the decision to speak with his grandfather that evening. *It feels good to at least have a purpose again.*

King Kortan sat in the main hall playing tafl with his attendant when a very disheveled prince entered the room. The young man looked as though his world would crash down on him at any moment. It was the same look he had held on his face since he returned from the home of those heathens. Kortan knew there was much more to the story the young man had told but chose not to press the point. He was just happy that Toren had returned without the slave. Now he could marry Morgan, and the old hag's vision wouldn't come true.

"Prince Toren," he said, smiling to himself that his tafl king was again going to escape Holan's men. "This is a surprise. I was sure you would still be resting after your ordeal."

"I must speak with you in private, Grandfather."

King Kortan quickly waved everyone out of the room except for Holan and beckoned the prince forward.

"Grandfather," Toren began, throwing Holan a dirty look. "One of the only reasons I was allowed to leave Seerling land was because I made a promise."

The king's mood suddenly soured as he waited for the rest of what the prince had to say.

"I promised that I would make certain that all of the Seerling slaves were released from their duty and allowed to go home." The boy hurried his words.

Is this all? King Kortan sat with a straight face not allowing Toren to see his thoughts. Those slaves had been more of a headache to him than anyone would ever know. Their very presence on his land reminded him of the witch who had entered his court and placed fear in his heart. He didn't care what happened to them.

Instead of stating his true feelings, the king pressed the issue with his grandson. "Toren, it has been a long tradition of ours to keep our prisoners as slaves. And if we release them, who will harvest our fields?"

"I made a promise, Grandfather." Toren threw back his shoulders in an annoying display of bravado. "I intend to see it carried out."

The king sat very still for many minutes contemplating his thoughts. Toren had to be ready to listen to reason. This was exactly what he wanted. "I will grant you this, my son, if you make me a promise."

He smiled slightly to himself as Toren's face darkened. He knew the young man didn't like to barter.

"You have put off your duties to this kingdom for long enough. I will release the slaves if you promise to marry Morgan as soon as the ceremony can be arranged."

Toren stood staring straight ahead. His face was emotionless as he slowly nodded his head in agreement. Kortan could not read his thoughts, nor did he care to. The boy had agreed. That was all he wanted.

"I will marry Morgan if she will have me." Toren's words sealed the deal. There was no going back on his word now, and they both knew it.

Kortan smiled at Holan, his attendant, in a knowing way. "Oh, she'll have you."

It didn't bring him pleasure to have Toren press his luck by saying, "I must insist that we give her the traditional engagement time to prepare." But he knew how finicky women could be, and he wanted Morgan's complete cooperation. She was the key to keeping the crone's words from coming true.

Nodding his head, he laughed and ordered the attendant to have the guards release all of the slaves before the end of the day. He noted the dark stare that emitted from Holan's eyes. *What's gotten in to him?* Kortan did not waste time contemplating his attendant's surly attitude. He had far too many plans to set in place for the upcoming marriage ceremony.

He watched Toren leave the main hall and smiled brightly. Finally, things were turning around in his favor.

"This will stop that old crone's prediction from coming true." His smile broadened as he went on, "I have had nothing but trouble from those slaves anyway. This barter will work to serve two purposes."

CHAPTER TWENTY-NINE

A stril sulked through the campsite, staring at the evidence of ritual animal sacrifice to the Great Goddess, yet another distraction in their quest to free the Keepers. The stench of death permeated the air. *This has got to stop,* she thought, kicking at the dust.

"This animal has only recently been killed," Keanu, a soldier in her army stated while examining the remains.

Astril scanned the site with a weary eye. "How long ago?"

"A day, maybe two."

Frustrated, Astril sat down on a nearby log. Behind her grew an abundance of angelica flowers. She broke a batch off and put them to her face, inhaling their sweet scent. The hill was covered with the yellow beauties. The time of sacrificing had always been when the weather became cooler, and the flowers fell asleep. Here the angelica were in full bloom and standing tall. How strange that an herb used to cure fevers and stomach ailments could encompass an area of death.

Astril shook her head, still staring down at the batch of flowers. "It isn't even the proper time that the sacrifices would have taken place." Turning to Keanu, she asked, "How do we convince them that this is not the right way?"

What Keanu lacked in height he more than made up for in brawn.

Only two days before, Astril was witness as he killed a mature male boran with his bare hands and then hefted the body over one shoulder.

He looked down on the smoldering embers of the campfire. "It's difficult to force change, Astril. There will always be those who rebel."

She shook her head in disgust. "I know that I need to be more patient. Everything is still so new, and it has to be hard for most of them to go without a leader."

"You're our leader!" he responded in shock. "And from my point, you are a better leader than your mother ever was."

Astril patted his overly muscled arm and smiled. "Thank you for the kind words, my friend." She continued to survey the campsite before adding, "You know this is the third site of sacrifice we've found this phase of the moon."

Keanu rubbed his thumb and forefinger over the yellow stubble growing on his chin. "I think it will be very good to have your priests come and train us. Perhaps their words can bring about a further change in the people."

Astril nodded. "Yes, I am so glad they agreed to come. It's my hope that Priest Augur and his attendants will help me train future leaders." She then smiled at Keanu. "Leaders like you and Raina."

The blush on Keanu's face spread all the way up to the hairline of his blonde curls at the mention of his new mate.

Astril couldn't help teasing the man further. "I hope she's not furious with me for taking you away from her so quickly after your marriage union."

Keanu turned toward her, his manner as serious as it always was. "My mate is very supportive. She believes in our quest." Earnest warmth filled his gaze. "We both believe in what you are doing, Astril."

"Come," she said with a smile. "If we spend all our day talking, we will not complete our task to rescue the Keepers."

"I cannot believe we were so terribly misled about their treatment. Long ago, my mother's own brother was chosen as a Keeper. Their entire family believed it was an honor for him to have been chosen. Now to find out what he has had to endure."

Astril placed her hand upon his arm and sighed. "I doubt that he is alive today, my friend. When I found my sister, she looked to be among the oldest living Keepers. Their life is hard and filled with sickness."

Both Astril and Keanu walked on with the other soldiers in silence. None knew what to expect once they climbed the steep cliffs, and they wanted to be prepared for the possibility of fighting the ancient mystic.

Nightfall was coming on fast when the company of Seerling soldiers finally made it up the rocky cliffs to the land of Keepers. It was a hard climb, and Astril had more than her fair share of rock dust to eat. Still they continued stealthily up the cliffs. Each soldier prepared for whatever met them above.

Swinging her leg over the last pile of rocks, Astril crouched low and helped another soldier over. Once they were all safe She looked around searching for a sign of her sister or anyone else. No noise came from the cave where she had originally found Elan and the others.

The mountaintop was almost flat and went on for a long while. There were a few small shrubs and plants but no trees to obstruct the view. The cave was the only prominent thing in site, and Astril shuddered to think of her sister slaving away in its sweltering dampness.

She made a sign for silence, and the party swarmed quietly over the mountain in search of the Keepers.

"Over here!" screamed a soldier from an open area behind the entrance to the cave.

Astril and Keanu, along with the others, rushed over to where the soldier's voice had come from. There they saw a small group of frightened Keepers huddled around the thin body of a young woman. Astril pushed her way through the group while Keanu and the other soldiers stood back in horror at the scene before them.

"Elan!" Astril cried, gathering the girl up in her arms.

"Astril?" Elan's weak voice whispered. "You came back for us."

Tears streamed down Astril's face as she held Elan close. "I came back for you, Sister. We have come to free you all."

Elan smiled softly and then turned her face away as her body was racked with a coughing fit. "Thauma left us here many nights ago. She said we would no longer work in the mines."

Astril smiled through her tears and held her sister even closer.

"You came back for us, Astril. I knew you would return." Another coughing fit engulfed her sister's emaciated body. "I waited for you."

"You are safe now, Elan. You will come home with me and be treated with honor for what you have endured."

Shaking her head slowly, Elan smiled up at her. "No, for me it is enough to know I am free."

"No, Elan. You will be well. I will heal you."

Elan raised her hand to her mouth as a loud, rattling cough convulsed her. Blood coursed between her fingers as the cough echoed from the hill. "I have my peace, Astril. I see a man, a beautiful, shining man. He stands with His arms open wide to me. I remember His name now. The name my grandmother used to call. He is the One." Her thin body was racked with coughing again, but she raised her head and held out her hand as if touching the sky. "He's calling my name, Astril. He tells me that He loves me, and that I am no longer deserted."

"Go to Him, sweet sister." Astril choked on her own tears. "Go into His loving embrace."

Elan's smile lit up the night as she stared into the darkening sky and reached her arms toward heaven. She gently laid her head back down in Astril's arms, took a sharp breath of air, then exhaled. Her poor, abused body stilled.

Astril held her close for a long time, staring up into the night sky and mourning the loss of her last sibling. Yet through her grief she praised the One True God for revealing Himself to Elan before her death.

The soldiers built a bed of rocks and topped it with a thick layer of dried grasses, upon which they laid Elan's body. They touched a burning torch to the pyre in traditional funeral rites while Astril stood by and watched. Keanu comforted the small company of Keepers and assured them that their families had not known of their ill treatment and were now anxiously awaiting their return home.

The next morning Astril, Keanu, the soldiers, and the Keepers left the mountain to return home to Seerling where they were greeted with much love and tears.

Life in Seerling was beginning to make sense to Astril. The Keepers were now home and safe with their families, and the slaves had been released from Harkan. Their return brought hope to the people and a strong readiness to serve a just and kind God. There was still much work to be done in destroying the many high places that her ancestors had made for the Great Goddess, but today all work ceased as several Harkonian carriages rolled into the clearing.

"Drinna!" Astril screamed, running toward the rotund woman clambering from one of the carriages. Grabbing her about the shoulders and hugging her tightly, Astril laughed. "I never dreamed you would come."

Drinna held her closely. "You know you can't get rid of me." Then hugging her again, Drinna added, "You've lost more weight. I'm going to have to fatten you up."

Astril laughed at the woman as she looked around for the priest. "Where is Priest Augur?"

Drinna searched the group that had arrived with her. "I'm not sure. I saw him a moment ago as we entered the clearing."

Astril continued to look through the crowd of thirty or more priests and attendants then smiled as she recognized the familiar brown eyes of the priest. *He has grown so old in such a short time,* she thought while surveying his short, gray hair and long white beard. The smile he gave her as he approached emphasized deep-set lines at the corners of his eyes and mouth.

"What a long trip," he said breathlessly as he held out his arms to hug her tight. "My, you have grown."

Astril stood back in astonishment. "What? Drinna says I've lost weight."

The priest raised his eyebrow and stepped back to look at her more closely. "I was not commenting on your physical growth, my dear." He smiled then and added, "I see a great source of strength from the One True God flowing through you."

"He has blessed me tremendously." Even while speaking the words, she remembered Toren and dropped her head in an attempt to hide the sadness that always tempted to overwhelm her.

The priest laid his hand on her forehead and sighed. "I also see much sorrow."

Astril forced a laugh in an attempt to show merriment. "I am so very glad to have you both with me. Thank you for coming."

The group turned and allowed Astril to show them to their huts where they rested through the heat of the day.

That evening, after their meal, Astril took Priest Augur aside for a walk.

She led him toward the site of where the Great Goddess's temple used to be.

"I debated for many days on what I should do with the temple." She glanced at him. "It seemed wrong to convert it into a place of worship for the One True God."

"Yes, I believe you are correct. This is a place of death and evil," he said, studying the large mound of rubble.

Astril smiled. "Do you believe it would be appropriate to have a house of worship for Him in Seerling land?"

"Astril, the One True God has done a mighty thing here. However, He does not need large houses of worship to prove who He is."

Looking down, Astril spoke slowly. "But the people do." She then looked up at him and added, "I feel that the building of a new temple, dedicated to the One True God, will help them grow in their faith and give them some tangible hope to hold on to."

"If you believe this is the right thing to do, I support you," the priest spoke comfortingly.

The two stood in silence for some time before he spoke again.

"Astril, what is it that troubles you so?"

She shrugged her shoulders and tried to hide the tears that spilled down her cheeks.

"You have made a large sacrifice to lead your people. Haven't you?" Priest Augur pulled her into a hug.

All of the pain she had hidden for months spilled over in a torrent of tears onto his tunic as she choked out, "I've lost the only family I had left, and I lost Toren. I have no one now, no one to love."

Augur allowed her to continue to cry and after a few minutes guided her to sit beside him on a large stone.

"I know the pain in your heart, my dear. I have also lost those I loved." Gently he stroked her arm and sighed.

His sudden admission shocked her out of crying as she gasped at his words.

He chuckled at her reaction. "Yes, I was once in love. It was a long time ago, but when I close my eyes I can see her standing before me." He shut his eyes, touched his finger to his lips, and whispered, "I can still feel the warmth of her kiss."

Astril continued to stare at him.

Priest Augur opened his eyes and sadly smiled. Turning back to the young woman he spoke, "That woman was your grandmother, Astril."

He ignored her shocked look. "I loved her more than I ever thought possible, but she had a choice to make just as you did. I wanted her to stay with me, but she knew that she had a responsibility to her people… a responsibility to her daughter."

Astril started to ask a question but was quieted when the priest continued his tale.

"It was a hot day, much like today, when she came to tell me she felt the One was telling her to leave. I begged her to stay and marry me and when she refused I told her I would give up everything and follow her to Seerling. She knew that her people would never allow a union between us. So in an attempt to protect me from my foolish self, she left in the seclusion of night. That was the last time I ever saw her."

A faraway look filled his eyes. "I never blamed her for leaving. I knew she had learned everything she could from me, and it was time for her to take that knowledge back to her people." He touched Astril's cheek and whispered, "She would have been so proud of you."

Smiling through her tears, Astril nodded. "She is the reason I am staying. The elders approached me and one by one told of all she had taught them. They told me of the secret hope she instilled within them all."

Priest Augur added, "The hope of a better life under the One True God."

Astril nodded her head. Sorrow flooded her again as her head filled with images of her own lost love. "I only wish my story had ended better than my grandmother's." She looked back at him sadly. "If only she could have had you at her side during all those long years of seclusion."

"She had her true love with her," he said softly, "and He is the only One who will never desert you." Then looking over and smiling he added, "And you do not know that your story will end the same as hers, my dear. The One True God blesses us through the sacrifices we make in His name."

Astril gave him a sad smile. "Perhaps one day Toren will understand."

CHAPTER THIRTY

T oren knew Morgan was standing there watching him, and it grated on his every nerve. *Why can't she just let me alone? I'm giving her what she wanted. Is it so much to ask for a little peace once in a while?* He sat at his desk intentionally ignoring her, hoping she would go away.

"Prince Toren," Morgan said interrupting his dark thoughts. "Might I speak with you?"

He couldn't ignore her any longer, so he looked up at the young woman and dismissed her with a wave of his hand. "Not now, Morgan. I'm just too busy." It was a lie.

She stood her ground and looked him over. *This is new.* Why wasn't she leaving? She'd always gone when he told her to in the past.

"Please. I have to speak with you."

Toren jammed the top on his inkpot, giving it a vicious twist. "What is it?"

She stood wringing her hands before him. When she failed to speak after some moments, he went back to staring down at the missive on the table before him, ignoring her again.

"Prince Toren, I... need to ask you something." She paused until he cast a wary glance at her. "I need to know if... do you love me?" The final words came breathlessly out of her mouth as several tears ran down her cheeks.

This was exactly why he didn't want to spend time with the girl. He knew this was going to come up eventually. She was such a needy person.

"Isn't it enough that I'm going to marry you tomorrow, Morgan?" He regretted the words even as they escaped his lips.

A small shudder coursed over her, and she turned her head away from him, letting out a cry. Slumping, Toren stood and walked toward her. He laid his arms on her shoulders but couldn't bring himself to pull her into an embrace.

"Please do not be distressed." He forced a smile, trying to set her at ease. "Why don't you go make some plans for a special getaway, just the two of us. I'll let you decide and after the wedding I'll take you there."

Then, having offered her the world, he turned and went back to his chair very pleased with himself. *That should solve the problem!* Once he had sat down again he looked up and noticed that she still stood in front of him even after he had dismissed her. *What does she want now?* He tapped his quill as he waited for her to speak.

"I…" she began then stopped. "Prince Toren." Her voice held a hard edge. "I have been in training for many years to be your wife. I have faithfully studied all of your likes and dislikes. It's the only thing I have ever learned."

He sat impassive looking at her. *So, I never told her to do all of that.*

"Our engagement time is almost over, and I can not pretend any longer. I never thought it was important that I love the man that I marry, but…" She began to weep, her words garbled by her hysterics. "I was never prepared to marry a man who is in love with someone else."

Toren sat staring after her as she ran out of the room wailing. He knew he should run after her and speak comforting words, but it was impossible for him to move. They both knew that she spoke the truth.

Toren had awoken the morning of his marriage dreading all that would take place. How could he marry Morgan when his mind was always consumed with Astril? He was so caught up in his thoughts that he didn't even notice that his intended bride never came down for the morning meal. In fact, the only time he looked up from playing with his food was when the King's guard entered the room and announced that she had run off with Holan, Kortan's main hall attendant.

"She did what?" roared the king, spilling his crushed apples from his spoon and onto his lap. "Bring them back!"

Before the guard could leave the room, Toren held up his hand. "Do not recover them." Looking to his grandfather, he said, "At least someone may find joy in his life."

"But Toren, she was your intended." The king screamed, "Her running off with my attendant brings shame upon us all."

Toren shook his head and braved himself up against his grandfather. He was glad she had gone. Her actions not only released her from the certainty of an unhappy marriage, but they also released his heart. "I did not love Morgan, Grandfather. It's unfair to force the girl to marry under those circumstances."

Kortan almost toppled the table over with the impact of his pounding fists. "You promised you would marry her."

Toren shook his head and grinned. "I promised I would marry her if she would have me. It's clear by her action that she will not."

He stood and quickly walked out of the room and back to his own chambers, grateful to Morgan for the enormous burden that had been lifted from his shoulders.

The sun had slid down the western sky, and Toren still sat in his chambers, wondering at the strange turn of events that had transpired. He knew that it was the conversation they had had the day before that led to the girl's running off. *I couldn't lie to her and give her false hope.* He smiled to himself. How could he have not noticed that she and Holan were becoming close? *I guess there are just some things I'm clueless about.*

Hearing a soft knock at his door, Toren rose and answered to see his mother standing before him.

"Toren," she said after hugging him close. "I am as shocked as you are. Are you all right?"

"I'm fine, Mother."

"But how can she have done such a thing?"

Toren sighed and told her of their exchange the day before.

"Then I suppose this is best for all." She smiled up at him with a look of relief.

It was for the best. Toren believed that Morgan would indeed be happier with Holan than she ever had been with him. He was greatly relieved to not have to spend any more time with her, so why was his heart so heavy? After all, hadn't he gotten what he wanted? *No, I didn't!* He shook his head in frustration.

"Tell me what bothers you, my son." His mother's ability to read a person's face was impressive. He had evaded her questions and concerns throughout the four-month engagement to Morgan and wanted to tell her again that he was doing fine. He wanted to be fine. He couldn't stuff his feelings away any longer. In the privacy of his chambers and in his mother's presence, he allowed the feelings he had locked away for so long to fall over his face. His shoulders slumped, and he felt as though he might fall over with grief.

"This is not about Morgan, I think." His mother held his hand gently. "Something else troubles you greatly. Please let me share your pain."

Toren turned to her and told the entire story of what had transpired between himself and Astril. He even told her what he had said and done in the meadow on their last night together.

Princess Emile listened quietly without interrupting until he was completely finished with his tale and was looking to her for advice.

She placed her hands together in her lap, and looking up at him calmly, inquired, "And you do look at her as if she were your slave, right?"

"No!" How could she question him? She knew him better than anyone except Astril. How could she believe that about her own son?

"But Toren, you do." She paused as he shook his head in anger then added, "I saw you that day when you brought her in before your grandfather. You were filled with rage. It was a look I have never seen on you before."

Toren gulped. "I was angry because of the way she had been treated."

"I understand that, Son. What I don't understand is why, when your grandfather gave you one gift to choose, you chose to take her as your slave instead of setting her free."

"It was my intent to set her free," he said quietly. "You saw me try."

Shaking her head, the princess continued, "No, my son, you did not really try. You told the king who she was. Deep inside, you knew he would never release her. You knew you would have to take her to the priests."

Toren sat shaking his head in disbelief of her words.

Patiently Emile reached out her hand and patted his. "The point is that you took her as your own instead of giving her freedom."

He shook his head and continued to look down at his hands. "I only wanted to protect her." Then looking to his mother he added, "Is it wrong for a man to want to protect the woman he loves?"

The older woman smiled at her confused son. "It is honorable for a man to want to protect, but I feel your desire to protect her led to a belief that only you could do that job. You left the One True God out completely."

Was his mother speaking truth? Could he have chosen a different path? The dawning of reality burned deep within him as he listened intently to her words.

"If you love her the way you say you do, then you have to give her to Him." He had been so afraid of losing Astril that he hadn't given her over to the care of the One. Now, here he sat without her anyway. His mother placed a comforting hand on his own. "That does not mean you will lose her forever, my child. It only means that you can not hold so tightly that you snuff out the very life that you love."

"But she chose her people over me," he whispered, still unable to understand. "I've already lost her."

Emile let out a small sigh. "It sounds like she chose the will of the One True God over you, my son. It was you who chose your people and your way over her."

How could he have not seen that? Astril had asked him to stay. She never once said she didn't want him. *I've been so foolish demanding my own way. I never saw that there was another.*

Emile pulled her hand away and stood at the bedside next to him. "Besides, if she truly is as you have said, I do not believe you have lost her."

He slowly rubbed his face with his hands. Even if all this was true, he had hurt her terribly. How could he ever presume to ask for her back? "Deep in my heart I know what you say is true, Mother, but I have failed her too many times to make anything good of this now."

She smiled down at him with a face of wisdom. "Give her to the One True God, Toren. He will make all things right."

That night, Toren knelt to the ground, laid his heart bare to his God, and asked for forgiveness for all that he had done. After unrolling his copied scrolls and reading for hours, he was finally able to give up his ownership of Astril and place her care in the hands of the One True God. He walked with deliberate steps toward the palace records room, found the slave records, and permanently struck out her name. No longer would Astril be a slave to anyone. She was a child of the One and would always have Toren's heart.

It was the first time in ages that Toren could remember waking up happy. He jumped from his bed feeling lighter for having shed the burden in his heart. Now he had only to go and ask Astril's forgiveness for all the wrongs he had committed. The thought of seeing her again sent his heart into convulsions, but he reminded himself that his trip was only to seek forgiveness. Once he was back in Seerling, he would let the One decide his future. *It feels so good to have direction again. Thank you, Lord.*

"I will go to her and ask her forgiveness," he said to himself while dressing. *First I have to tell my grandfather.*

He rushed to get to the morning meal and let his family know of his plan.

He entered to see his grandfather and mother were already seated. The meal went by uneventful with barely a word passed between any of them. It was not until the final course that Toren was able to convey his plans to return to Seerling land and beg Astril's forgiveness.

He sat quietly waiting for a response and wondering at his grandfather's unusually calm demeanor.

Did he hear me? he questioned himself while keeping a carefully guarded eye on his grandfather. The man had been so unpredictable recently.

Many quiet minutes passed as the three sat. Toren looked up at his mother, who shrugged her shoulders slightly. He noticed that her eyes held a hint of fear.

"Grandfather, did you hear me?" Toren asked slowly.

King Kortan raised his head so Toren was able to see the clouds that had crossed over his eyes. He stared at the unexplainable rage that began to rise throughout the old man's body and was quick to duck out of the way as the king sent a bread knife sailing toward his head.

His mother cried out in fear, grabbing the arm of the king. Kortan stared without recognition at her then pushed her hand away as he rammed his chair backward. Toren jumped out of the way as the king lunged for him and grabbed for his throat.

Toren leapt to the side and was almost out the door trying to avoid his grandfather's second attack.

Frustrated and panting, the king screamed, "You will not bring that heathen back here to rule over my realm." Then hands outstretched, he rushed toward Toren once more. Toren shoved the king aside with his elbow and spun around before fleeing the room.

His mother screamed.

His grandfather bellowed a curse on Toren. "You are banished, Prince Toren. You are never to return to Harkan again."

CHAPTER THIRTY-ONE

Toren raced straight to the stables and saddled and mounted his horse. He did not stop for food or clothing in his flight from Harkan. He rode hard for three days, barely resting at night. The entire way to Seerling land, he prayed for his grandfather.

"I know now that I can not return to my homeland until my grandfather forgives me," he spoke aloud while preparing a short meal of berries. It had been foolish to travel so far alone, especially since there were still reports of attacks between the Seerling and Harkonian peoples. But after the display in the dining hall, he knew he fared better at Astril's hands than those of his grandfather.

"And to think, I was always taught that it was the Seerlings who were heathens."

Toren was glad that he had paid attention while traveling with Astril. Riding from landmark to landmark, he was able to enter the Seerling clearing only three days after his journey began. He jumped down from his horse and ignored the many fair faces that stared in disbelief at his arrival.

Recognizing Raina, a young woman who had given him food the last time he was there, he asked, "Where's Astril?"

Raina stared with her mouth agape then quickly pointed to a hut off to the left.

Toren smiled at her and strode in the direction that she had pointed.

After knocking on the door, he was surprised to be greeted by a familiar rotund face. He gave Drinna a giant hug and asked what she was doing in Seerling.

She endured his hug and gave him a slow nod along with a noticeable cold shoulder.

"Astril sent for Priest Augur to help train the people. I came to serve her."

"Priest Augur is here?"

She raised her eyebrows in his direction and snorted her reply.

"How is Astril doing?" He couldn't stop fidgeting his fingers as he stared around the clean but sparsely decorated room. Why wouldn't the woman just let him see Astril?

Drinna turned angry eyes upon him, pointed her finger in his chest, and accused, "You don't have a right to know!" Her voice quieted, and she turned away from him. "That poor thing has done nothing but love you, you stubborn fool."

Toren nodded and gulped back his pride. He knew she was right. "I'm sorry."

Barely acknowledging his apology, Drinna continued her tirade, "Yes, you are sorry, coming here to see her so soon after your own marriage. You should be ashamed of yourself."

She then turned to walk into a side room, still raving, "If you think you're going to come here and try and… and seduce her…" Then turning around, Drinna screamed, "She's not that type of girl."

Toren tried hard to hide the smile that played at his lips as the large servant paced back and forth, spitting out angry ravings.

"Please, Drinna." He held up his hands in surrender. "I have not come here to treat her unkindly. I came to ask for her forgiveness." He paused and smiled. "And I did not get married."

Drinna stopped her diatribe and walked back over to him. She reached out her hand and laid it forcefully upon his chest. "Prince, do not hurt her again."

Toren recognized the sadness in her voice and the reality of her words and nodded his head. He knew he didn't have a right to ask for Astril's forgiveness after everything he had done to her, but he needed it. He bent down and gave the heavy woman a long hug.

"Now, if you are finished taking me to task, I would love something good to eat."

She laughed at him and scurried to get the food.

After he sat down, she began to prattle on about all the good things Astril had accomplished in the name of the One True God.

"Where is she now?" he asked before taking huge bites of the bread and herbed meat she had offered. He savored the tender meat. Drinna was such a good cook.

Drinna smiled and rounded the corner in the room with a wheel of cheese.

"Oh, she's off again destroying the ancient high places that were dedicated to the Great Goddess. I hear they are numerous and hidden well. There certainly seem to be a lot of them at any rate."

"She has accomplished much then," Toren whispered. How he wished he could have been there to help her.

Looking as though she were the proudest mother in the world, Drinna stated, "That girl can do anything."

Toren spent the next four days hunting and helping the men with the building of a temple, which they said was to be dedicated to the One True God. He also assisted them in the building of three additional huts. It seemed the Seerlings were always busy building something.

Every day's hard work invigorated him and brought a new meaning to the pampering Drinna provided in the evening. She knew exactly which salves to put on his sore hands and how to rub the tightness from his left shoulder.

Toren also had plenty of time to spend at the side of Priest Augur, who faithfully taught the men and women from the ancient scrolls. They all seemed eager to learn more about the One who had saved them from the tyranny of the High Priestess. Everyone was so happy and content. It was a different Seerling than he remembered.

Astril, Keanu, and their company of soldiers galloped their steeds at full speed through the final length of forest and into the clearing of their land. They had been gone longer than anticipated, mainly due to a skirmish between themselves and a few hardy Gernons, who had learned of the demise of the High Priestess. Without her magic, the Gernons felt they could attack, trying to take the women. Astril had personally had to beat down four Gernon warriors to rescue one of her female soldiers.

Seerling women had always been prepared against the lust-filled heathens, but attacks were rare under the rule of the High Priestess. Astril resolved to make sure every female knew exactly how to handle a staff and dagger.

Despite the ambush, they had been successful in tearing down the last of the ancient high places, at least all that Astril knew about. Her heart was filled with joy upon entering her homeland and seeing her people hard at their daily work.

"We did it!" She cried at the top of her lungs while entering the clearing. "The final high place has been destroyed." Her soldiers let out their war cries and raised their staffs in celebration. Those nearest to the forest rushed toward the group, yelling their joy. Astril and the soldiers steered their steeds passed the people and ran deeper into the village.

Once they entered the main circle she yelled out to all who could hear, "Tonight we celebrate." Still rejoicing at the victory, Astril searched the faces in the courtyard for Priest Augur and Drinna. In front of her hut a young, dark-haired man at Drinna's side raised his hand in a tentative salute. She shook her head in disbelief. *Could that really be him?* Her mind reeled. She had been told that he was to celebrate his marriage to Morgan only a few days ago yet here he stood smiling at her.

Instead of merely sliding off her mount, Astril threw her leg over the steed's head so she could jump down with a flourish. At that same moment the animal decided to stretch his neck, and her foot stopped short of its goal, throwing her off balance. Her body jerked forward, and she fell face-first to the ground, landing in an ungraceful heap. Keanu was quick to jump to her aide, grabbing her waist and pulling her upright again.

Astril's face flamed with embarrassment. "I'm fine, let me be." Had they all seen her foolishness?

Keanu looked in her eyes, still holding her close and said in a low voice so only she could here, "I have never known you to not be able to manage your own steed before. Are you sure you are all right?"

She quickly disengaged herself from his grasp and beat the dust from her tunic with her fists.

"Tell the elders that we will celebrate tonight, and have the families prepare for a large feast. I'm famished." Then turning, she walked toward her hut just in time to see Toren's back disappear inside.

Toren slammed the door shut behind him and growled at Drinna when she turned toward him. "Why didn't you tell me she has a man?" he screamed at the poor woman.

The door opened behind him, letting in a cool breeze. He stood growling in Drinna's direction even though he knew it was Astril who had entered.

"Toren, I can't believe it's really you." He turned angry eyes upon her. Her mouth popped open. "What's wrong?"

He looked away as she walked closer and touched his arm. He jerked away from her touch then glared back at her. "Is that your mate?"

"What… who?" She stared at him. "What are you talking about?"

He turned back toward her and gestured with his open hand toward the closed door. "That muscle man that was holding you so close. Is he your mate?"

Shaking her fist in his face, Astril screamed right back at him, "You're the one who left and got married. How dare you come to my home and accuse me of anything." She then turned from him in anger and shouted, "No one asked you to come back."

Toren growled his response and huffed from the room. He felt like such a fool. Here he had waited all these days just to apologize to her and now she had a mate. He stormed to the stables to get his steed. *There's no way I'm sticking around here to be made a fool of.*

The long walk to the stables helped cool him off, and he began to realize that he had no right to expect anything out of her. After all, hadn't she always been his friend? Was this what the One True God expected of him, to be Astril's friend but not her mate, her lover, her protector? *Is that what's going to happen here?* He stared up at the wooden ceiling of the stable and breathed in the familiar scent of horses and hay. A few men were unharnessing the steeds the soldiers had used. They went about their work in quiet, ignoring him. It was a gift he was very thankful for.

With shaking hands, he took down his saddle. No matter what his feelings were, no matter whether he could live up to the task set before him, he knew he needed to go back to her and apologize for all he had done. *Okay, I'll go back after I saddle my steed, but then I'm out of here.*

"Go after him, Astril," Drinna said from the table where she sat preparing beans.

Astril was in no mood to be told what to do, and she certainly didn't want to look at Toren even once more. "How dare you let him come in here?"

Drinna took the abuse with blinking eyes.

"Astril, Prince Toren did not marry Morgan. Go after him before he leaves."

"I can't. He has done nothing but cause me pain." Then turning around she began to walk into the next room. There was no way she was going to allow him to hurt her again.

For a fat woman, Drinna moved quickly, and before Astril knew it she was taken by the shoulders and turned about like a disobedient child. The older woman's eyes pleaded with her. "He was jealous because he saw Keanu holding you."

"Keanu picked me up when I fell because I tripped over my own horse making a fool of myself to get to Toren." The pouting tone in her voice made her cringe.

Drinna gave her a maternal smile. "I know this, but he doesn't." She took Astril's hand. "The One True God is giving you a second chance, child. Don't ruin it with your pride."

"But, Drinna, how do I know this is a second chance. Maybe it's just another test, and I'll have to give him up again." She shook her head sadly.

"Oh, child, you can't expect love to be perfect. Sometimes we give everything we have, and we get hurt, and sometimes we are rewarded. Don't you want to know what it feels like to be rewarded?" Drinna's words made a lot of sense. She did want the rewards of being held in Toren's arms, of being loved by him.

Drinna smiled down at her. "Don't let fear and pride keep you from the greatest gift the One True God may be laying at your doorstep.

Could Toren's return truly be a gift from the One? Astril knew there was only one way to find out so she turned from the large woman and ran from the hut.

It didn't take her long to find him standing in the stable preparing his horse for the long trip back. She quietly motioned for the few men who were tending the horses to leave.

"I'm sorry for screaming at you," she murmured from a corner stall. *Why do I suddenly feel so shy?* She berated herself for her cowardice.

He turned around and gave her a shaky smile. "Please forgive me for being so angry when I saw you in that man's arms." He looked down at the reins that were in his hands. "I have no right to be jealous over another man."

It took all of her strength to walk toward him, but she wanted all that the One might be providing.

He was concentrating hard on the animal's reins. "I wish you the greatest happiness, Astril. He looks like a fine man."

Warmth surged up her neck into her face. The urge to kiss him was overwhelming. He looked so broken, so hurt, but there was a difference about him. He was letting her go. *Well, I'm not going to allow you to let me go, Toren.* Flinging her arms around his neck, she pulled him down until they were face-to-face. "I believe Keanu's wife, Raina, also thinks he's a fine man."

"You mean…"

She rubbed her nose against his and grinned. "Keanu tried to help me when I fell off my horse. I made a fool out of myself because I was trying desperately to get to you."

"So… you have not taken a mate?"

Shaking her head no, Astril stood on her toes to kiss him.

Chapter Thirty-two

Every Seerling that could be found from all thirteen tribes was invited to partake of the celebration feast that evening. In honor of the event, Astril had asked Priest Augur to give a special victory speech.

Standing in the middle of the assembly he began, "Followers of the One True God, today a great victory over evil has been achieved. You have all worked hard and have opened your hearts up to a new way of believing."

Looking around the group, he smiled. "And I am so very proud of you all. This is a momentous time in your history; a time when good has triumphed. You can now live your lives in peace, knowing that your children will not have to suffer under the heavy hand of an evil ruler. You now have the freedom to walk in the light of the One True God away from the tyranny of evil.

The priest raised his palms toward the sky. "Today, you have done a great thing for Him."

Everyone present cheered at the words of peace that were spoken by the priest.

Astril looked over at Toren, who had turned and was speaking with Keanu. She smiled at how quickly the two men had taken to one another.

Although they were physically as different as night and day, each possessed a quiet strength and was a strong leader for the One True God.

Everything was as it should be. The evil age of the Great Goddess had passed, and she and Toren could pursue a future without condemnation. The only time that Astril could remember feeling so much peace was when her grandmother had sung over her as a child. She looked up to heaven and gave a quick prayer of thanks for all the One True God had done in her life, then quietly slipped away from the party.

She felt the cool of the night breeze as she walked and chuckled remembering the argument she had earlier with Drinna about wearing a dress. She laughed at the remembrance of Drinna bringing all those Harkonian dresses out of her trunk. Astril didn't have the heart to fight her, but knew she had to put her foot down fast, or the woman would have her dressed in silly clothing every day. So to pacify the older woman, Astril called for a traditional Seerling gown to be brought in for her to wear for the special occasion. She had smiled to herself when Drinna commented that the simple green gown was quite lovely and functional.

Finally, a compromise, she thought.

Astril continued her stroll, ending up at the quiet pool that sat behind the rubble of the former temple. Bending over, she took a fallen leaf and swayed it back and forth in the water, gazing into the depths and remembering a time when she and Gallian had shared the pool as their own private haven. It wasn't long before she felt the weight of Toren's stare on her back. Every time he was near, her heart fluttered before her eyes even saw him

Not moving an inch she spoke aloud, "I used to swim in this pool with my sister when we were young."

Toren walked closer to her and kneeling down asked, "How do you always know it's me without turning around?"

"My heart tells me." Then splashing him lightly with the water, she laughed. "And you have big, loud feet."

Toren laughed and splashed her back. Then taking her hand in his, he helped her stand.

"Astril, I have learned so much while away from you," he began. "I want to ask you to please forgive me for being selfish and for trying to control you. I also want to let you know that I have erased your name from the slave records. You are no longer owned by anyone but the One True God."

There was a time when she thought she would never hear those words spoken. It filled her with joy to see how much he had changed, how much he had grown.

She lightly cupped his face in her hand as he continued to speak. "I know now that you were not rejecting me. You were accepting your calling, and I should have stayed to help you." He held her hand to his mouth and kissed her fingertips in a way that always sent a spark up her arm before asking, "Please forgive me for being so foolhardy and selfish."

Astril draped her arms around his neck, loving him even more. "I've been praying for you to find your way, Toren. I never want to come between you and Him."

"Does that mean you forgive me?"

She smiled and nodded her head.

Pressing his luck a little further, Toren kissed her cheek and whispered in her ear, "Will you take me as your husband?"

Pulling away, Astril stared up at him and smiled through her tears before kissing him softly on the lips.

"Astril, does that mean yes?"

Her heart had never felt so light. She had found love, and she now had a family. The One had given him back to her. Breathlessly she answered, "Toren, it means forever."

It felt so right to sit next to him knowing that their future was secure. The One was going to bond them together. Astril's happiness sparkled almost as bright as the stars they sat looking up at.

The moment was so perfect, but she still couldn't help but wonder if their differences might be difficult for them to manage. The first thing to conquer was the vows themselves. She had heard tales of Harkonian traditions and ceremonies. Would the vows be filled with a lot of details? Seerling marriages were so simple.

The two sat in silence for a long time before she built up her nerve to ask, "How do Harkonians take mates?"

Toren chuckled and put his arm around her shoulders. "Oh, they wait through at least four phases of the moon. Then there is a huge ceremony that lasts many hours where a priest says a blessing over the couple. All day long the wife and husband are attended to by family who force them to change their clothing every few hours, which symbolizes the changes that take place in a marriage. After that, everyone in each family and throughout the country comes and celebrates for three days. The husband and wife often take a marriage trip to some remote area where they stay for a few days. When they come back, they are married.

Astril dreaded the idea of having Drinna change her into so many different oufits. "That is very different from the way Seerlings take mates."

"How do Seerlings?"

Smiling mischievously back at him, she answered, "Well, first they seek permission of the leader. Once permission is granted, the leader takes a length of leather rope and binds it about each of their wrists while speaking a blessing. Then they enter into a hut and… and become husband and wife."

Toren laughed, "It's that simple?"

Nodding her head, Astril smiled and reiterated, "It's that simple."

Toren kissed her fingertips and produced a devilish grin. "It's too bad we have no leader besides you to grant us permission tonight."

He was teasing her, but it did probe a concern. How could she grant permission and perform the vows for herself? An idea hit her head like a brick. She jumped up and sprinted back toward the celebration.

"Astril, where are you going," he called, trying to catch up.

She stopped and turned around. "Priest Augur can perform the vows." Then seeing the astonished look on his face, she asked, "Or would you rather have a traditional Harkonian service?"

"What?" He still looked very confused.

Raising her hands above her head, Astril shouted, "Toren, a Harkonian priest can perform the Seerling ceremony tonight. That will make it legal in the eyes of both our peoples."

She placed her hands on her hips and smiled sweetly at him. "You aren't going to make me wait through all those phases of the moon to get married, are you?"

"Let's go find that priest!" He rushed past her toward the party, and she raced to catch up with him. They locked hands and ran full force toward their future.

Bible Scriptures used in *Seed of Seerling*

CHAPTER 1

May you be blessed by the One True God, the Maker of heaven and earth.
(Psalm 115:15). Paraphrased in prayer by Sallian.

CHAPTER 2

Let them praise His name with dancing and make music to Him with tambourine and harp. For the One True God takes delight in His people; He crowns the humble with salvation (Psalm 149:3–4). Paraphrased by Sallian.

CHAPTER 16

"O our God, will you not judge them? For we have no power to face this vast army that is attacking us. We do not know what to do, but our eyes are upon you" (2 Chronicles 20:12). Read aloud by Priest Augur.
"The One True God will deliver them to you. Be strong and courageous. Do not be afraid or terrified because of them, for the One True God goes with you; He will never leave you nor forsake you." (Deuteronomy 31:5–7). Paraphrased by Astril.

CHAPTER 22

"O our God, will you not judge them? For we have no power to face this vast army that is attacking us. We do not know what to do, but our eyes are upon you" (2 Chronicles 20:12). Quoted by Astril.
In You, O Lord, I have taken refuge;… Save me in Your unfailing love (Psalm 31:1–5, 14–16). Sung by Astril.

CHAPTER 25

"The One True God will deliver them to me. Be strong and courageous. Do not be afraid or terrified because of them, for the One True God goes with me; he will never leave me nor forsake me" (Deuteronomy 31:5–6). Paraphrased by Astril.